QUEEN OF KATS

QUEEN OF KATS

JOHN G. HARTNESS

PART I
BETRAYAL

CHAPTER 1

Remarin's feet slid on the slick cobblestones as he rounded the corner, threatening to send him sprawling into the street and under the wheels of a cartload of whiskey barrels. Scrambling madly and bowling over a rotund matron loaded down with laundry, the slight thief regained his footing and dashed off down an unlit alley. He ducked into a darkened doorway as four mailed, spear-toting guards barreled down the street. Remarin sagged with relief but kept to the shadows as he crept slowly to the mouth of the alley.

Remarin peered back the way he'd run, ducking back into the shadows as two more heavyset guards came into view at more a trot than a sprint. They clattered past, chainmail and breastplates shattering the stillness of the night with their cacophonous rattle. Remarin stayed frozen until they were long past, then exited the alley and walked back the way he'd come, affecting a casual swagger to hide the adrenaline-fueled trembling in his legs.

That was close, Remoron. The voice in his head was dry as burnt toast, and Remarin glanced down at his belt. The black hilt of a dagger hung there, a ruby set into the pommel. In the heart of the ruby, a small light flickered as if there were a flame dancing within the gem.

"Trand, you're back. I thought I left you in the belly of the first guard," Remarin whispered, long practice allowing him to converse with the dagger with the barest hint of lips moving.

I'm not that easy to get rid of. We're stuck with each other until you're dead or I'm released from this stupid curse.

"Or I smelt you down into earrings for that good-looking tavern wench I met last week. What was her name again?" The dagger didn't answer. Grateful for the rare silence, Remarin turned a corner off the main merchant's thoroughfare and headed toward the poorer section of Bravis, capital city and principal port of the kingdom of Veosia.

Here on the cheap streets one could find a pub with a room to let, a man in an alley with goods of undisclosed provenance, or a good street brawl if that's what one was looking for. Tonight Remarin was in search of none of that. He found what he was looking for just a few short blocks from the merchant's district in a nondescript building nestled between a bustling pub and a shuttered laundry. He knocked twice on the door, waited for three breaths, then knocked twice more.

The door opened and a wizened man of maybe five feet in height stepped back to allow the thief entrance. "Welcome back, Remarin. I trust you have my goods?"

"I have the jewel, Salvar. I assume you have my money?"

"I have everything you're entitled to, thief. Hand over my gem, and I'll fetch your payment." Something in the little man's tone rung false with Remarin and out of the corner of his eye, he saw the gem flash brighter than normal in the dagger's hilt.

"Not to be suspicious, Salvar, but let's see the payment first." Remarin stepped slowly back until he could feel the door against his back heel. He couldn't hear anything out of the ordinary, and that alarmed him even further. At this time of night, the tavern next door should be raucous, full of the sounds of drunken fighting and off-key warbling from the horrible bard they kept chained up by the fireplace. But tonight, nothing. Not a scrape of a chair, not a single slurred bellow for more ale, not even the twang of an out of tune lute.

Something's amiss here. The voice in his head now sounded worried, as though the dagger actually cared what happened to Remarin.

"Really? And here I thought the tingling along my spine just a draft," Remarin whispered.

Salvar, for his part, was playing the role of affronted partner to the hilt. "Why, Remarin, I'm amazed at your lack of trust! How many times have we done business? How many times have I moved merchandise of questionable ownership for you? And how many times have I given you fair market value for goods that I couldn't move for weeks, even months? And *now* you choose to mistrust me? I may as well turn my back on you so you can pull the dagger out and stab me through the heart again!"

"It's not that I don't trust *you*, Salvar. It's that I don't trust anyone. A trusting thief very quickly ends up as a dead thief, and I have no interest in becoming a dead thief. Now where's the money?"

The corrupt little pawnbroker fidgeted for a long moment before reaching behind the counter. His hand came up with a dagger and Salvar let out a yell. "Help!"

Remarin whirled around and shot the bolt on the door. He grabbed the heavy wooden plank that leaned against it and set it into the two iron holders, securing the front entrance for a few moments at least. He turned back to Salvar and drew his own dagger. "You know you can't best me in a knife fight, Salvar. Why even try?"

"Because I'm being paid very handsomely to deliver your dead body, and if I don't kill you, I don't get paid," Salvar said, waving his dagger around in an almost-convincing display of knife work.

"I admire a man who sticks to his principles, Salvar. Even if those principles are killing me. For that, I'll let you die quickly." Remarin changed his grip and flicked the dagger across the room. The ruby-hilted blade tumbled end over end to bury itself in the hollow of Salvar's throat. "Sometimes it's very useful having an enchanted weapon around."

Are you claiming that there are times that it is not *useful to have me around?* Trand's voice echoed in Remarin's mind as he crossed the room to pull the dagger out of Salvar and wipe it on the dying man's tunic.

"Yeah, Trand. Like when you're talking. I could definitely live without talking to my weapons."

You're just mad that I've got a bigger vocabulary than you do. And there are two of them behind the door.

"I knew that," Remarin grumbled, pulling open the door that led to Salvar's storeroom. A pair of surprised mercenaries stood there, hands on sword hilts and shields at their sides. Remarin drew his rapier and ran the first one through the throat in one fluid motion. The second charged the slight thief, knocking him over and adding to his growing collection of bruises. Remarin grabbed the man's ankle and dragged him to the floor before he could reach the front door and open it for his reinforcements, then clambered up the man's back and slit his throat with a spare dagger he drew from his boot.

"Is that all of them?" Remarin gasped. Trand remained silent. "Trand, are there any more of them?" Nothing. Remarin sighed. "Fine. I'm sorry. I didn't know there were two of them in the storeroom; I could only hear one. You saved my ass. Again. Are you happy now?"

No, but if you let me stab something else, I might be able to recover from your appalling lack of faith in me. There are four outside but no more in the building.

"Then I've got enough time to loot the place and sneak out the back way," Remarin replied. He wiped his dagger down, slid it home in his boot, sheathed his rapier, and commenced to pilfering any valuables the mercenaries might have had on their persons. He gathered up a couple of necklaces, three good rings, and one jeweled earring, understanding that most mercenaries kept their savings in jewelry since it was easily portable.

Salvar's body proved as worthless as the man's loyalty, yielding nothing worth stealing, but Remarin knew where the pawnbroker stored his gems and gold. The thief moved soundlessly up the stairs to Salvar's bedroom and flung open the door. He stepped quickly to the center of the room, flipped back the corner of the rug, and pried up the false floor at the edge of the bed. He'd cased Salvar's home and shop many years ago when they first began to do business, just in case something like this ever happened. "Better safe than sorry, I always say."

No, you don't. You always say something remarkably stupid like, "What's the worst thing that could happen?" Well, you could end up dead or trapped inside a magical dagger for a thousand years, that's what could happen!

"Shut up, Trand," Remarin said, filling his purse with jewels and what coins he had room for. He barely felt the air shift above him but dove for the floor in time to avoid the brass candlestick swinging at his head. The startled burglar flipped onto his back and got his arms up in time to block the return strike before his brains got smeared all over the floor. The blow had little force behind it, and Remarin easily disarmed his attacker and sprang to his feet. He drew back a fist to continue the fight but froze when he saw the dirty face of a young boy staring up at him.

CHAPTER 2

"What in the Seven Hells is this?"

That is a child, Remoron.

"I hate you. You know that, right?" Remarin hissed.

He turned his attention back to the child that had almost bashed his brains out. "Who are you? What are you doing here? And why did you attack me?"

"I'm Kit," the child answered, jaw set and fists tight at his sides. "Salvar had me tied up here, dunno why. And I attacked you because that's what you do to thieves. You bash 'em."

"Well, let's have a little less bashing and a little more talking." Remarin looked the boy up and down. His blond hair was dirty and longer than was the fashion, and his clothes were little more than rags, but there was intelligence shining in those blue eyes, and a ferocity that Remarin found . . . well, amusing if he were to admit it to himself.

"Nothing to talk about. Salvar's dead. There are men beating down the front door to kill you and I think they'll probably do that or worse to me. Can we run away now?" Remarin revised the boy's age upwards at his words, then heard the loud crash of a door splintering downstairs.

"Yes, I think running away now is a grand idea. Do you have good boots?"

"No. I was barefoot when—when Salvar nabbed me." Kit pointed down, and Remarin looked at delicate feet that didn't look like they'd ever run barefoot before. Oh well, the child was about to get a survival lesson.

"That's fine. We're taking the High Road, and barefoot is better than bad shoes up there. Now come on." Remarin flung open the window and looked out into the street. So far their little adventure hadn't attracted any outside attention. More likely, Salvar had paid off anyone he thought would scream for the watch, so as long as the fighting stayed in the house, no one was going to say anything. He stepped out onto the narrow ledge and stretched for the eaves. His fingers found the slimmest purchase, and he pulled himself up onto the roof. He lay flat on his stomach, reaching down for the boy.

"Kit, can you grab my hand?" Remarin whispered.

"I . . . I think so." The child's voice quavered. Remarin didn't blame him. If he slipped, the boy would fall to a hopefully quick and definitely painful death on the cobblestones below. Kit stood on tiptoes on the ledge, then on one foot as he strained to grab the thief's dangling hands, then their fingers locked and Remarin pulled the boy to safety.

"You're heavier than you look," Remarin panted as they lay on the roof.

"You're just weaker than you thought," Kit replied. The boy scrambled to his feet and said, "Which way?"

Remarin pulled himself up to a crouch beside Kit and pointed off to the east. "That way. We'll follow this line of buildings all the way to the docks, then hop over a couple of alleys and into the attic of a man I know."

"You mean a thief," Kit said. Remarin looked at the boy, startled by the accusation in his eyes.

"Not everyone I know is a thief. This man happens to be a shade, I'll have you know." Remarin started off across the rooftops, walking toe to heel to keep his steps silent.

"What's a shade?" Kit asked, matching his steps to the larger man's.

Remarin sped up to get ahead of the boy, hoping to hide his flush. "A shade is someone who buys stolen goods from thieves."

"Oh, but he's not a thief, *oh no*, mustn't think *that*."

"Shut up, Kitten."

"It's Kit. Don't call me Kitten."

"If you're going to follow me around like a puppy, I should call you Spot."

"Well, what am I supposed to call you? Mr. Thief seems a little silly." Remarin held up a hand and they slowed their march across the rooftops as they crossed a house that the thief knew belonged to a light sleeper with a crossbow and a willingness to punch holes in his own roof in an attempt to skewer "squirrels."

"Call me Remarin, Prince of the High Road." He tried for a grandiose bow but almost lost his balance on the pitched roof and had to frantically windmill his arms to regain his balance.

Call him Remoron, King of the Jackasses.

The boy's eyes flew wide and he whirled around, looking for the unseen speaker. "Who said that? Where are you?"

"Wait—you heard that?" Remarin put out a hand to steady the boy, whose balance had grown precarious, as he looked for the source of the voice in his head.

"Of course I heard it. Someone making fun of your name. But where is he? I don't see anyone."

"He's my dagger," Remarin said simply. Kit gaped at him, then stared at the dagger with its softly glowing red hilt.

"Your dagger?"

"Yeah, his name is Trand. He's trapped in the dagger for a thousand years because he managed to irritate a powerful wizard."

I irritated him? I seem to recall there being two of us in the wizard's tower that night.

"Yes, but I'm not the one trapped inside a knife for an eon," Remarin replied.

Only because I got caught.

"Proving that I am the Prince of the High Road," Remarin said, bowing. This time without the balance troubles. "But that doesn't explain how you heard Trand talking. Who are you?" He peered more closely at the child, who ducked his head at the scrutiny.

"I told you. I'm Kit. I'm nobody special. And aren't we still on the roof that you were worried about?" Remarin's eyes widened as he heard a commotion from below.

"Dammit! Run!" The thief and boy sprinted across the slate roof, sending loose tiles to skitter down the rooftop and shatter in the courtyard below. A crossbow bolt erupted through the roof just in front of Kit, causing the boy to skid to a halt and look around wildly.

Remarin dashed back a few steps and grabbed the boy's arm. "Don't stop! He needs time to reload. Better to be somewhere else when he does." The pair reached the end of the row of connected homes and Remarin hung a hard left, pulling Kit after him. No longer running across the relatively level ridge beams, now the thief and the boy bounded up and down the pitched sides of roofs and leapt from building to building. Remarin looked back once and was relieved to see the terror in the boy's face had faded to exultation as he reveled in the night's chase.

This is the best part of the job, he thought. *The night air, the freedom, the cash . . .*

The people climbing up on the roof ahead of you with swords that want to chop you into kibble. . . Trand's dry voice snapped Remarin back to the task at hand, and he looked ahead at the pair of guards trying to find their footing in their heavy, hobnailed boots. The chain mail restricting their movement was bad enough, but they didn't stand a chance of catching anyone with those silly boots on.

Remarin reached into a pocket on his pants and pulled out a string of firecrackers, lighting one and flinging the string at the guards. The small poppers burst into life, blinding the guards and startling them with the flashes and bangs. The first guard snatched the string of explosives out of the air, then threw it back over his shoulder as a pair of firecrackers went off in his hand. He clutched his injured fingers, lost his footing, and tumbled over the edge. Remarin never looked back to see what happened to him, just assumed from the resounding crash from the street below that it didn't end well. The second guard fared a little better, keeping his feet until the firecrackers stopped exploding in his face. By the time the smoke cleared and he could focus on anything other than not falling off the roof, Remarin and Kit were out of sight.

The thief and boy sprinted across the rooftops, silent as the night itself. Remarin listened for any other signs of pursuit, but heard nothing. Moments later, he waved Kit to a stop and knelt in a shadowed corner on a sloped rooftop of a nondescript building near the docks. Remarin knocked three times on the roof, waited a moment, then knocked three more times. After a long pause, he repeated the series of knocks once, then twice.

Finally, after several minutes of rapping, a section of slate roof several feet away slid open and a bald head poked out. The old man grinned like a skeleton through a mouth of missing teeth. "Remarin, are you ever going to learn which section of roof to knock on? You're driving my wife crazy pounding on the roof of her bedroom."

Remarin dashed over to the man, motioning for Kit to follow. "Gaither, are you ever going to divorce that harpy? You know she hates me and all the rest of your suppliers."

"Aye, but she's got great . . . tracts of land." The man finished hurriedly after a glance at the boy. "Who's the brat?"

"I dunno—"

"I'm Kit," the boy said, holding out his hand to shake. Gaither shook it, then looked at the boy, brow furrowed. "You look familiar, boy. Have you been here before?"

"I don't even know where 'here' is, so it's not likely, sir." The boy slipped past Remarin into the attic. The thief followed, and Gaither closed the roof entrance behind them. The "attic" was little more than a landing at the top of a flight of stairs. Gaither picked up a lit candle and led the pair down the stairs into his storeroom. This was Gaither's "private" storeroom, where he received and catalogued his more exotic items, as well as items of undocumented provenance, like the gems that Remarin started pouring out of pouches and pockets.

"Now hold on there, Remarin," the old man protested. "I don't know that I got any use for all this, much less the time to sort it. Why don't you run this stuff through Salvar? He usually handles your bulk trade. You know I only like dealing in currency or rare artifacts."

"Salvar's dead," Remarin replied, never pausing in the unloading of his packs. "I killed him an hour ago. He betrayed me and this kid to somebody who wants me dead. Don't worry, they're not very good."

"How not good are we talking about?" Gaither didn't flinch at the news, just started picking up the jewelry and gems Remarin was unpacking, weighing each stone in his hand then dropping it into a velvet-lined box he pulled down off a shelf. The jewelry he examined more closely, wedging a small glass circle in front of one eye to magnify the details and maker's mark.

"They tried to follow me across the rooftops in full armor. It didn't go well," Remarin said.

They're pretty stupid, but the ones in Salvar's place seemed well equipped.

"Hello, Trand." The shade nodded at Remarin's belt.

Hello, Gaither. How is the wife?

"Irritable. So let's try not to cause a disturbance."

Talk to the idiot that still has arms and legs.

"As opposed to the idiot trapped inside a dinner utensil."

Try to carve a turkey with me. I dare you.

"Gaither, what's all this garbage worth?" Remarin waved a hand over the assortment of gems and jewelry scattered across the counter. "Salvar came down with a bad case of the deads before he could pay me for swiping a gem, and now I've got to find someplace to foster this kid, too. I need some cash, you know it's all marketable stuff, even the jewelry, so let's skip the part where you lowball me, I threaten you, we argue, Inelle wakes up and screams at us both, and you finally give me a fair price so I'll just leave and you can go back to bed. Let's jump right to the fair price bit, Inelle will never know I was here, which means she'll never know *Trand* was here, which means she won't be depressed for a week about him being trapped in a dagger, and you get the idea."

"You're a bastard, Remarin."

"And you sell stolen shit for a living. Now that we've got that out of the way, what's it worth?"

"Twenty rulls. That's my best offer."

"Twenty-five," Remarin replied without pause.

"Done." Gaither handed out twenty-five octagonal gold coins, then tossed a silver to Kit. "For luck, boy. You'll need it if you're throwing in with this one. Don't forget what happened to his last partner." The old man nodded at the dagger flickering on Remarin's belt.

"Trand was more than my partner. He was my best friend."

I still am.

"He was *my* wife's little brother," the shade shot back.

I still am.

"I'll get it fixed. Somehow." Remarin didn't meet the older man's eyes as he spoke.

"Get out. Let me get back to my bed." Gaither turned a knob by the counter and a piece of paneling slid open into the candle shop that was the legitimate business hiding his less-legal enterprise. Remarin and Kit followed him into the front of the shop, then out the front door. Remarin heard the sound of the door locking behind him and a bolt being thrown as he looked up and down the street, making sure they weren't observed.

He looked at the lightening sky to the east and took the boy's elbow. "Come on, Kitty-cat. We need to find a safe place to rest for the day."

"Kit. I told you not to call me that."

"Get over it, kid. Let's go." Remarin led the way through the twisting streets and alleys of the Poor Quarter, where the streets were so narrow that two wagons could barely pass side by side, and not at all in some places. They passed through the stink of the Tannery Row, the open Market that dominated the Poor Quarter, until they came out into a wider, cleaner street that bounded on the Merchant's Quarter. The buildings here were cleaner than in the rest of Lowtown, but still shabby. The sky was growing lighter by the moment, and the door of a house near the pair opened and a nervous-looking man stepped out, looked from side to side, settled on Remarin and Kit, then quickly glanced away as he scurried up the street into the Merchant's Quarter.

"What is he afraid of?" Kit asked.

"I'd guess his wife," Remarin said dryly.

"What do you mean?" The boy looked up at the thief, who just shook his head.

"You'll see, kid." Remarin went up to the door the man just came out of and knocked softly. Kit stood on the street, looking up at him. After a few moments, a beautiful blond woman opened the door, her body shrouded in luxurious silks that displayed more than they hid. She smiled at Remarin and threw her arms around him with a high-pitched squeal. She held their embrace for perhaps a second or two longer than absolutely necessary, and Remarin's face was flushed when he turned and gestured to Kit.

"Oh!" the blond woman exclaimed when she saw him. "How adorable! Come in, come in, dear. We'll find the two of you a nice, quiet room to rest in."

Remarin and Kit followed the woman inside, and Kit looked around in wonder. Everything was draped in silk and other soft fabrics, even the candle-globes. It gave the rooms a gentle, soft feeling, like walking through a dream. Everything smelled nice, too.

"What is this place?" Kit asked. "Is this an inn?"

Remarin blushed again, and the pretty woman chuckled. "Not exactly, Kit," the thief said. "People don't usually sleep here. I have a special arrangement with the . . ."

"Proprietress," the blond woman added as Remarin stumbled over his words.

"Proprietress. That's a good one," Remarin agreed. "I have a special arrangement that I can rest in one of the unused rooms whenever I need to in exchange for performing certain errands for the girls that work here."

"What kind of errands? I thought you were a thief," Kit asked.

"Sometimes people . . . receive services here and don't want to pay for them. Or they need to be persuaded to pay. I take care of that."

"Oh," Kit said, his voice small. "So you're a basher."

"I prefer the term Payment Specialist."

Kid's right. You're a basher.

"You keep quiet," Remarin said to his dagger.

"You're a basher with a talking knife," Kit said. "I don't think I like you."

Remain found himself stung by the child's casual condemnation, and he wasn't sure why, but he found the need to defend himself. "I don't think I care. I think all I care about is keeping us both alive long enough for me to figure out what to do with you, then getting the hell out of town for a little while. I don't know who paid Salvar to kill me, but the fact that there are a lot of people to choose from makes me realize that I should probably be somewhere else for the foreseeable future. But I can't get out of here tonight. I'm tired, I'm hungry, and I have to take care of you. So we're sleeping here, and we'll figure everything else out in the morning." The blond woman stopped in front of a door at the end of the hall, a small smile playing across her face.

"You shut up, Karin," Remarin said. He knocked on the door, waited a few seconds, then opened it and walked in. The room was an exquisitely appointed bedroom, with a separate sitting area and a huge canopied bed swathed in silks. The sitting area contained a small two-person sofa, a small table, and a comfortable-looking chair, all in matching dark woods and burgundy cushions. On the table sat a tray with several sandwiches, a bottle of wine, two glasses and a small glass of cold milk, chilled enough that water droplets were forming on the sides. A beautiful woman in her thirties sat on the sofa in a gown almost the same color as the cushions, but with a brighter, more blood-red tone. Her dark curls spilled down across an expanse of exposed cleavage, and even at the late hour, her face was made up perfectly.

Remarin walked in and sat on the couch, reaching for the wine, and turning the bottle up. He took a long drink and wiped his mouth with the back of his hand. "Good stuff, Marie. Thanks for the food."

"You're a barbarian, Remarin." The woman chuckled as she took the bottle from him and poured herself a glass. She looked up at where Kit still stood by the door. "Come in child, I don't bite. At least, I don't bite babies." She gave him a grin that seemed a little less innocent than it should be, and Remarin broke out in a laugh.

"Leave him alone, woman, the poor boy's blushing. Come over here, Kit. The food's good, the milk is for you, and we're safe here. Marie has helped me out of a few close spots over the years. I trust her more than anyone."

Anyone still human, he means.

Remarin glanced down at the dagger. "Yeah, anyone except Trand. Now sit. Eat." The thief took a sandwich and shoved half of it in his mouth, then took another long swallow of wine to wash it down.

Marie elbowed him. "Leave the child alone. He's shy." Turning her attention back to Kit, she said, "It's all right, child. I haven't altered the food or drink in any way. If you'd like, I'll taste the milk so you know it's fine." She smiled at Kit kindly, and he stepped slowly over to the table, looking every second like a scared rabbit.

"No, thank you, ma'am. That won't be necessary. If Remarin trusts you, well . . . he saved me, so I have to trust him." Kit sat on the edge of the chair and began to eat a sandwich. The boy was obviously ravenous, so once the first sandwich was gone, he looked to Marie, who nodded at him. He almost inhaled the second sandwich, then drank down his milk in two big gulps.

"Thank you, ma'am. I appreciate it," Kit said when he was finished.

"You're very welcome, young man. What did you say your name was?" Marie asked.

"It's Kit, ma'am. What is this place?" The boy looked around at the silks and the finery.

Marie and Remarin shared a look. Remarin gave a little shrug as if to say, "I'm not telling him," and Marie sighed. "This is a pleasure house, child."

Kit's face took on a frightened look and he sprang to his feet. "A brothel?"

"Yes, son. It's a brothel." Remarin grinned at the boy. "You're a little younger than most of the customers here, but I don't think you need to be quite so alarmed. Sit down, child. No one's going to hurt you."

"But that man, Salvar. He talked about trying to sell me to a brothel. He said they'd pay top dollar for . . ."

"I don't want to know what Salvar said, child," Marie cut in, her voice hard. "I just want to know that he's dead." She looked over at Remarin, who nodded.

"Good," she continued. Marie looked at Kit with a stern expression. "Now let me be very clear. I do not keep children in my house. And I don't cater to men that like children. That is abhorrent, and I will not tolerate it. You are as safe here as in your mother's arms, and probably safer. You and Remarin can sleep here tonight, and tomorrow we'll figure out somewhere for you to stay. But it won't be here. I can't have a child roaming about learning things he shouldn't learn at your age. Now you two rest, and I'll be back to bring you some breakfast in the morning. The water closet is next door on the right. *Don't* go into any other rooms." Marie stood in a rustle of silk and satin and swept grandly from the room.

"Thank you for the food," Kit said softly to her back as she left.

"Well done, Kitten. You just annoyed the woman who is solely responsible for keeping us alive for the next day. Hope she wasn't too offended." Remarin started taking off his boots, then stood and took off his sword belt. He hung the belt on one of the bedposts, then finished disrobing.

The thief stood in the middle of the room in his black leggings and nothing else. Kit could see a long scar across his ribs, and a puckered circular scar on one shoulder. "What?" Remarin asked. "Get undressed. Unless you want to sleep in your clothes. I don't care. I'm going to bed." He climbed into the canopied bed and flopped his head down on one of the pillows. "Blow out the candle when you're ready to sleep." Moments later, the thief was snoring.

Kit sat up for a long time, wondering exactly what had happened. The night had started ordinarily enough, but veered off course somewhere after dinner.

Are you going to say something? The voice in Kit's head was somehow quieter than other times the dagger had spoken, and he knew that Trand was speaking only to him.

"No," Kit whispered.

Why not? It's not like he'll do anything bad to you. Remoron's a good guy, if kinda stupid.

"He seems like a good person. But I don't know who I can trust right now. How did you know?"

I'm made of magic, remember?

"Well, I'm not telling him, and I'd really rather you didn't either."

Fine, I'll keep your little secret. But don't blame me if it gets you both killed.

"I think if I get killed, I won't be able to care." Kit stood, blew out the lamp, and curled up on the sofa amid the sounds of giggling from the rooms beside them, and Remarin's snoring.

CHAPTER 4

ake up. Marie's bringing breakfast. Kit started awake at the voice in his head and almost fell off the sofa. A ew seconds later, a gentle knock came on the door, and it opened softly. Marie slid into the room, almost silently, carrying a tray loaded down with eggs, bacon, and bowls of porridge. She set the tray down on the table and motioned for Kit to keep quiet. A sly smile flickered across her lips as she crept slowly toward the bed where Remarin lay snoring. She leaned over the sleeping thief's face, then let out a surprised squeal as Remarin came to life and wrapped his arms around her.

"Good morning, love." He grinned and pulled her into the bed with him, kissing her soundly on the lips and the neck.

A-hem. Children present. Trand's voice pierced everyone's mind, and Remarin froze with his lips on the woman's collarbone. He let go and Marie slid out of bed, straightening her mussed skirts and bodice.

"I hate you sometimes, Trand."

And good morning to you, too, Remoron. Marie. Kit got the mental sense of the dagger giving a mock-courtly bow to the woman, who blushed and gave a half-curtsy in response.

"Good morning, Trand. Kit." Marie nodded in the boy's direction, and Kit gave her a little seated bow.

"Well, now that we're being insufferably polite, let's eat. Maybe if we're all being polite, Trand won't fart at the table." Kit giggled, and Marie covered her mouth with her hand.

"Excuse me, ma'am. Which room did you say was the washroom?" Kit asked quietly.

"Out the door and to the right, love. It's the room right next door," she replied. The child was gone for a few long moments, then returned, out of breath and flushed. He darted inside and pressed his back to the door. Remarin didn't look up from his plate, but Marie noticed the boy's crimson cheeks at once. "You went into the wrong room, didn't you?" she sighed.

Kit just nodded.

"Well, I suppose you already knew what kind of place this was, didn't you?"

The boy hesitated, then shook his head. "I knew it was a brothel, but I didn't know exactly what that meant." He blushed again as Marie's laughter spilled across the room.

"Oh dear. Remarin, what are you doing bringing an innocent child here?"

"This is one of the safest places for a child I know, Marie," the thief said around a mouthful of egg.

"For his body, maybe, but you seem to have struck the poor child dumb with the sights in the hall." Marie smacked Remarin playfully on the back of his head.

"You're not hurt, are you, child?" Remarin asked, a flicker of actual concern darting across his features.

"N-no," Kit managed to say after a long pause.

"Good, then. So you saw some things that maybe you shouldn't. You'll learn all about that sort of thing soon enough. Now have some breakfast." Remarin waved a hand at the untouched plate beside him. Kit sat beside the thief and tucked into the meal. It was better than expected, truth be told, and he soon polished off the entire plate, and some of Remarin's extra bacon besides.

"You were hungry, child," Marie remarked carefully.

"Yes, ma'am."

"You're awfully polite, even now that you know what we are here." The woman raised an eyebrow.

"I was taught that you should treat everyone with respect, and they will be more likely to treat you the same way," Kit replied.

Remarin snorted, but Trand's dry voice filled Kit's ears. *That's a fine way to go through life, child. Too bad some others don't agree.*

"Shut up, silverware," Remarin said.

"What's next?" Kit asked after Remarin finished the last of his coffee.

"What do you mean?"

"I mean what's next? Last night a man you trusted tried to kill you, so you stole all his valuables and sold them for enough money to get far from here. But you rescued me and brought me here. I don't think you brought me here to sell because the lady said this isn't the kind of place that takes . . . boys, or children at all, so I think you're just stopping here to figure out what's next. So what's next?"

"Marie, did I ever tell you how much I hate smart kids?" Remarin said.

"No, but since you hate almost everyone, I just assumed."

"Well I do. I hate smart kids. I hate anyone smarter than me."

Which encompasses a tremendous number of people, Trand interjected.

"And at least one overgrown toothpick," the thief shot back.

Remarin looked at Kit, and his face was serious. "You're right, Kitty-claws. I don't know what's next, but I know I've got to get out of here. I stole a gem last night from the king's brother, and while that wouldn't usually worry me, when I tried to hand it over to the guy who hired me to steal it, I got ambushed. And had to kill one of my best clients. And then I rescued a kid from his bedroom, which I don't regret, but which will certainly complicate matters."

"Thank you for that, by the way," Kit said politely.

"Happy to help. Anyway, I don't know what's going on, and I don't really care. I've got enough money to get halfway across the world, so that's where I'm going. But I need to figure out something to do with you. Because I can't just leave you in a whorehouse, no matter how educational it may be. And I don't think I can just leave you out on the street, either. Something tells me you aren't really a street kid, so that wouldn't be right."

"Can't I just come with you?" Kit asked.

"No, kid. I'm sorry, but you can't. I don't know exactly where I'm going, or how I'm going to get there. So I can't take you with me. And besides, I hate smart kids. So put on those boots that Marie brought you, and let's figure out where we can deposit you that you'll be safe from whores, thieves, and other unsavory characters like us." He grinned at the end to take some of the sting out of it.

Kit opened his mouth to say something, but his eyes filled with tears and he found himself unable to speak. He tried again, but as he drew in breath to speak, the door flew open and a girl not more than a few years older than Kit came in, breathless.

"Guards, Madame Marie! There are City Guardsmen at the door, demanding entry. They claim that you're harboring a known fugitive from the King's Justice and they'll burn the house down if we don't let them in." The girl's eyes darted around the room as though looking for an escape route.

"Did they happen to mention who this fugitive might be?" Marie asked calmly. She'd never risen from her seat, but Remarin was already up and belting on his sword and dagger. Kit was hurriedly shoving his feet into the new boots when the girl pointed.

"Him, ma'am. The guards are after him." Marie followed the girl's finger as it wavered between the two thieves.

"Remarin? Well, that's nothing new. The Watch is after him almost monthly."

"No, ma'am, not Remarin. They said he might be with the fugitive, but he wasn't important," the girl replied.

"Hey!" Remarin objected.

"Then who are they looking for?" Marie asked.

"Him, ma'am." The young whore pointed straight at Kit. "The boy. They're after him."

Pounding feet echoed down the hallway after the girl, and Remarin slammed the heavy wooden door shut and pulled a table over to block it. He threw back a rug from the center of the floor and opened a secret door there.

Kit's eyes widened. "How did you know that was there?"

"As much as I hate to admit it, this is not the first time I've had to run away from a whorehouse," Remarin replied, pointing down the ladder into the darkness.

"Although it may be the first time that a disagreement over payment is not the reason." Marie smiled sweetly and Remarin gave her a quick kiss on the lips before roughly shoving Kit toward the hole.

"Let's go, Kitten."

"I told you, don't call me—" The child's words cut off as the pounding feet in the hallway stopped and changed to pounding fists on the door. Kit scampered down the ladder with Remarin right behind. The dimness shifted to absolute blackness as Marie closed the trapdoor, and Remarin drew his dagger.

CHAPTER 5

The pale crimson glow of the dagger's gem gave them some light to see by, but very little. Remarin led the child through twisting tunnels mostly by memory, trying only to remember the way out, not to dwell on the things that he'd seen and done in these tunnels in years past.

"Where are we—" Kit began, but Remarin clapped a hand over his mouth.

The thief pressed his lips almost to Kit's ear and breathed, "Shut up. Everyone involved in anything underhanded in the city knows these tunnels, if not quite as well as I do. But none of them know who you are. Let's keep it that way a little longer, shall we?"

Kit nodded, and Remarin took his hand away. They continued through the darkness for a little while, making numerous right and left-hand turns. Remarin never hesitated, following an unseen path as if he'd walked it a thousand times before. After an interminable time, they came to what looked like a dead end. Remarin felt around on the apparently solid wall, then rapped three times sharply on a particular stone. He waited for a count of five, then rapped three times on a different stone. The stones rang hollow, and after another five-count, a deep grinding noise came from the other side of the wall, and the stones separated to reveal a dimly lit chamber.

Remarin slid through the opening in the stones like a shadow, and Kit followed close on his heels. The child looked around the room, taking everything in. The room was maybe thirty feet on a side, with two visible hallways leading out. Four men sat around a small round table in one corner, barely looking up at the new arrivals. A long bar took up one wall, and a bartender so tall he almost had to stoop from hitting his head on the low ceiling polished the gleaming wood surface with a spotless bar rag while two patrons stared into their empty beer mugs.

"Remarin, you bastard, you owe me money!" A bellow came from one of the hallways, followed by a stout man with flaming red hair and beard. He brandished a dagger and a scowl, but Remarin never batted an eye.

"Gortan, I owe everybody money, get in line. But I need you, so come over here." The thief waved the angry man over to a table and held up two fingers to the bartender. The giant cocked his head at Kit, and Remarin nodded. Kit sat at the table with Remarin and the redheaded man as the bartender brought over two beers and a mug of water. Remarin and Gortan clinked mugs together, and Remarin passed three of the golden rulls across the table.

"Now we're square, right?"

"Well, we'd be square except for—"

Gortan's next word never made it from his lips because there was a ruby-hilted dagger pressed tightly against them. "Think carefully before you answer, Gortan. I've had a long night and I'm not in a mood to be jerked around."

The redheaded man's eyes widened, and he nodded slightly. Remarin pulled the knife away, and Gortan said, "Yep, we're square. If anything, I owe you a copper, so I'll pick up the price of the beers. Sound fair?"

Remarin leaned back in his chair, the dagger vanishing as quickly as it had appeared. "Fair. I need passage out of town."

"To where?"

"Gorix." Gortan let out a low whistle.

"That's a long way to travel, Remarin. Should I wonder why?"

"You shouldn't, but you will. And you can wonder, but I won't be telling you. How much?"

Gortan thought for a minute, then started counting on his fingers, then pulled out a knife and started rough calculations on the scarred surface of the table. After several strikethroughs and muttered curses, he raised his head. "Seventeen rulls. I'm sorry, Remarin, but that's the best I can do. If you can double up as a guard, I can get five of that taken off, but the kid makes it expensive."

"Fine. Make it happen. I'm not going to play guard, though. Just book it for seventeen, and keep it quiet. Is there somewhere here we can hole up until the next wagon leaves?"

"I'll put you up at my place. Serenia has forgotten all about the last time." Gortan motioned for the bartender, who brought two more beers.

"I hope so. She threatened to cut off my privates if she ever saw me again."

"She didn't mean that." Gortan buried his face in his beer. Remarin stared evenly at him over the lip of his own mug. "Okay, she meant it, but she told me a couple weeks ago that she might not kill you if I brought you home for a visit again."

"As long as I stay away from her sister." Remarin took a long drink and smiled as Gortan sprayed beer all over the table. The men finished their beer in quiet conversation. Kit tuned them out, preferring to examine this underground pub, or safe house, or whatever it was. After a few minutes looking around, Kit went back to Remarin and tugged on his sleeve.

"What's up, Kit?" the thief asked.

Shit. Trand's mental voice spoke to them both as Kit began to whisper.

"I think we should go. I think we're in a lot of trouble."

"Why would you think that?" Remarin asked. "I trust Gortan here with my life, and I've known half these cutthroats even longer. If we're not safe from the Watch here, we're not safe anywhere."

"Then we're not safe anywhere. Look around, Remarin. The bartender hasn't poured a drink since ours, and he's polished that bar so clean it squeaks. The men playing cards stopped betting as soon as we walked in, and even the whore behind you is wearing knives."

The kid's right, Remoron. You've walked right into a trap.

Remarin's gaze went slowly to Gortan's face. The round little man held up his hands to protest, then his shoulders sagged. "Sorry, Remarin. The money was really, really good."

"I hope Serenia enjoys spending it on your coffin, you bastard." Remarin growled and flicked a hand out at Gortan's face. The fat man's head snapped back, a small throwing knife buried in one eye. Remarin leapt to his feet, kicking the table over in front of him as the bar erupted in chaos. The card players all drew swords and started to move in while the whore barred the door and drew a pair of knives from holsters on her legs. Remarin drew his rapier in one hand and Trand in the other, then turned to face six well-armed men charging across the room.

He looked down at Kit. "Can you fight?"

"N-no."

"Then try not to trip me!" Remarin handed Kit a knife and turned back to the fight. "Don't stab me, either!"

That would be my doing, not the child's, a dry voice echoed in their heads. Kit took a good look at the blade and gaped. *Close your mouth, child. It's unseemly.*

"Why you?"

Because I'm the best chance you've got of staying alive. Now just relax and let me do all the work. Kit tried to relax, which was hard to do in a barroom full of thrashing bodies and flashing steel, but eventually felt a consciousness pushing outward from the dagger, pushing to be let in. Kit focused on pulling the consciousness in, and in a matter of seconds *felt* Trand, like they were suddenly sharing a body.

Which they were, and it suddenly became a body that knew how fight. Trand took over as the whore stabbed at Remarin's back, ducking under the woman's arms to slash tendons in the elbows, then dance around behind to hamstring her and cut her throat. The woman bled out onto the hard-packed earth floor, but Trand had already moved Kit's body away and into a new fight. The dagger's consciousness blotted out all of Kit's fear, all of the horror at the bloodshed, all of the panic at being chased by armed mercenaries. All that remained was the fight, and it was *glorious.* Cut, parry, thrust, slash, stab, dodge, kick—all parts of the deadly dance that Trand performed in Kit's body.

Remarin was no less an artist once Kit's safety was assured. His sword and dagger flashed again and again, and time and time blood flowed from his blades. He took down all but one of the attackers and was poised to block and return a dagger thrust through the heart when a cold voice behind him said, very simply, "Stop."

Remarin and his opponent froze, a slow smile spreading across the mercenary's face. Remarin turned to see a slender man dressed all in black holding Kit by the collar. He had a knife at the boy's throat, and the child's eyes were wide with terror. Remarin put away his weapons but turned to cast a warning look at his nearest opponent, who instantly stopped his approach and stepped back, hands high.

"What do you want?" Remarin asked through gritted teeth. He locked eyes with Kit and shook his head slightly as the child struggled. The mercenary delivered a casual slap to the head that crossed Kit's eyes.

"I have what I want. I have the child. Now I want to kill you, but that's just a bonus. Men, destroy him."

So much for long speeches, Trand's wry voice cut into Kit's head as the dagger suddenly appeared in the child's hand.

How? Kit thought.

I'm magic. I can return myself to my wielder's hand. Now wield me. Kit didn't hesitate, just stabbed backward with the dagger and felt Trand sink through the mercenary leader's leather armor like butter. The black-clad assassin let out a small *oof,* then collapsed to the floor. Kit jerked wildly away, and the sound of ripping fabric pierced the silence of the room as Kit's ratty tunic finally gave way and fell to pieces, still clutched in the merc's dead fist.

"Uh. . . Kit? Is there something you wanted to tell me?" Remarin asked. He had a very confused look on his face, matching the baffled look of the mercenary he'd just skewered.

"Tell you about what, Remarin?" Kit asked in a sugar-sweet, too-innocent voice.

"Uh . . . those." He pointed to Kit's chest, where a pair of small but well-formed breasts sat high in the middle of her ribcage.

"What about them?" Kit asked with a saucy grin.

"They're . . ."

"They're breasts, Remarin. I'm sure you've seen them before. After all, we did just flee a whorehouse." Kit was obviously enjoying the thief's discomfort, but she finally took pity on him and retrieved the pieces of her tunic and arranged herself in some semblance of propriety.

"Why do you have breasts, Kit?" Remarin asked when his mouth worked again.

"Because I'm a girl, Remarin. Now can we leave? I think I know who wants to kill me, and I'd really rather not be here if he sends more people."

"And who is 'he'?"

"Uncle Alexander. I think he wants to kill me."

"Uncle Alexander. As in Alexander Rutvor, Prince of Veosia?"

"That's the one. I think you broke into his house last night and stole a gem? That was all part of the plan. I was spending the night there with my cousin Alexi, and I was supposed to be killed by this terrible thief who stole Uncle's precious gem. Except the assassin he sent in murdered Alexi instead while I slept in Alexi's bed, then it all went pear-shaped, I had to run out in the middle of the night, I ended up captured by the assassin who took me to your friend Salvar's house to be slaughtered, which you were still to be blamed for, by the way, and then you showed up and things got *really* bad."

"Who are you that he wants you dead, Kit. Wait . . . Kit . . ."

Wait for it. Wait for it.

"Son of a bitch!" The words exploded from Remarin, and he sat down on a nearby unbroken chair.

"Yes. I'm Crown Princess Kitarina Rutvor. My father is dying, and I'm supposed to be queen once my eighteenth birthday arrives. In three weeks. But my uncle thinks I should be dead by then instead. Now can we run away, please?

CHAPTER 6

Remarin swore. He swore loudly and creatively, and for quite a long time. He ran out of the usual swear words after insulting Gortan's family, his heritage, his religion, his sexual prowess or lack thereof, and all generations of his family yet to be born. Then he moved on to all mercenaries in general, royal families, smart-arsed little girls, double-crossing royal bastards, politics, and then all the gods in particular, one after the other.

Kit sat calmly on a stool at the bar while the enraged thief went through his litany of curses. After several minutes of watching the small man stomp around at an impressive volume, she glanced down at the bloody blade in her hand. *Is he likely to be at this for a while?*

Oh yes, Trand replied. *Once he gets a head of steam on him, he can rant for hours. I once knew him to swear for a full day once when a job went south on us.*

I don't suppose it could go much more south than learning that all your trusted friends have sold you out and that you're probably being hunted by one of the most powerful men in the land.

Probably not. You should find something to amuse yourself with until he's done. And maybe a rag to clean me with? I hate getting dried blood in the crease between my blade and my hilt.

Kit slid down off her stool and knelt by the mercenary she had stabbed. She carefully wiped Trand off on the man's sleeve and set him on the bar. His sheath was still around Remarin's waist, but Kit wasn't quite in the mood to hand the thief a blade at that moment. She searched the body of the dead mercenary, finding nothing more interesting than a purse with a few silver coins in it and a nicely crafted dagger. Kit sighed at the state of her clothing and moved over to the dead whore. Her cut throat had bled spectacularly, but most of it had missed her blouse, so Kit stripped the woman, apologizing under her breath at the immodesty she was leaving the corpse in, but after some wrangling of skirts and blouse and tying knots in things to fit her slim frame and cover up a few bloodstains, the girl was more or less dressed. At least in something better than the slave rags she had been in. The whore had a gold piece stamped with the likeness of Kit's father on one side to go with her couple of silvers, and Kit sat down for a moment, just looking at the golden image before her.

It was her father in his glory, strong chin, wavy hair tied back, and a stern look on his face. She remembered that look from countless scoldings and from times she had seen him deal with his Councilors. Her father was a hard man, a warrior forced off the battlefield and into the throne room, but he was always fair. She looked at the lines of his face, mentally comparing her uncle Alex to his older brother. Alex's jawline would be hidden by his floppy jowls, and his chin was so weak it had to bring a few friends along. Her father's brother had always enjoyed the trappings of power, but had never worked to earn it.

Until now, she corrected herself. Now he was working to steal what should be her inheritance. And her life as well. Well, not if she could help it. Not if she and Remarin could . . . Her attention snapped back to the ranting little thief who would stomp off and kick a corpse for a minute before returning to yell at dead Gortan some more and slap the turncoat's body around some more. Thankfully, dead Gortan did not respond. She smiled as she studied her unlikely savior. He was so . . . *small*. Half a foot under six feet tall, he was slender enough to almost slip between the bars of a jail cell. And that face, that strange little ferret-face, with his long, pointy nose and shock of black hair sticking everywhere atop his head. It looked like he had never met a comb. He had a strong chin, though, which was currently stuck out in an obstinate glare as he looked around the room for something else to punch or kick. His beady green eyes flicked over Kit, then back to land on her.

"What in the Nine Hells are you smiling at, Kitty-cat? You've gotten me killed, sure as the world. I'm a dead thief, and it won't even be my fault! I tried to do something good for a change and see where that left me! Dead! I'm dead, I tell you. They'll have me strung up outside the city gates with a pike up my arse and a rope around my neck. They'll kill me at both ends! They'll, they'll—*OW!*"

Remarin cut his rant short as Kit slapped him smartly across one cheek, then the other. "Are you quite finished? Because I'd really like to have less whining and bitching and more running and hiding, if that's quite all right with you."

"And where exactly do you suggest we go, Princess?" He said "Princess" as though it were a new word for "idiot."

"I thought we were going to Gorix?"

"That was when I thought we could get on a caravan. Now we can't, and we can't travel alone."

"So your friend Gortan was the only person in Bravis that hires people out for caravan guards?"

"Well, no, but . . ."

"But what?" The girl had moved to stand in front of Remarin by now and had her hands on her hips. She was tall enough to look the little thief in the eye without stretching too much, so she gave him her best challenging stare. It had always worked when her governesses hadn't wanted to do something her way.

It worked on men, too. Remarin held her gaze for a moment before looking away. "So we go to the caravansary and I job in as a guard. Won't be as good a rate as Gortan would have gotten me, but—"

"But it won't come with that pesky side of trying to kill you, either."

"That's fair enough, Little Princess."

"Who's calling who little, thief?" She reached out and ruffled his hair, surprised to see the older man blush at her touch.

❧

The next morning found Remarin sitting on the front steps of the Temple of Asentra, Goddess of the Fortunes and adopted patron deity of thieves and rapscallions. Remarin munched slowly on an apple as he watched the third caravan of the day depart by the Southern Gate for Gorix. Their fortunes had seemed bountiful when they arrived at the caravansary that morning—there were five caravans leaving that day for Gorix, more than Remarin could remember ever seeing in one day. Unfortunately for them, the word had gotten around that it was a good day for sell-swords and hangers-on, so the caravansary was teeming with grim-faced men and women bristling with steel. Remarin's slight build and Kit's mere presence had gotten them laughed out of the tent of the first two caravan leaders, who could little imagine what a "puny runt with a pig-sticker and a brat fresh off the teat" could do to keep their caravan safe. The third man had at least met with them, but Remarin beat a hasty retreat after seeing the man's head guard peering a little too closely at Kit for comfort.

The princess was back in her disguise as a boy, if you could call it that. Remarin had stood uncomfortably with his back to the girl as she wrapped her breasts in a long linen cloth, binding them tight to her chest before slipping on a loose tunic that morning. Her hair was chopped haphazardly, as if a blind man with only three fingers had been her barber. None of this could hide the high cheekbones and good teeth that marked her good breeding, but Remarin artfully smeared dirt all over her face, arms and hands and told her under no circumstances was she to speak to anyone. Her cultured accent and educated speech would give her away more surely than the chin she shared with her father, a chin that graced one side of every coin in Veosia.

"What now?" she asked. "Aren't there more caravans we can talk to?"

"What's the use?" Remarin stared out across the town square. "I've got as much chance of getting added to your uncle's High Council as I do of convincing a caravan to take me on as a guard. And they're right. You don't want little sneaky bastards like me for guards. You want big, burly brutes that will scare off the bandits from a hundred yards away. I don't scare anyone, I just sneak up behind them and slit their throats before they even know I'm shaving them."

"Then why not be a scout? Don't caravans use scouts? When we traveled outside the city, my father always sent men to scout ahead, and they were always the ones who were fastest and could think on their feet, not the big guard types."

"Aye, that might be worth a try. Perhaps you're not such an idiot after all, boy." Remarin tossed her the half-eaten apple and stood up, brushing the dirt from the seat of his pants. He glanced back at the temple and nodded. "And thank you, my Lady, for giving this idiot child one good idea to save one of your faithful."

CHAPTER 7

Remarin strode back into the huge tent that housed the caravansary for all of Bravis. Caravan leaders sat at the dozen or so large tables scattered about the room, and those wishing to join the wagon train approached with either money or hat in hand. If you were a merchant with a shipment of supplies, you paid the wagon master and took his credit chit for safe passage of your goods. If you were a guard, cook, wagon wright, or driver, you came as supplicant to these masters of their dirty rolling fiefdoms. Each table sat under a tall pole with various badges hanging from it, advertising what the caravan needed and where it was going. Some had arrows with one head, indicating a one-way trip, some had two-headed arrows, showing that the wagon train would pick up cargo at its destination and return to Bravis. Those were the prized passages as a guard hired for a round trip wouldn't have to look for return passage from his destination. They were also the rarest trips and the hardest to latch onto.

Remarin had no interest in returning to Bravis, at least in the near future. Almost everyone he'd liked had tried to kill him in the past few days, in no small part thanks to the dirt-encrusted little girl following in his wake. And that was another thing. She wasn't quite as little as he'd first thought. When he pulled her out of Gaither's upstairs room, he'd thought she was a boy, maybe twelve years old, but she was a princess, and almost eighteen, only a few years younger than Remarin. And certainly not shy about giving him a glimpse of her legs, or whatever else might come into view.

Get your mind out of the gutter, thief. She's so far out of your league as to not even be in the same game.

I know, Trand, but I have to think about her, don't I? It's my job to keep her safe.

It's your job to get us all the hell out of Bravis right now, Remoron. Keep your eyes on the prize.

The "prize" this time was a corpulent greasy man seated at a table with two hook-nosed thugs sitting beside him. Over his head was a sign indicating a one-way freight caravan to Gorix leaving that afternoon. But there were no hiring placards on the post, not even for a cook-helper. Remarin was useless in a kitchen, but even he could manage to wash wooden bowls without breaking too many of them.

"Can't you read, lout? I'm full." The fat man didn't even look up from his lunch, just continued shoveling rice into his mouth with dirty fingers. He picked out a piece of some unidentifiable meat and sucked it down, then reached for a tankard of ale.

"You need me." Remarin stood motionless in front of the table, the scowl on his face hiding the nervousness he felt.

"What do I need an undergrown sell-sword for? I have the Druckan Brothers." He waved a rice-covered hand, and the two guards stood up slowly, giving Remarin plenty of time to absorb exactly how enormous they were. Both men stood nearly seven feet tall, and they had mirror-image scars running from above one eye across their nose down to the edge of their mouth, pulling it up into a permanent sneer.

"How did you get those, cut yourselves shaving?" Remarin cocked the brothers a grin but got only stony silence in return. "All right, so you've got plenty of guards. But what about someone to keep you from needing so many guards?"

"What are you talking about, little man?" The fat man scowled up at Remarin.

"I'm talking about a scout. A pair of scouts, actually. My nephew and I make our money by securing yours. We ride out a few miles ahead of your caravan and clear the way. We take care of . . . obstacles, shall we say, and protect your caravan from attacks."

"That's what we do. You trying to put us out of a job, shrimp?" The larger of the Druckan brothers, if that was even really a way to discern between the two, glared at the thief.

Remarin held up his hands and gave the giant his very best "please don't eat me" smile. "Not at all, not at all. You see, in this day and age, a caravan must have guards. The roads are not safe, especially at night when not even the best scout can see the dangers that live outside the sanctity of our city walls. But with a good scouting team, like Kit and myself, you can use *fewer* guards. That way you save money and your cargo is still protected."

"So I hire you and the brat, and I don't have to hire two other guards? Doesn't sound like much of a bargain to me." The fat man brushed a few grains of rice off his enormous belly and waved for Remarin to go.

"It wouldn't be, if we just replaced two guards. But a caravan like yours must be traveling with what, eight to ten guards? A good scouting duo can easily replace four guards, and I am a master of the blade, so Kit and I can replace nearly five other guards of inferior quality. Obviously, you would want to keep the Gargantuan Brothers here employed, because of their obvious skill and wit, but you could dismiss almost half the rest of your force with us on board."

"Half the other guards are our cousins, runt. You want us to get them fired?" The smaller giant spoke.

"Of course not!" Remarin spread his hands wide but quickly returned one to Trand's hilt. "I want you to fire the guards you aren't related to! And maybe that one cousin you don't really like. You know, the stupid one."

The Druckans looked back and forth at each other, then down at the fat man. After several long seconds, the larger one spoke. "What do you think, Uncle? We let Ikan stay here and work in the kitchen, take Jakob, Drake, and the midgets here, and we all make more money?"

The fat man closed his eyes for a moment, seeming to contemplate the idea. After a few seconds, he began to snore softly, little rumbling fat man snores that blew rice and fetid breath across the tent. The smaller Druckan reached out and tapped his uncle on the top of the head. The man awoke with a start. "Wha? I have considered your proposition and have deigned to accept you into the service of Jaram's Caravan and Delivery Service as guards. You will serve under the leadership of my nephew Aram." He pointed to the larger brother. "He will kill you and bury your body in the desert if he decides he doesn't like anything about you."

Aram smiled down at Remarin, who suddenly had visions of his desiccated body buried under a sand dune. "Do a good job, little scout, and I won't have to dull my blade cutting through your neck. Besides, selling little boys in the slave markets of Gorix is a nuisance." With that, the giant turned and walked out of the tent, his brother close behind.

Remarin looked from the giants to the fat man and back again. Jaram glared at him, then flapped a fleshy paw at him to follow the brothers. Remarin and Kit hurried out into the sun, shielding their eyes from the dazzling glare as they looked for the caravan.

"I think it's that one," Kit said without an ounce of hope in her voice. Remarin looked across the open marshaling yard where the smaller Druckan was arguing with a huge dim-looking fellow. The dim one, apparently the fired Ikan, threw up his hands and stormed across the yard toward Remarin and Kit. He stopped in front of the pair, his shoulders heaving and his fists clenching and unclenching rapidly. He was at least half a foot taller and a hundred pounds heavier than Remarin, with a shaved head and a scar running down the side of his face, marking him as one of Jaram's guards.

I wonder if they all go to the same hoodlum to get their matching scars or if they do it in a mirror? Trand mused silently.

"You!" the big man bellowed. Remarin ducked aside as a fetid mix of onions, peppers, and beer breath cascaded over him. "You stole my job! Now I don't make any money! How am I supposed to eat now? I kill you, I get my job, and I get to sell the boy! Prepare to die, thief!"

"You're very excitable, aren't you?" Remarin said without moving for his weapon.

Ikan lifted a huge scimitar high over his head and brought it down with a rush of air. Remarin stepped aside and the blade buried itself into the packed earth of the marshaling yard. Remarin continued around behind the huge swordsman and flicked a knife out, just nicking the man's leg right behind the knee. Ikan spun around, moving fast for a heap of muscle piled on muscle, but far too slow to get a blade on the nimble thief. Remarin ducked under the looping slash, drawing a thin line of blood across the big man's ribcage. A second knife appeared in Remarin's other hand, and he tapped Ikan lightly on the side of the neck and danced a few steps backward.

"I could have killed you three times in the last five seconds, Ikan. I chose not to do so because you're upset, and we all make bad decisions when we're upset. But that was your warning. If you raise that stupid sword against me one more time, I'll leave you lying here bleeding out in the dirt, and I'll still have your job. The only difference is, you'll be dead. I just need to make one run. After that, I'm gone, and you can go back to thumping heads and banging camp followers. Here's two silver. That should keep you drunk for about the next week. By then, you'll have forgotten how much you hate me, and I'll be gone anyway. Now pick up your money, put away your sword, and get the Hells out of my sight before I open you up and show everyone what you had for breakfast."

Ikan glared at Remarin, but it was a different thief standing before him. Gone was the light-hearted nimble jester and second-story man he'd attacked. Standing before him was an ice-veined killer, with death in his eyes for anyone who crossed him. The crowd that had gathered when they thought they might see a big guy smash a little guy was gone, replaced by a lot of face-down not witnesses scurrying about their normal business watering horses and loading wagons. Ikan stood frozen for a long moment, then he nodded without a word and put away his sword. The stocky man picked two silver coins out of the dirt and walked away.

Aram, the larger of the giant Druckan brothers, walked up to Remarin and Kit. "Good job. I would have been put out if you had killed my cousin. Not angry, mind you, just a little put out. Do you have horses?"

"No." Remarin's face was stony.

"Take two from the picket line. Wear this badge, both of you. It will identify you as Jaram's men." He handed them each an octagonal piece of metal on a leather thong. On each side, it showed three diagonal slashes in blue through a yellow circle.

Aram turned to go, but Remarin grabbed his elbow. The big man turned slowly, looking down at the thief. Remarin stepped in very close and spoke, his voice low but steady. "I know you told your cousin if he killed me you'd give him his job back, and that's fine. But if you do anything to put this boy in jeopardy or make even the first joke about selling my nephew into slavery, I'll feed you your brother's balls while he watches. Do you understand me?"

Aram looked down at Remarin, and whatever he saw in the thief's eyes made him pale and step back. "I understand. You're part of the caravan. You are under my protection and my leadership. As long as you hold up your end of the bargain, I'll hold mine."

"And as long as that happens, I'll keep your goods and your brother's balls as safe as I can. But I make no promises about that cook's helper." Remarin nodded toward a pretty girl that Aram's brother was staring at.

The giant laughed and clapped Remarin on the shoulder. "I like you, little scout. You have more guts than brains, but I like that in a fighting man. Too much brains makes the sword slow. Now get your horses and gear from the quartermaster. We ride in a quarter hour."

CHAPTER 8

"I hate the desert," Kit said.

"I hate sand," Remarin replied with a grin.

"I hate the sun," Kit fired back.

"I hate scorpions."

"I hate eating beans for breakfast."

"I hate eating beans for everything." Remarin's grin almost touched his ears by now.

"I hate sleeping on the ground."

"I hate sleeping with sand in my butt crack."

"You win." Kit waved a hand at the thief. "I'm not going to talk about any of the uncomfortable places I've got sand, especially not with you."

"I wouldn't even dream of princesses having those places, Kitten, much less allowing sand or anything else to ever enter those hallowed fields."

"I told you, don't call me Kitten." The pair rode several miles ahead of the main caravan, keeping their eyes focused on the horizon for dust clouds where they shouldn't be, dunes that looked too perfectly formed, or any other indication that they weren't alone in the desert. The first eight days of the trip had been uneventful, except for the cook chasing Aram's brother Karam around the camp with a cleaver after he caught the giant and his helper/niece "washing the dishes" together after supper one evening.

Remarin laughed and opened his mouth to reply when suddenly he froze. "Stop," he said, holding up one hand to Kit. She reined in her horse beside him and looked up ahead.

"What is it?"

"There's someone out there." Remarin pointed to the dunes off to their left.

"What do you see?"

"See the line at the top of the dune?" He pointed again.

"Yes, but it looks like sand."

"It is sand, but it's sand covering something. The line is too straight; it doesn't look like the wind has blown the top off the dune there. There's probably a dugout in the back of the dune with a pipe through the front so they can see out."

"Have they spotted us?" Kit's head spun around as if expecting an attack from any direction.

"Almost certainly." Remarin's voice had slipped into that icy calm that Kit had only heard once before, when he threatened Ikan back at the caravansary.

"What do we do?" the girl asked.

"Normally I'd ride past, circle around and kill them in their blind, but this group seems a little better prepared than that. So we're going to do what they least expect."

"Which is?"

"We're going to let them spring their trap. As long as we know it's a trap, they'll be the ones caught in it. But first, I'm going to need an excuse to stay right here while the wagons catch up." With that, Remarin vaulted from the saddle and stormed around, waving his arms wildly and mouthing curses. He gestured at the sky, then at the horse, then back at the sky, never looking back to see if his quarry was watching.

"What the hell are you doing?" Kit asked, jumping off her horse to stand next to him.

"Look at my horse."

"What? Your horse is fine."

"Nope, he just pulled up lame. Must have been the heat and not enough water. He can't go any farther for a little while. We'll just have to stay here and wait for the rest of the train to arrive."

"Oh!" Kit's face lit up as understanding dawned, but she quickly turned it into a frown and a shake of her head.

"Exactly. Now we wait. And curse our ill fortune." Remarin pulled a tarp off his horse and set up a small lean-to beside a nearby dune.

It was less than an hour before the first of the Druckan brothers rode into view at the head of the caravan. The giant held up a hand to halt the wagon train, then rode ahead to where Remarin and Kit were sitting under their makeshift shelter.

"What's wrong? Why are you stopped?" The big man glared down from the back of his horse at the thief, the difference in their sizes made all the greater by the addition of a very sad horse. Remarin spared a moment to feel bad for the poor animal, who not only had to suffer through the desert heat, but also had to bear the bulk of the Druckan on its back. Remarin was pretty sure it was Aram who sat astride the beast, his feet almost dragging the ground.

"My horse pulled up lame," Remarin said, shaking his head at the huge man. Aram's eyes widened as he looked down at Remarin's hands, which were hidden from the bandit blind by his body and were gesturing wildly at the big man. The little thief mimed pulling his dagger and stabbing himself, then Aram, then pointed backward to the ambush point. Aram nodded his understanding and turned back to the caravan. Aram walked back to his brother at the last wagon, waving and gesticulating back at Remarin.

"When it all starts, get to cover in one of the middle wagons. The first wagon and the last one are the attack points; the three in the middle are safer. There's likely to be a lot of blades flying around, so keep your head down and help keep the children hidden."

Kit nodded and looked to the horizon. "I think it's all starting now." She pointed and Remarin turned. A plume of dust rose in the distance, less than a mile away and moving in their direction.

Remarin swore and ran to his horse, yelling for the Druckans as he did. Kit ran right behind him, then jumped on her horse and brought it back into the quickly forming circle of wagons. She pulled a long tube from her saddle and hopped into one of the wagons.

Remarin leapt onto his horse and rode toward the plume of dust, whipping his horse into a gallop.

What exactly are you doing, Remoron? Trand's dry voice echoed in his head.

I'm trying to see how many of them there are and then get back to the caravan before they reach us.

There are seven, with two holding back at the ambush point.

How do you know that?

I'm a mind-reading magical knife with the soul of a thief. I have certain abilities that I didn't have when I still had my body. I still don't think it's a fair trade.

I would probably agree with you, but right now I think you're way more useful than you were as a second-story man and relentless philanderer. Remarin wheeled his horse around and galloped back to the Druckans.

"There are seven of them," Remarin gasped.

"How do you know that?" Aram asked. He had a pair of curved scimitars at the ready and his reins looped around one wrist. His brother was similarly armed but with a pair of short axes instead.

"I wouldn't be much of a scout if I didn't, would I?" Remarin drew a short sword from his scabbard and faced the oncoming marauders.

"Defend your cargo and your women!" Aram yelled at the wagon drivers. He raised one sword high and bellowed, kneeing his horse into action as the raiders came close.

The seven raiders found themselves riding into a prepared fight instead of a stunned ambush, which helped even the fight. The arrow that caught the lead rider in the throat evened things out far more, as two of the front riders pulled up hard when their fellow crashed to the ground in front of them, sightless eyes staring up at the sky as he toppled from his saddle.

Remarin spun around to see Kit standing in the back of a wagon, a short bow in her hands. She smiled down at him. "I took archery for years. I suppose it's time to put it to use." She quickly loosed another pair of arrows, bringing down another rider and narrowly missing a third.

Then the fight was upon them. Aram engaged two raiders, one on each side of his horse. Karam, the smaller Druckan brother, lost his axe when he crushed the skull of the first rider he swung at, but the second proved more of a challenge. Remarin danced around one attacker for several seconds, deflecting his blows with his slender short sword until an arrow sprouted from the man's neck and he crumpled to the ground.

"About time!" he yelled at the wagon.

"Took you too long to get out of the way!" Kit yelled back.

Remarin stood up in his stirrups and flung Trand high in the air. The dagger arced up, up into the sky, ruby hilt flashing in the afternoon sun, then came whirling down in a wicked curved flight to bury itself in the eye of one of Aram's attackers. The startled Druckan brother spun in the saddle and cut his other opponent nearly in half with his scimitars. Karam was hard-pressed to dispatch the last raider until his brother joined the fray, then it was over in seconds.

Remarin pulled his horse alongside the wagon where Kit was standing and looked up. "Jump on."

The girl hopped on the back of the horse without hesitation. "Where are we going?"

"There are two more of them. We're going to go kill them before they tell the rest of the bandits how many are in our party and where they can find us. If they just don't come back, we'll likely be left alone. If they go back with intelligence, we'll never make it to Gorix. Lash yourself to me."

Kit unwound one of the long desert scarves that kept the dust off Remarin's head and tied herself to him, back to back.

Trand, to me. Remarin sent his thought out and seconds later the blade appeared in his belt. *Thanks.*

Don't thank me, I'm stuck with you until we break this spell or you die. And since I like pestering you better than serving as a toothpick for either of the Dumbass Brothers, I'll try to keep you alive for now.

Your affection overwhelms me.

Try not to get weepy. Your sobs will screw up the girl's shooting.

"I'm going to try to overtake them and kill one with my knife. You shoot the other one as I ride past," Remarin said over his shoulder.

"Shouldn't be a problem."

She was right; it wasn't a problem. Remain spurred his horse into a gallop, and as he topped a low hill a few hundred yards from the site of the supposed ambush, he found the two marauders at a crossroads, arguing with each other. They never even noticed him riding up until it was too late. Remarin struck one raider a fatal blow in the neck as he rode by, and Kit dropped the other one with an arrow in the chest.

Nice shooting.

"Thanks. Remarin, can we stop for a moment before we rejoin the others?"

"Sure," the thief replied. "I want to search the bodies anyway." He reined in his horse, untied the sash binding Kit to his back, and slid down to do just that. The girl dropped to the ground beside him and hurried off into some tall bushes beside the road. Remarin found nothing of interest on the brigands' bodies, just a few pieces of silver and one decent boot knife.

He turned to hop back onto the horse when he realized that Kit was nowhere to be found. Cursing under his breath, he stomped off into the underbrush in search of her, only to draw up sharply when he found her on all fours on the ground in front of a pool of vomit, weeping as though her heart would break.

"Hey there, what's all this?" Remain asked, kneeling beside the girl. "Are you hurt? One of them didn't get you with a lucky shot, did they?" He started to pat her down, looking for injuries, then suddenly remembered that not only was she a young girl, but royalty to boot, and he drew back as if stung.

"I mean, are you hurt anywhere? Do you need anything?"

Kit turned her face up to his, and he saw rivulets of tears running down her dirt-smeared cheeks. "Those men," she started, then blew her nose on her sleeve and started again. "Those men...they wanted to kill us. They were trying to kill us!"

"Kitten," Remain said, his voice uncharacteristically soft, "there have been men trying to kill us for days. Lots of them. One of them is your uncle. I thought you'd be used to it by now."

"That's not it," the girl said, leaning back to sit on her heels. "I didn't kill any of the other men. But I killed these. I took their life, without so much as a thought. I just put an arrow to the string, and loosed it, just like they were a turkey or a deer. But they weren't. They were men. Maybe they were bad men, but what if they weren't all bad? What if they had wives and children and they were just stealing to provide for them. I mean, you're a thief, and you're not really *bad*, right? Maybe they weren't bad, either. Just...I don't know. I've never killed anyone before. Does it get easier?"

Remarin took a deep breath and moved around to sit cross-legged on the ground in front of the young princess. "I wish I could say it doesn't. I wish I could say that every time you take a life, you have to run off and toss your breakfast and weep for what might have been. But that's not the world. The world is an ugly place, and sometimes you have to do ugly things to avoid having ugliness done to you. Those men were thieves, yes, but they were nothing like me. I am a member in moderately good standing, depending on the day and to whom you direct the question, of the Thieves' Guild of Bravis. I am bound by my oaths to the Guild never to take a life except in self-defense or the defense of others. I am bound not to steal from the poor, but only to rob those what can afford to lose a little, and I would never, ever be caught dead ambushing wagon trains in broad daylight. It lacks anything of the style that a true robbery should possess.

"So yes, little Kitten, those men were robbers. Those men were rapists and murderers who would have slain all the men, abused all the women until they were tired of you, then either sold you into slavery or simply slit your throats and dumped you on the side of the road for the buzzards. So yes, they were very bad men, indeed, and deserved everything you did to them, and much, much more."

"I know that, but why does it feel so bad?" Kit asked.

"Because you are not a bad person, Kitty-cat. And that means that you understand that killing has a cost, and we all pay it. They paid with their lives, and we pay with a little piece of our soul. You have to guard those little pieces of your soul because it's all too simple to cast away more of them than you can live without."

"You know they were bad people?" she asked, sniffling.

"They must have been so, for they sought to deprive the world of our company. And that would be a travesty, indeed, would it not?" Remarin stood with a flourish and reached down to help her stand. Kit took his hand, and together they walked back to where the bodies lay by the road.

"What should we do with their bodies?" Kit asked.

"Well, I've already robbed them of anything valuable, so that's done." Kit glared up at him. "What? It's a time-honored tradition—if you kill someone, you're allowed all their belongings. Besides, they've no further use for the few things of value I pilfered. But you should take that horse. It will endear us to the Brothers and you won't have to hold onto me as we ride back."

Kit adjusted the stirrups on the horse Remarin indicated and hopped into the saddle. The two of them rode back to the caravan in almost silence.

Nicely done, Remoron. I didn't think you had it in you.

"Thank you, Trand. I appreciate anything resembling a compliment from you."

Don't get used to it, idiot. I don't plan on making a habit of it. Remarin sighed, Kit giggled, and they returned to the caravan with a new horse and a few extra pennies in their pockets.

CHAPTER 9

The caravan rolled into Gorix four days later without further incident. Remarin and Kit spotted a couple of advance riders off in the distance, but no one approached them. Gorix was a compact city, contained within high walls with sturdy gates. The caravan queued up in a long line of wagons and horses awaiting inspection and admittance to the city in the height of the mid-afternoon heat, and it wasn't long before entrepreneurial Gorixans approached with oxen towing water wagons.

"Fresh water!" the water peddlers yelled. "Penny a dipper! Quarter a skin! Fill up out here, it's cheaper than beer!"

Remarin chuckled at the rhyme. "He neglects to mention that the beer is mostly water, too." The thief stiffened in his saddle and suddenly motioned one of the water-bearers over to his side. "Give me a dipperful, my good man, and fill both our skins." He tossed two silver coins to the man, who scurried over to stand next to Remarin's horse. The water-bearer looked like all the other men selling water to caravans, skin burned a deep bronze from the sun, his clothing the loose natural linens of the desert people, with folds of fabric draped around his head and neck to keep the worst of the sun off. Kit noticed his beard was more neatly trimmed than the other peddlers, and his hands showed none of the calluses a life of hard work brings. If she had to guess, the man had never worked a day in his life before this one.

Remarin leaned down beside his horse's neck and drank deeply from the dipper, nearly draining it, then pouring the rest over his head. He hung there letting the water drip from his head and beard and said, "What in the Nine Hells are you doing here?"

The peddler looked around and pressed himself up to the horse, whispering. "Apparently I'm waiting for the slowest damned thief in all the Kingdoms, and maybe the stupidest."

There's no question about the stupid part, trust me, Trand chimed in. Remarin thumped the gem on top of the dagger, and Trand flickered out.

"Well, now you've found me, so tell me what you want before someone in the caravan starts wondering why I'm having a longer conversation with a water-bearer than I've had with any of them in the past month," Remarin said.

"Marie's had me out here every day passing out water to caravan guards and merchants to give you this message, so it better be good," the little man said.

"Well, then give me the message, idiot, and you can get back to your whores," Remarin grumbled.

"Marie says keep the cat hidden, there are many dangerous dogs about," the man recited. He obviously had very little idea of the meaning of his message, and he just as obviously didn't care. "There, the message is delivered, and I just have to finish this day and get back to my real work." He turned back to his ox and resumed half-heartedly shouting "Water!" up and down the line of wagons.

Remarin looked to the heavens and said, "Why me? Why does it always have to be me? It was supposed to be a simple job. Steal a gem, deliver it, get paid. Nobody said anything about princesses. Nobody said anything about treason, or murder, or fleeing from an angry usurper king. These are the things I want to know before I take a job, not after I've done the stealing part." With a heavy sigh, he turned to Kit.

"We've got trouble," he said.

"I gathered," Kit replied. "I suppose I'm the cat they're looking for."

"I assume the very same," Remarin said. "We need to find another way into the city."

"Is there a gate that's less guarded?" Kit asked. "I've never been to Gorix, and when I traveled previously, we never waited in lines. I fear we were the cause of a great many people waiting in lines, and now that I see how unpleasant it is, I shall endeavor not to make people do so in the future."

"That's lovely of you, Kit, but there are only five ways into Gorix. Two main gates, the one we're in line for and the one on the opposite side of the city. These are the caravan and wagon entrance points, and everything that goes in is taxed. That's why there are such delays. Each caravan must be searched, all the contraband found, taxes levied, bribes paid, taxes paid, and only then can the wagons move through."

"Wait, did you say contraband? And bribes? Are we expected to bribe the city watch?" Kit asked, her eyes huge.

"No, no, no, Kitty-cat. We don't ever try to bribe the Watch; they're much too stiff-necked to accept bribes. We bribe the customs officials. Those are men who understand the workings of the world. And yes, contraband. Every city and nation has its quirks. Some don't allow tabac, some don't allow pleasure slaves, some don't allow cocaina powder. There's a great deal of money to be made just in buying things legally in one place and selling them in another place."

"Illegally," Kit said, arms crossed across her chest.

"Well, technically, that's true. But why should it be that men in Gorix can partake of tabac whenever they like, but men in Radina cannot? It's not fair, is it, to deprive Radians the pleasure of a nice relaxing pipeful of tabac? So sometimes we bring things across the border that the guards wouldn't necessarily approve of. And that adds to the time at the gates. There's another gate at the north entrance to the city, but it's only for foot traffic, and the searches there are even worse. Then there's the slavers' entrance at the south entrance, but that's nowhere we want to go near."

"You said five entrances," Kit prodded.

"I did indeed," Remarin replied.

"Is the fifth gate an option?"

"Oh, it is. It just isn't a very pleasant one."

"It sounds like it's the only one we have."

"I was really hoping you wouldn't come to that conclusion as well."

"Well? What is it?"

"You understand how cities work, right, Princess? When you get a lot of people together in one place, certain things are produced in great quantity."

"Yes, but I don't see where you're going with this."

"Well, one of those things produced in great quantity is waste products. And it takes a network of tunnels and aqueducts to remove all that waste product from the city. And that, dear Princess, is the only unguarded entrance into Gorix. The sewers."

"Oh no, Remarin!" the girl protested, and for the first time, Remarin thought of her as a girl. Not a boy, not a thief-in-training, not a liability, but a scared girl. "I'm sorry, but I have to draw the line somewhere, and creeping through a sewer is definitely where I start drawing! I am not going through that sewer."

Remarin pulled his horse off to the side of the slow-moving line. Kit drew up next to him and followed his arm where he pointed at two guardsmen searching wagons a few dozen yards ahead of them. "Do you see that, Kitten?"

"Sure, it's a couple of guardsmen searching for contraband, like you said."

"What is the captain on the horse holding?"

"I don't know. It's a piece of paper. Maybe instructions, or a list. Something like that, I suppose."

"Do you suppose that a guardsman who searches wagons every single day needs a list of what to look for? Do you think the captain of the guard has to be reminded of what is and is not allowed into the city?"

The girl's face grew somber. "I guess not."

"So what do you think is on that piece of paper, and could it have anything to do with the way all those people are lined up against the wagon?"

"It's a picture," she said. "And the guards are searching for whoever it's a picture of."

"Feel any different about going in through the sewers?"

"I suppose so, but how are we going to get out of line without being noticed?"

"Go pee," Remarin said.

"Excuse me? I don't need to relieve myself right now, and it's none of your…oh, I understand."

"I was hoping you'd get the general idea," the thief replied.

Kit slid down from her horse and walked off into the trees beside the road. There was a steady stream of people coming and going from the woods as nature called throughout the day. Remarin clucked his tongue at his horse and rode to the front of the caravan. He fell in beside Aram and clapped the huge man on his shoulder.

"Well, Aram, my friend, it appears this is where we must part company. I know that you will view my departure with all the sadness you can muster, but I behoove you to endure this hardship with strength."

"What are you babbling about, Remarin? I'm not paying you early, so get that thought out of your head. I told you we'd settle up tomorrow at the Dancing Rabbit, and I'll not change for you nor that sweet-cheeked little boy you're running with."

"Yes, about him," Remarin said. "He's the reason I'm leaving your service a few hours early. You see, his father is a wealthy man in Gorix, and he doesn't approve of certain aspects of his son's relationships."

"You mean the fact that he's sleeping with you?"

Remarin put on his best offended face. "Were you but a gentleman, you would understand that Kit and I have a relationship that is far from physical. I have never laid a hand on the boy, but care for him as though he were the most precious diamond. His father, however, is an abusive thug of a man who beat Kit's mother to death and now wishes to relegate the boy to a life of bare servitude. That is why we must leave your company, to protect him from the evil lackeys of his dreadful father. Please, I implore you not to mention Kit or myself when your wagons are inspected, or you could doom the child to more beatings, not to mention what they would do to me."

Aram looked Remarin up and down. "I don't understand half of what you're saying thief, but I think you're not near as smart as you think you are. I don't think anyone is more than half as smart as you think you are, but I'll help you. You and the boy were never here, and I won't be at the Rabbit tomorrow dispensing everyone's pay."

"Then I most certainly will not see you there," Remarin said, sliding out of the saddle and grabbing his pack off the horse. He took Kit's pack off her horse and strode into the woods, whistling.

CHAPTER 10

"I hate to sound like a whiny little princess, but for Yanna's sake, Remarin, when are we going to get out of these thrice-damned sewers?" Kit asked.

"I know, Kitten, it's wet, it stinks to high heaven, and there are chunks of things unfortunately not nearly unimaginable enough floating by. But the fact of the matter is, I haven't been to Gorix in some years, and I don't really remember exactly where all the safe places to stick my head aboveground are, so I'm—" He stuck out an arm and slammed Kit against the wall, pressing himself tight to the stones as a thin beam of light pierced the blackness ahead of them.

"Come on out, my pretties, I heard ya, so there's no point trying to hide. Somebody's down here using the Low Road without applying for passage, and Mocking Joe Jessup needs to know who's splashing about in his pond, don't he?"

Remarin let out a long breath and stepped out into the tunnel. "What are you doing splashing about in other people's shit at your age? I would have thought they'd retired the old Master of the Low Road by now."

"Remarin? Is that you, you incorrigible bastard?" came a wavering voice.

He definitely knows you, Trand quipped.

"I'm back, and I beg for safe passage. I have a young apprentice and we got in a bit of trouble over in Bravis and had to make a run for it."

"Does this have anything to do with that missing princess I been hearing about? The reward on her and anybody that's helping her is almost enough to make me go straight." The old man shined his thieves' lantern over the pair. Kit squinted against the light, but Remarin went further, closing his eyes and covering them with his hand.

"Come on, Jessup, get that light out of my eyes or I'll be blind as a bat down here!" Remarin said.

The old man chuckled and shuttered the lantern, cutting off the narrow beam of illumination. "Well, you really are who you say you are, at least you, Remarin. I don't know the boy."

"Like I said, my apprentice. I don't remember what his father called him. I mostly call him Lion because he's like a scared kitten all the time. Another year or two and we'll get him his own name, but for now, just call him Leo."

The man laughed, his fetid breath cutting through the stench of the sewer. "I like that, Remarin! Leo! That's a good one, it is. You always was a funny one. I hope you still are. The new master likes a good laugh, and he's left orders that anyone coming into Gorix by the Low Road comes to him first, even if they got a pass from another Guild."

"That makes a lot of sense, Jessup. You want to inspect new players in the territory, right?" Remarin replied.

"I'm glad you feel so reasonable, Remarin. You wasn't always known for being reasonable."

That hasn't changed, Trand said.

"Well, what are we waiting for? Let's go see your Chief." Remarin looked at Jessup, who didn't move.

"You need hoods."

"Hoods?" Kit asked.

"Blackout hoods," Remarin replied. "They're worn when you don't want the people your taking somewhere to have any idea where you're taking them. It's a custom that's usually waived with thieves from other Guilds. As a gesture of professional courtesy," Remarin explained, pulling a silver medallion out from under his shirt. The three-sided medal hung on a leather thong and was obviously worn.

"I know you're from another Guild, Remarin. I'm one of the men who voted for your transfer, remember? But that don't matter none. The boss specifically said that you had to wear the hood if you ever set foot in Gorix again."

"That's ridiculous! Who's the boss now that would care enough about…tell me, no. Tell me it's not him." Remarin shook his head.

"It is, lad. Xamos is Guildmaster now, and he hasn't forgotten what you did to him before you left town all those years ago."

"I did to him? I seem to recall there was some pretty mutual doing to going around right before I left, and I got done to a few times myself."

"Aye, but nothing like your last night here," Jessup said.

"What did you do, and why are we having to deal with it now?" Kit asked, a note of command entering her voice.

"I don't think I like your tone, *apprentice*," Remarin said.

"I don't think I care very much, *master*," Kit replied. "Part of your job is to keep me safe, and you're doing just a grand job of that so far, aren't you?"

"Xamos and I had a disagreement about a woman. Most of the disagreeing was on his part, as the woman and I were both pretty agreeable toward one another."

"Is there a woman in every one of your stories of poor judgment and horrific consequences?" Kit asked.

Pretty much, not that I have any room to talk, added Trand.

"Yeah, there might be a couple where there are no women, but generally I try to keep a couple around to make things interesting. Anyway, this woman and I saw ourselves as something of a couple, and Xamos saw himself as more of a beau to the young lady than she or I thought, and he went around us to make sure that he could approach her."

"What did he do?" Kit asked. "Go to her father?"

Jessup laughed and Remarin gave Kit one of those smiles that he trotted out when she needed to know that her pampered upbringing had left her woefully unprepared for life outside a castle. "In a manner of speaking," Remarin said. "Angel was a whore, so Xamos went to her madame and bought her contract. He released her from whoring, on the condition that she marry him. She did, and I decided to leave town to avoid any further unpleasantness between myself and a man with the political savvy to go far in the Guild."

"That's a kind way of describing you running through the sewers like a dog chasing a rabbit with nothing but your sword and dagger. And you might have left out a few gifts that you left for the happily married couple."

"There's no proof that I put a rotting salmon under the floor of their bedchamber. There's certainly no proof that I loosed a sackful of honey and Kardalian fire ants into their wedding bed. And it would be completely impossible to prove that I paid a hedge wizard to brew up a potion of impotence for the groom and a potion to increase ardor to almost unbearable levels in the bride. So shortly after they retired to their infested marriage bed, Xamos found himself unable to perform the very deed that he'd gone to so much trouble to be allowed to do. There might also have been a note left on his new bride's bedside table reminding her that she knows where to find me should any aspect of married life not live up her vigorous expectations."

"You did all that because a man stole your girlfriend?" Kit marveled. "You must have loved her."

Remarin paused, then stared at Kit for a moment. "I suppose I did," he said, voice soft. "I suppose I did. I also hated Xamos with a blazing passion, a sentiment that was—"

"Still is," Jessup chimed in.

"A sentiment that is completely true. He's a thug of a man, no subtlety in his soul, no artistry in his thefts, not a drop. He's a mugger, a basher, a purse-snatcher of the worst degree."

"And now he's the head of the Gorix Thieves' Guild," Kit added. "And he still hates you."

"Both of those statements are very likely true," Remarin agreed.

"Oh don't worry, Remarin," Jessup said. "He certainly hates you. He had a crude drawing of you posted across the main meeting room from The Big Chair, and he likes to sit and throw knives into your face from across the room. Just think how thrilled he'll be when he can throw knives at the real thing again."

"Fine, give me the hood," Remarin said, then pointed to Kit. "But you make sure nothing happens to the boy, Jessup. I'm holding you responsible."

"That's a lot less frightening since I know that you're more likely than not going to be dead within the hour." Jessup pulled the hood down over Remarin's eyes, then did the same to Kit. The old thief took Remarin by the arm and turned to Kit.

"Reach out with your hand, child," he said. He guided Kit's hand to the back of Remarin's belt. "Now don't get lost. If you take off hood before I give you permission, I or another Guild member will have to kill you."

Don't worry, youngling. I can see everything, and I can get us out of here if need be. Just put on the hood and go along with them for now.

Kit did as she was told and put her hand on Remarin's belt. Jessup led them down a winding, twisting, turning route, and Kit was convinced that they had doubled back on their trail at least once. Finally, after was seemed like hours but was most likely fifteen minutes, Jessup stopped them and took off their hoods.

Remarin looked around, marveling at the changes in his time away. What had once been little more than a hovel was now a bustling, vibrant underground market and city, complete with a vendor selling fresh fruit that was anything but native to Gorix. The thieves had built dozens of buildings, stretching several stories above the sewer floor. Remarin considered, and realized, this must have been one of the old pumping stations, far below the city. There were several stories worth of room to build up in those, and that was what happened here, with warehouses on top of the sewers for access to street level.

Torches and gaslights flickered around the common area, and Jessup grinned back at Remarin. "Whattaya think, eh? A whole lot different from when you was here."

"It certainly is," Remarin agreed. "But isn't it a little much? Don't you worry that the people overhead will become curious when they hear the sounds of a market under their feet?"

"They would," said a smiling Jessup, "if this market weren't built right underneath the city market! That way there's no chance of being overheard. But let's go, the Big Man is waiting, and you know how much he likes waiting."

"Don't remind me," Remarin said.

Jessup led them into the bottom floor of one of the more ornate buildings. This one had doors rather than silks and music playing low in the background. The room was dark and smoky with a long bar running down one side of the building. A large bald man with multiple gold hoop earrings in each ear and his nose polished a glass as he stared at the newcomers. Kit stared back, trying to count all the rings in the man's face.

"Why does he have so many earrings? And why is he wearing them in his nose and eyebrows?" she asked Remarin, pitching her voice low to not be heard under the general murmur of conversation in the bar. She knew at once that she'd failed when the man smiled at her and flashed ten fingers twice, then six more, indicating he wore twenty-six pieces of jewelry in his face.

"That's Mond. He's the bartender, bouncer, settler of disputes, and cleaner of problems for the Guild. Each of those rings represents someone who didn't have money to pay their bar tab but had a piece of jewelry. You should see his hands and wrists."

"A man wants to wear all that jewelry?" Kit marveled.

"Mond isn't like most men," Remarin replied. "And neither is his husband." Remarin motioned over to the slight man playing guitar in a far corner of the room. He sat perched on a small stool, his slight legs twined around the rails of the stool. He looked as if he'd blow away in a good wind, sharp contrast to Mond's massive size.

"Those two?" Kit asked.

Remarin nodded. "I know it's hard to believe looking at him, but Zemtriss is one of the most dangerous assassins that I've ever heard of, much less met. And here's our adoring host."

Remarin gestured toward a large man with a full brown beard and curly brown hair seated on a couch on a dais at the back corner of the room. His position was elevated, defensible, and overlooked by half a dozen guards, all clad in black on black with gleaming swords and daggers at their waists. Black steel knife hilts peeked out of their boots, and each man had a garrote wound into a bracelet on one wrist.

Xamos leaned back on a pile of cushions, but the way his eyes darted from Remarin to his bodyguards told Kit that the man was frankly terrified to have the other thief in his lair.

Trand? she sent out a thought.

Yes, girl?

Why is Xamos afraid of Remarin? she asked mentally.

A great many people are, my dear. Remarin, for all he's not a very good thief, is one of the greatest assassins this realm has ever seen. He talks a good game about how scary Zemtriss is, but he neglects to mention who trained the little bard.

Everyone wears masks, don't they, Trand?

Everyone everywhere, little kitten, including you, if you remember. Kit almost felt the smile along the connection she shared with the enchanted blade.

"Remarin, my old friend!" The bearded man stood and held his arms out wide, as if to hug the entire room. "I am so glad to see you back in Gorix *for a visit*. We have all missed you very much."

Remarin stepped up and gripped arms with the bigger man. "I doubt that very much, Xamos, but it's good of you to say." Under his breath, where no one outside the dais could hear, Remarin said, "I invoke Guild passage and protection."

Xamos's eyes went wide for an instant, but he quickly brought himself under control. "Granted, your safety is guaranteed. I pledge my own life as surety," the big man whispered. He turned to the room, pulling Remarin to his side. "The bar is closed!" Xamos shouted. "I am having a private party to welcome our prodigal friend Remarin home! Everyone out!" The dozen or so patrons looked around, confused, then began to protest.

"Your drinks are on the house," Mond said in a low voice that nonetheless carried perfectly to every seat in the room. "You owe nothing. Now get out." The last was said in a low growl that left no question to his seriousness. Within seconds only Jessup, Xamos, Zemtriss, and Mond remained. Remarin took a seat with his back to the door, leaving the couches to Xamos and his thieves.

"That's new," Zemtriss remarked. "The Remarin that left here never would have left his flank exposed."

"I trust you to watch my back, Zem. Always have," Remarin replied with a grin.

"Just his back, Z, nothing else," Mond said, mock-growling.

"Don't worry, lover. Remarin has the flattest ass in all of Veosia. Must be from sliding around all those rooftops on his butt," Zemtriss replied.

"What's going on, Remarin? What have you done that's so bad you have to invoke Guild protection?" Xamos asked after the laughter had settled everyone's nerves a bit. The other thieves looked around at their leader and each other.

"I'm sorry, boss," Jessup started. "I had no idea—"

"Don't worry, Jessup," Xamos said. "I'm sure you didn't. If this was like any of Remarin's other plans, he had no idea he was going to invoke sanctuary either until half a second before the word left his tongue."

"Close, Xamos, but it was when I saw a Veosian spy sitting in your front row that I realized I needed help, and no matter how much it pains me, you're the only man in Gorix that can provide it."

"What do you want me to do?" Xamos asked.

"I need you to help me overthrow a country," Remarin said. "Kit, if you please?"

The princess stared at Remarin in shocked silence. "This is your plan?"

"I think it's actually your plan, Princess. I'm just changing the timeline."

Kit stood up. "Gentlemen, I am Princess Kitarina Rutvor, Crown Princess of Veosia. My uncle has stolen my throne, destroyed my reputation, and is in the process of turning Veosia from a thriving center of world commerce to an insular, backwater nation that can see no farther than her borders. I need you to help me take back my throne."

"See, I told you, Zem," Mond leaned over and said in a low voice. "Things are going to get exciting now that Remarin's back in town.

CHAPTER 11

"Princess Kitarina, eh?" Xamos said, scratching his chin. "I suppose I can see a little resemblance. You don't look much like that picture of you on the money, though, do you?"

"I was five when that portrait was done, so no, Mr. Xamos, I do not bear much resemblance to that child any longer."

"And your uncle wants you dead, eh?"

"You seem to say 'eh' a lot, Mr. Xamos. Do you not hear well, or are you simply not very bright?" Kit asked. Remarin laughed, a short bark that wouldn't be contained.

"Yes, Mr. Xamos, my uncle needs me dead. As long as I live, his claim to my throne will be in jeopardy. Even if he produces an heir, my claim has greater legitimacy than his, so he will stop at nothing to see me dead."

"And what makes you think I won't turn you over to him for the money?" Xamos asked.

"In the first place, he hasn't offered a reward because he's put forth the claim that I'm already dead. Killed by your old friend Remarin, here, as a matter of fact. So anyone trying to ransom me to him would just be opening themselves up to murder, since they aren't supposed to know I'm alive in the first place. In the second place, while you have a reputation that spans the continent as a rogue, thief, and smuggler, you aren't known to be a murderer, or particularly interested in politics."

"Right you are, girl. I don't care who sits a throne or lives in the High Mayor's house, long as things are stable. Too much turmoil can be bad for business. But a peaceful, prosperous city? That's a place a man of my talents can make some money."

"Absolutely, Xamos," Remarin chimed in. "The richer the city, the more need for rent boys that can be had by the hour!" Remarin laughed, looking around the room to see who was laughing with him. No one else was laughing.

"Hmmm," he mused. "Perhaps this is another one of those times when my wit has outpaced my audience."

"Or you just made another stupid joke that nobody thought was funny," Xamos said.

"I'll allow that as a possibility. But please, go on." The thief gestured for the two of them to continue their deliberation. "Pretend I'm not even here."

"As impossible as that typically is, today I'm not even interested in attempting such a feat." Xamos smiled and clapped his hands together twice. A pair of half-naked serving girls materialized from behind some dangling silks and passed out goblets of wine to everyone.

"Don't worry, little princess. I am not going to sell you to your uncle for him to murder. I have need of some of Remarin's skills, and I do not mean his uncanny ability to make everyone in a crowded room hate him."

"Very funny, Xamos. What's the job?" Remarin said with a scowl.

"There is a priest here in town who promised to imbue some of my equipment with the protection of his deity. He reneged on his end of the bargain, so now I am out a great deal of money and have no enchanted weapons."

"What do you want me to do?" Remarin asked. "Force him to magic you up some weapons? I don't think it works that way."

"Not only would I not trust any weapons enchanted under such duress, I doubt I would trust you, of all people, to provide me with enchanted weapons, Remarin. No, I want you to break into the

Temple of Ketsin and steal the holy symbol of their goddess from the shrine in the sanctuary. You'll bring it to me here, I'll ransom it back to the High Priest of Ketsin for twice what he stole from me, and everyone will be happy. Unless you get caught, in which case you'll almost certainly be killed and spend your afterlife in unending torment for defiling the temple of a goddess."

"Isn't Ketsin the Goddess of Death and Murder?" Remarin asked.

"As well as burial, rivers, and snakes. Oh, yes, that's something you should probably be careful of."

"What's that?" Remarin said, glaring at Xamos.

"Snakes. They're sacred to Ketsinites, and they hold them in holy places throughout the temple. But sometimes they get out, and it's considered an offense against the goddess to harm a snake in her temple."

"So you want me to break into a snake-infested Temple of the Goddess of Death and steal a holy symbol from the most sacred part of the building, all without harming any snakes, being seen, or killing anyone. Did that pretty much cover it?"

"I don't actually care if you kill anyone in the temple or not, but otherwise that's a pretty good assessment of the situation." Xamos leaned back in his chair and steepled his fingers, smiling broadly at Remarin.

"And in exchange for this service, you'll help Kit here regain her throne?"

"In exchange for this service, I won't turn your little Kitty-cat over to her uncle and slit your throat in the middle of the Gorix town square. How does that sound for help?"

"Sounds about like what I expected from you, Xamos. Is there somewhere here that we can clean up and rest? I think I'll smell a little less appetizing to the snakes if I wash some of the sewer off before we begin."

R emarin waited for the guard to pass beneath him before he took a small ball of gluetree sap from his pocket and pressed it to the skylight. Then he drew Trand from the sheath on his belt and reversed his grip on the dagger.

I do not approve of being used in such a manner, the dagger said in Remarin's mind.

Then you shouldn't have let them put such a nice glasscutter into your hilt, the thief replied.

How many times do I have to tell you it's a ruby? Trand asked.

Until I remember? I already do. Until I care? I don't know, keep trying. Remarin pressed the pommel gem of the dagger into the glass and scribed a small circle around the lump of adhesive. When the circle was complete, Remarin rapped on the glass a few times, then lifted the circle from the rest of the skylight using the sap. The resulting hole in the skylight was barely big enough to fit Remarin's hips; his shoulders would never fit through the space. So he gritted his teeth against the pain he knew was coming, wedged his hand between his knee and the roof, and pulled. With a loud *POP!* Remarin dislocated his left shoulder and let it hang loosely by his side. Using only his right hand, he slid very carefully through the hole and down the rope into the sanctuary. He dropped the last few feet, then walked over to a marble pillar on the side of the room.

With a grimace, he took a couple of running steps and slammed his shoulder into the pillar, knocking it back into place. Remarin sank to his knees, tears springing unbidden to his eyes and a string of profanity running through his head. He managed to keep his noises down to one low groan, then got to his feet and surveyed his surroundings.

The skylight entry deposited him into the nave of the main sanctuary, just outside the seating area for the temple. Dark gray marble surrounded him in its cold austerity, the stone seeming to press in on him from all sides. The air was cool and dry, with none of the incense-laden fumes of other temples Remarin had visited. There was a hint of musk in the air, and as he pressed his ear to the sanctuary doors, a soft rustling sound was all that greeted him.

The skylight provided ample moonlight, and Remarin opened the large carved wooden door into the sanctuary. He took care to open the door in one smooth motion, the better to keep the hinges from creaking. The rustling sound increased in volume, and as the door swung wide, Remarin realized what was causing the noise. The entire sanctuary, from the door to the pulpit, was carpeted in snakes of all sizes. Tiny adders wove in and out of enormous constrictors, as colorful desert vipers raced up and down the aisles with mottled wood rattlers. Remarin froze, drawing in a sharp breath at the tapestry of reptiles in front of him. His was the only sound in the room, and every snake froze, then turned in unison as though looking at the door.

Hundreds of forked tongues licked the air, and the nearest serpents began to move in Remarin's direction. His heart raced for a moment until he realized why the snakes were coming toward him. *They're cold-blooded animals, and I'm the warmest thing in the room*, he thought.

I don't think that means they just want to cuddle, though, replied Trand.

Even if they do, I think that cuddling with a ten-foot constrictor would be near the top of my list of bad decisions.

And there's a lot of competition for the top of that list, thought the dagger.

Remarin looked from side to side, then up at the rafters. The beams were wide and close together, perfect for running from the front of the sanctuary to the back. Except there was no way to get there, and Remarin had snakes closing in from all sides. He leapt to the nearest pew, then hopped up on the back of the bench when he nearly stepped on a coiled adder sleeping on the pew. The nimble thief pinwheeled his arms for balance, then hopped forward to the next pew. He stopped, peered through the dimly lit sanctuary to the back of the next pew, then hopped again. He repeated this process a dozen times until finally he stood on the back of the front pew, less than twenty feet from the pulpit, with its repository of holy relics and, presumably, his quarry.

But to get there he would have to find a way across twenty feet of solid snakes. Once they had lost track of his warmth, the snakes returned to doing whatever it is snakes do in a church dedicated for them, which in many cases seemed to be working on making more snakes. Remarin looked around for a way across, his eyes finally lighting on a burnt-out torch in an iron wall bracket about halfway between the pew and the pulpit. He dashed to the end of the pew, building up a head of steam as he ran. As he reached the end, he planted one foot on the pew's armrest, pushed off, and flew toward the wall sconce, arms and legs flailing. He smacked into the cold stone wall and started to slide down into the roiling mass of scales. Glancing down, Remarin saw the fangs below and caught the iron sconce with his fingertips. That was all the purchase he needed to swing himself up onto the iron bracing and launch himself at the pulpit. He landed on the raised dais, dropping to one hand for balance.

Remarin looked around the platform, marveling at the lack of serpents. He saw them writhing by the thousands on the main floor of the sanctuary, even on the pews and going up the stairs to the balcony, but not a one to be found on the pulpit. As he looked around the raised platform, he felt a cold prickle on the back of his neck, and all the hairs on his arms stood up.

Trand, is there something terrible that I've missed?

Probably, but I can neither see it nor sense anything that's going to kill you.

But you feel that, too, right?

That sense of presence? Yes. But we are in the heart of the Death Goddess's temple. It might just be Ketsin herself looking down upon you with disapproval.

Disapproval I can live with. Anger, probably not.

Remarin focused once again on the task at hand and knelt behind the pulpit. There were no doors or drawers or open spaces, no obvious hiding places where one would store a bejeweled holy symbol. Remarin felt around the back of the podium lightly, his fingers searching for any crack or crevice that could hold the emblem. Finally, after several minutes of searching, he felt a spot on the podium give with a *click*, and a small drawer slid out from the back.

Within the drawer, nestled in a bed of black velvet, lay the triangular holy symbol of Ketsin, Goddess of Death. Set in the center, representing the ever-present Eye of Death, was a polished onyx three inches across. Seven diamonds alternated around the Eye with glittering emeralds and sapphires. The entire piece was cast in platinum and polished to a miraculous glow. The Eye sparkled so much in the low light that it almost seemed to glow from within.

Remarin tucked the symbol into a pocket inside his shirt and readied himself to dash back across the sanctuary the way he'd come. He stood on the edge of the dais, took a deep breath, and just before he leapt, heard a voice from behind him ask, "Just where do you think you're going with that?"

CHAPTER 12

Remarin froze, barely keeping from tumbling headfirst into the writhing mass of serpents below. He spun around and saw a man clad all in black crouching and leaning against a wall on the far end of the platform.

"Who are you?" Remarin asked.

"These aren't really the times when we introduce ourselves, are they? Isn't this one of those times when I just kill you and deliver the Eye of Death to the man who paid me very handsomely to bring it to him, no matter what obstacles I found in my way."

"Xamos double-crossed me," Remarin said with a shake of his head. "I expected something like this, just not quite this method. I expected something a little less subtle, like him bashing me in the head after I delivered the goods to him."

"Not enough style for Xamos these days," the man said. "I hear when you were in town he was more a basher, but since he took over running things, he's got a flair for the dramatic. That, and you're still pretty well-liked by some of the boys, so it had to look like an accident, like I was just sent to back you up, and when you fell into this pile of extremely poisonous snakes, you threw me the Eye so I'd help your little protégé."

"Nobody would buy that. I'm not that magnanimous," Remarin said, sizing up the man for openings. He saw none in the way the other thief held himself, and there were no visible weapons, so he kept his gear tight.

"Thieves don't have to have a good story; they just need a story that could possibly be true. And that one could possibly be true, so it'll be good enough. They probably won't even see the holes I leave in you." The man's hand flicked out, and Remarin dove to the left, away from whatever the other thief threw and the snakes crawling all over the floor.

Remarin looked behind him and saw a small dart quivering in the wood of a nearby pew. "Poison?" he asked.

"From one professional to another, yes. It's one I made up myself, from the root of the Xingwin tree, only found in one forest far from here in the country of Tingzai. It paralyzes you from the outside in, starting with fingers and toes and working its way in to the heart. Once it freezes the heart, you die."

"Seems exotic," Remarin said. "I've always been a fan of a knife in the throat myself." As he spoke, he stood up from the floor and flung Trand at the other man in one smooth motion. The knife tumbled end over end, straight for the assassin. He flung himself backward and kicked the knife out of the air to spin harmlessly off the platform and bury itself into the wood.

"That was my favorite knife," Remarin grumbled.

"That's the problem when you throw away your best weapon," the man replied, flicking his wrist at Remarin several times, sending a volley of darts in his direction.

Remarin whirled around and grabbed one of the matching banners of Ketsin from a corner of the stage. He spun around behind the banner and heard the soft *thwap thwap thwap* as the darts buried themselves into the fabric. Remarin reached up, tore the fabric free of the pole, snapped the base of the banner off, and advanced on his adversary, twirling his newly made quarterstaff over his head. The other thief's eyes went wide, then he dashed to the edge of the stage, grabbed his own banner, and followed suit. He got his staff around to block just as Remarin swung for his skull, and the modified flagpoles met with a *crack* that echoed through the sanctuary.

"I thought you assassin types were supposed to be subtle," Remarin said, slamming his staff into the other man's defense.

"I thought you thief types were supposed to be nimble," the other man said as he parried a blow and responded with a sweeping shot at Remarin's knees. Remarin planted his staff and swung around it, throwing kicks at the man's face. He ducked, then kicked the staff out from under Remarin, bringing the thief crashing to the dais.

Remarin shook his head to clear the stars from his vision, then rolled out of the way as the other thief struck at his head again and again, each strike booming through the sanctuary like thunder. He pulled up sharply at the edge of the platform, staring down at a small cobra gazing up at him, then reversed course, still trying to scramble to his feet. He finally regained his footing, just in time to catch the assassin's fist on the point of his jaw. Remarin staggered back, then dropped to one knee, dazed from the blow, or at least dazed until the assassin came within reach.

Trand, to me! Remarin sent desperately. The dagger materialized in his hand, and Remarin sprang upward, slicing his foe open from belt to throat. The black-clad man gaped at Remarin as he stepped backward, his entrails spilling across the pulpit as he did. The assassin stared at Remarin, eyes wide, and collapsed in the ornate chair behind the altar. He let out a long, slow hissing breath as his lifeblood poured out onto the floor. Remarin watched the man die, then walked over and cleaned his dagger on the dead man's shirt. He patted the dead assassin down, reaching into his shirt to withdraw a heavy purse and a piece of paper with a rough black and white sketch on it.

"I'm not sure which I find more insulting—that the price on my head was so low, or that they sent out such an ugly picture to go with it," he mused.

Be upset over the bounty, the picture is actually flattering, came Trand's voice in his head.

"Thanks for the save back there, old friend," Remarin said.

Again.

"Again," Remarin agreed. "I know this is all impossible for you, trapped inside that thing. I swear, I'll find a way to fix it if it's the last thing I ever do."

I know, Remarin. I know.

"Now, do you know a way out of here that doesn't involve dancing with a thousand reptiles?"

A new voice boomed from the back of the sanctuary. "Who dares defile the Temple of Ketsin?"

"Oh come *on*," Remarin sighed. "Haven't I been beaten enough for one night?"

He turned his attention to the back of the room, where an emaciated man in sagging ceremonial robes thrown on over a nightshirt was storming down the aisle, snakes parting before him like waves before a warship. His bare feet stuck out from under the robes on spindly legs, and his gait was unsteady, but his eyes were clear and his voice boomed with the vigor of a man who has spent many years behind a pulpit. He carried a scepter in one hand and a heavy-looking mace in the other, and judging from the ropes of sinew twining his arms, he knew how to use it.

"Infidel!" the priest shouted. "Defiler of the Death Goddess's realm! I shall smite you and send you to meet Ketsin face to face! You will pay for your sins, evildoer!"

"I don't doubt that, Your Worship, but I don't think that's going to happen tonight," Remarin said. He darted back and forth along the pulpit, looking for a side entrance or at least a window he could break that wasn't covered in priceless, centuries-old stained glass.

The priest stopped short of the pulpit and waved his arms, beginning a spell. Remain paled, then reached out with his flagpole-turned-quarterstaff and poked the scrawny priest in his ribcage. The old man stuttered in his chant, then started over, again trying to call down the wrath of his god on the thief.

Remarin thumped him on the head with the staff and said, "I can do this all night, old man. You're not going to cast a spell, and unless there's a potion to cut forty years off your life, you're no match for me physically, so why don't we just both go to sleep and forget we ever met tonight? I'll get the army I need for Kit, you'll get a good night's sleep then pay Xamos what you owe the bastard, and all will be right with the world."

The old priest froze in mid-incantation. "Xamos? Is that who sent you? And he told you that I owe *him* money? Oh, sweet Ketsin, Mother of Night, that's rich! I caught that bastard breaking into my strongboxes two months ago and told him if he ever showed his face around my temple again, I'd unleash the real wrath of Ketsin upon him and he'd learn a new definition of pain. That cowardly shitball ran out of here like all the snakes of the Goddess were pursuing him." The old man laughed, then fell sober. "But he sent you, and you not only have broken into our most holy place and stolen the Eye of Death, you've perverted the most holy rite of our faith—death—by committing murder right here before Ketsin and all her subjects!" The priest gestured around himself to the snakes, who writhed and hissed at the words.

Remarin couldn't tell from the hissing if the snakes were irritated at him for killing the assassin, at the assassin for dying out of their reach, or at the priest for disturbing them in the middle of the night. And frankly, he didn't care.

"Look, Your Worship, I'm sorry about all of this. Especially the mess in your chair. I know from experience that it's just going to be better to throw the whole chair out—some smells just won't ever go away completely. But Xamos, idiot, traitor, and overall scum that he is, has something that I need very badly, and I need your holy symbol to get it from him. So I'd really appreciate it if you'd either tell me where there's a back way out of here or clear the aisle of snakes for a couple of minutes while I leave. It's been a very long night, and the last thing I want to do is hurt a priest."

"Don't worry, thief. You won't. Hurt me, I mean." The priest laughed and raised his scepter over his head. It glowed a blinding white, and when Remarin could focus his eyes again, the wizened old man in his nightshirt was gone, replaced by a hale and hearty grandfatherly-looking man clad in chainmail of the deepest black. The same piercing pale blue eyes looked out at Remarin from beneath bushy gray eyebrows, but all hint of decrepitude and fragility was gone. The priest strode the last few yards to the dais and charged Remarin, his mace held high to strike.

Remarin planted his staff and hopped backward, using the wooden flagpole to block the heavy mace. The wood held for three good parries, then shattered in Remarin's hands, leaving him with two short sticks too small to do anything with. He tossed them at the priest's head, then leapt from the pulpit to the first pew.

"I really don't want to fight you, old man. I just want to do the job I came here for and leave," the thief said.

"Well, that's too bad because I really want to smash your head flat and paint my altar with your brains!" The priest stomped down from the pulpit and came after Remarin, snakes parting at his every step.

"That's not a very nice sentiment from a holy man," Remarin said, jumping from pew to pew backward to stay out of the old priest's reach. "What would your goddess think about—oh yeah." Remarin fell silent as he remembered who he was talking to. The priest stopped several pews ahead of Remarin and began another incantation. Remarin looked around for an exit, any exit, but all he saw were the rafters high above.

Throw me, Trand's voice came into his head.

"Where? Up there? I fail to see where you being stuck in the rafters would help anyone...oh." Remarin paused as he considered Trand's suggestion. "Fine, but just the hilt, okay? I don't want to kill a priest." He drew the knife, flipped it over so he gripped it by the point, and threw it at the priest. The bejeweled pommel struck the priest right in the forehead, silencing him in mid-spell. Trand bounced off the old man's head, then blinked out of existence and returned to the sheath on Remarin's side.

Done and done, came the satisfied report from the knife.

Remarin could see how effective the knife was as the priest slowly toppled backward, unconscious before he hit the floor.

Time to go, the dagger spoke in Remarin's mind. *Use the distraction to get past the snakes.*

"What distraction?' Remarin asked, then he saw what Trand meant. All the serpents that were giving the priest a wide berth before were drawing near, testing whatever magic protected the old man from them. A six-foot rattler was the first to breach the former barrier, darting forward and striking the priest on the thigh. His armor deflected the bite, but the snakes grew bolder when no magical reprisals came down on them. An asp struck, then a viper, then a different rattler took its turn attacking the felled priest. Eventually a banded adder latched on to the man's cheek and he jolted awake with a scream.

"Help me!" the priest howled. Remarin shook his head and left the sanctuary the way he came, very gingerly walking the backs of the pews as the priest screamed his last behind him.

CHAPTER 13

It was several blocks before Remarin managed to get to a sewer entrance that wasn't guarded. It seemed like every member of the City Watch was out in force. His suspicions were further reinforced when he got into the sewers and had to dodge guards at almost every junction. He navigated the sewers as far as he could but came aboveground several blocks away from the Guildhouse when the tunnels became too crowded with people who weren't thieves, at least as far as Remarin could tell. He slid from the sewers up onto the street behind a fruit stand and began to mingle with the crowd as best he could. When he got to within a dozen blocks or so from the abandoned warehouse that the Guild was using as a hideout, his heart began to quicken. The number of people on the street was far above what should be out in the middle of the night, especially in a warehouse district.

Remarin fell in behind a crowd heading in the correct general direction, then began walking faster as he caught sight of a yellow glow above the line of rooftops. He thought about taking the High Road, but if traffic was as heavy across the rooftops as it was in the sewers, he wanted nothing of it. He walked, then jogged, then ran along the streets with the citizenry until he fetched up sharply after turning a corner. It was as he'd feared, the Guild Hall was ablaze, the entire building fully engulfed in flames.

"Kit," Remarin said under his breath and sprinted toward the Hall.

He covered no more than twenty yards before something caught his eye. He stopped and turned to the alley, where a thin woman motioned for him to follow her. He stopped, torn between Kit and the Guild and his own curiosity. As always with Remarin, curiosity won out and he stepped into the alleyway.

"Good," the woman said. "Marcus is two blocks down and he has orders to stop you from exposing yourself no matter what, so you saved yourself a beating coming in now. Follow me." She turned to go, and Remarin grabbed her sleeve.

"Excuse me, but I'm not going anywhere without some information. First off, who are you? Second of all, what the hell happened at the Guild Hall? And lastly, who the hell are you?"

"I'll explain everything, but I'd rather do it in the safety of my home than in the streets where anyone might hear us. Having too many people around while discussing sensitive information is likely what got your friend Xamos killed."

"If you knew anything about Xamos, you'd know that there are a lot more reasons than loose lips that people want him dead, and that he and I were far from friends. Wait a second, how did you know he's dead? And who killed him?"

"Inside," the woman said. She led Remarin down a seemingly blind alley, then pressed a series of bricks in succession. A segment of wall slid open, and she left him into a well-appointed sitting room with several couches, tapestries on the walls, and a serving girl moving between the couches passing around pitchers of water and beer to the men and women. All were dressed in some assortment of blacks and gray, and almost all were slight of stature and kept their eyes in motion at all times.

"Welcome to the League of Assassins, Remarin. My name is Taryn, and I am the chief assignment agent in Gorix. Please surrender your blade and any other weapons you have on your person. No one goes armed within our Hall." She held out a hand, and Remarin unsheathed his knife and laid Trand across the woman's palm.

"I don't usually give away my knife until we've at least had dinner together," he quipped.

"Don't worry. It will be well cared for," Taryn said.

"As attached as I am to my knife, I'm rather less concerned for its well-being than my own. I had a little encounter with one of your people earlier this evening. At least I assume he was one of yours. He certainly made a valiant attempt at killing me."

"If he was one of ours, he was working an unsanctioned job, and I'll have to speak with him most harshly about that. Please describe him."

"Wore a lot of black, terrible sense of humor, knew Xamos, had about eighteen feet of guts lying around his feet last time I saw him, so I don't think you'll need to worry about that conversation."

"We didn't take any jobs from Xamos. Ever. He had a bad habit of not paying his debts. I don't know who you killed and don't really care. Everyone I value within my Guild is within these walls, and the others are disposable, many of them holdovers from previous regimes. Why did Xamos want you dead?"

"Let's just say that I am a debt he really wanted to see paid. But why did you bring me here?" Remarin asked.

"Because I asked them nicely," Kit's voice came from behind him. Remarin turned and stared at the image that stood before him.

They'd traveled together for weeks, and with all that time in disguise, Remarin almost came to believe that Kitarina really was his nephew Kit. But now, dressed in dark gray leathers and a slim-cut blouse, he realized that the young princess was actually quite a striking woman. Her hair had been washed and trimmed into an attractive cut instead of the hack job Remarin did on it every couple of weeks, and her time riding through the countryside to Gorix had bronzed her skin to a healthy glow. A pair of knife sheaths rode low on her hips, and matching sheaths sat in the top of her boots as well. Per Taryn's orders, she was unarmed, but there was a new confidence about her that Remarin hadn't seen before. She looked much less the terrified princess and more the confident young woman.

"Who are you, and what did you do with the Kitten I left behind?"

Remarin asked, giving the young woman a hug and an appraising look.

Kit blushed and smiled up at the thief. "Well, since the very few things I still owned burned up inside Xamos' Guild Hall, I decided that it might be acceptable to let the kitten burn as well."

"And out of the ashes comes a full-grown cat? I think it's supposed to be a phoenix," Remarin quipped.

"Fair enough," Kit said. "But with Xamos dead, everyone back in Bravis will think the assassin was successful, and I can stop dressing like a boy all the time."

"Don't worry," Remarin said. "No one will mistake you for a boy in that getup. And what exactly are you planning on wearing that for? Are you becoming Princess of the Assassins now?"

"Queen," Kit said with a completely straight face.

"Queen of what?"

"Queen of the Assassins, not Princess. Taryn and her people have sworn fealty to me. They are now my kingdom in exile, and they are the first people pledged to help me get my throne back."

"You and a dozen assassins are going to overthrow your uncle and reclaim your kingdom? Are you insane?"

"I don't think so, but I also don't think I'd know if I was insane. But it doesn't matter. I have a kingdom to reclaim, and my people will help me. Just like you."

"Okay, let's all calm down a little bit. I appreciate everyone's enthusiasm, but can we back up for a moment? What happened tonight? Who killed Xamos and burned down the Thieves' Guild? Do we know anything about survivors? Do we know for sure that Xamos is dead?" Remarin fired off questions in rapid sequence, never giving anyone a chance to respond.

"I can answer most of that," Kit said, "and I believe Taryn can handle the rest. I killed Xamos."

"What?" Remarin exclaimed. "I left you there under his hospitality! He was supposed to protect you! What happened?"

"I think Xamos had a different idea of hospitality than you and I do. At least when I was taught the rules of hospitality, sleeping with your host wasn't part of the bargain."

"That bastard," Remarin said. "I'm sorry, Kitten, if I'd known he would have tried to stoop that low, I never would have left you there."

"Don't feel bad, Remarin. Fighting off Xamos was probably what saved my life. If he hadn't been such a bastard, I would have been asleep when the assassin came creeping in to slit my throat."

"Wait a moment, Kit. First you tell me we trust the assassins with our lives, then you tell me one of them tried to kill you a little while ago. Which is it?"

"It's both," Taryn said. "The man who took the contract on Kitarina was a rogue, not working under Guild authority. We were offered the contract several days ago, but we don't kill children, so we turned it down. I knew the man was still in town, offering up the contract to likely freelancers. When I found out someone had taken it, I sent a team into the Thieves' Guild Hall to eliminate the assassin and make our apologies to Xamos. The apology was obviously unnecessary. The rogue was an idiot, underestimating both Her Majesty and my crew, so while he died a most horrible death, he managed to catch the Hall on fire while he did so. Completely coincidentally. I'm sure, a squadron of the City Watch was dispatched to the sewers outside Lowtown, and two more squads began patrolling the streets above. They managed to pick up dozens of men and women fleeing the fire, many of whom had outstanding warrants with the Watch."

"Yes, coincidental indeed," Remarin mused. "So someone sent an assassin after Kit, sent another after me, and staged three squadrons of the Watch around the Guild Hall just to see if we'd flee right into their trap. Sounds an awful lot like that fire was no accident, but set by the assassin to flush the Guild into the hands of the Watch."

"We had the same idea, and for some reason Her Majesty felt kindly toward you and asked us to prevent you from being caught up in the sweep, so here we are," Taryn said.

"Yes, here we are. Now what are to do about it?" Remarin thought aloud. He paced the sitting room for a few moments, sipping on fruit juice from the serving girls. Finally, he turned to Kit. "Kitten, I need something of yours."

"What?"

"I don't know, but something that wouldn't burn up in the fire and is unmistakably yours. Something that the corrupt bastards in this town can wail and weep over, then turn over to your uncle as evidence that you're dead."

The girl thought for a few seconds, then reached behind her neck and took off a necklace. On it hung a round pendant with an image of Castle Rutvor, and on the reverse the seal of house Rutvor, a pair of crossed swords with knot work between the points. "This was given to me by my grandfather. It has been in my family for three centuries. Uncle Alexander will recognize this as mine."

Remarin handed the necklace to Taryn. "Here's where you prove yourself."

"We have proven our loyalty to Her Majesty's satisfaction—"

"Now prove yourself to me. Get someone into the Guild Hall. Find a dead girl about the right age to pass as Kit and put this on her. Then we can figure out where to go."

"Go?" Kit asked. "We just got here!"

"And we've already been found out. We have to get out of here, and quickly. But first I have some business to attend to."

"What's that?" Taryn asked.

"You said the man who tried to hire you was still in town?"

"At least this morning he was, yes."

"Then he's almost certainly still here, probably waiting for some type of proof of death, like the proof we're going to provide him. We'll give him time to send a message back to Alexander, then he and I will have a little conversation."

CHAPTER 14

The door opened to the small room, and the man stepped inside and bolted it behind him. He lit a lamp by the bed and swallowed a short scream as he saw Remarin sitting in the shadows of the corner.

"I am very unhappy with you," Remarin said.

"W-what did I do?" the man asked. He was a pudgy man of about forty years with a mustache and thinning brown hair. Not very tall, not very short, not very handsome but not terribly ugly, he had the look of a man who faded from memory minutes after he left a room. A useful skill in an assassin, Remarin thought, but not quite as useful as the ability to actually kill the right person.

"I was becoming fond of the young lady who died in that fire tonight. A fire you set, I understand."

The man stood up to all his very mediocre height and spluttered at Remarin. "I-I had nothing to do with any fire! I-I just went to help, to see if anyone needed my assistance."

"And to make sure you heard the reports of the dead, so you could make sure your clumsy assassin actually got your target, no matter how many others were injured or killed in the process."

"If that were true, why would I come back here? Why am I not on my way to Veosia with news of the death of Princess Kitarina?"

"I didn't tell you the princess was the young girl I meant," Remarin said. "In fact, no one knew Kit was actually the princess. Nobody but the man who killed her and the man who sent you here."

"So now what?" the man asked, reaching behind his back to draw a dagger. "We fight in this tiny room, draw the attention of every knuckle-dragging buffoon in the city, leaving the survivor a very uncomfortable set of questions to answer."

"No," Remarin said. "I'm going to kill you, but not tonight. Tonight I'm going to send you back to your master with your tail between your legs and a message for 'King' Alexander. Tell him that it's over. Tell him the girl is dead, that I'm leaving Gorix, and as long as he leaves me and mine alone from here on out—"

"And if His Majesty doesn't think he needs to take orders from a cut-rate thief halfway around the world?"

"Then one night he'll step into his bedroom, light a lamp, and find me sitting in a chair in his room. It'll be the last thing he ever sees. And we don't even want to talk about what will happen to you."

"Fine, fine," the man said. "I'll deliver the message. Now get out of here, I have a long ride tomorrow."

"You mean tonight," Remarin corrected.

"My coach leaves in the morning," the man insisted.

"Your horse is saddled and waiting downstairs. You've made a great many enemies in Gorix tonight, and there are still a few thieves that weren't in their Hall when you burned it to the ground. And I may have let your description and whereabouts slip into conversation with one or more of them."

"You're a regular bastard, aren't you?

Remarin laughed. "I like to think of myself as a very uncommon bastard, but no matter. Get out, and if I ever see you again, I'll wear your balls for earrings."

The man picked up a pack by the door, put a few items of clothing in it, and headed out the door. As he exited into the hallway, he stopped and turned to Remarin. "This isn't over, thief."

"For your sake, you'd better hope it is." Remarin watched the assassin leave, then looked out the window and saw the man get on a horse and ride off into the beginnings of a glimmering sunrise. Remarin stepped back from the window and said, "You can come out now."

The wardrobe along the wall opened and Kit stepped out. "It smells like rancid cheese in there," she said, wrinkling her nose.

"Be glad that's all it smelled like," Remarin replied.

"Now what?" The girl sat on the bed cross-legged and looked up at Remarin.

"Now we get the hell out of Gorix, Kitten. We find some place safe to hole up for a while and start building an army. If we're going to take your throne back, we're going to need more than a dozen assassins and one spectacular thief."

"Ooooh, when do I meet this spectacular thief? He sounds fascinating!" Kit joked.

"You wound me, Kitten. And to think I was hoping to be Grand Vizier when you're finally Queen."

"Remarin, do you even know what a Grand Vizier does?"

"No idea," he admitted.

"Then let's get on the road so you can find out someday." She slid off the bed soundlessly and moved past Remarin to the door.

"Lead on, O Queen of Kats. Lead on."

CHAPTER 15

King Alexander the First of Veosia looked out the window at the moonlit night. He stood naked in the starlight and beheld the capital of his kingdom, pale light casting his flabby body in a less than flattering image. The city slept beneath his gaze, with only the occasional candle in the window or light streaming from the door of a pub spilling out onto the cobblestones as another over-served patron walked, crawled, or was thrown out to make his way home the best he could, dodging working girls and cutpurses on his way to sleep it off for a few hours before returning to work in the morning.

"It's yours, Majesty," came a low voice from behind him. A woman with long red hair walked up and stood beside him, her pale skin almost glowing in the little reflected light. Her beauty was other-worldly, ethereal yet lush. She trailed a finger along Alexander's powerful shoulders, traced the line of his bicep all the length of his arm. She took his hand and brought it to her lips, kissing his palm and running her pale pink tongue around and around his fingers.

"Velisande, what news from Gorix?" Alexander asked.

"The girl is dead," the red-haired woman replied. "The thief has escaped, but the child burned to death with the other trash."

"Good," said Alexander. "Now we may move forward with our plans."

"Not yet, my love," the woman purred as she wrapped her arms around his hard torso. Her fingers danced along the muscles of his abdomen, then trailed lower, gripping him tightly. The king turned to her and kissed her, one hand rising to cup her heavy breast.

"Of course, I will serve out the mourning period for my idiot brother and his bitch of a daughter, but then we shall be wed, and I will move on Gorix in force. By year's end, I will control the two largest kingdoms on the continent, and you will be pregnant with my heir." He leaned in and kissed her, forcing his tongue between her lips and mauling her breast. She endured this treatment stoically, her mind, as always, on her true objective.

"And I will have reclaimed the blade that thief stole from my family. You will have your kingdom, and I will have my revenge." She smiled up at Alexander, then pulled him to her and kissed him again, a wicked smile playing across her lips as she thought of a dagger with a ruby-topped hilt.

PART II
SURVIVAL

CHAPTER 16

The slender black shadow floated across the rooftops, clinging to the ridgeline, keeping her shadow tight to the shale roofing tiles, minimizing her silhouette in the bright moonlight. Noise floated up from the courtyard as she drifted overhead, making not a sound as her soft-soled shoes provided purchase on the slippery tiles.

The girl reached a spot on the roof and stopped. She counted windows across the courtyard, came to the right number, and unspooled a thin black rope from around her waist. She tied one end to a three-pointed hook that she unfolded from her left boot top and wedged the grapple firmly in the corner between a nearby brick chimney and the roof. Playing the rope out between her hands, she edged backward toward the lip of the roof. This was her most exposed moment, cast in moonlight as she leaned backward and wrapped the free line around her leg for a brake. She didn't dare rush. One false move would splatter her brains across the cobblestones far below, ruining the Solstice celebration and doing far worse harm to her evening.

She finally rotated around the eaves to a fully upside-down position and slowly lowered herself down the line to the window below.

Pressing her feet together locked her position on the line while freeing up both hands to pick the lock on the window. It was a simple latch. Most people don't do much to secure interior courtyard windows four floors up inside a seemingly impregnable castle in a kingdom at peace for the past five decades. That just made her life easier. One slim piece of metal slipped silently between the ill-fitting shutters, and a flick of her wrist lifted the latch with only the tiniest of efforts.

She pulled the shutters open and pushed off from the building, swinging once, twice, three times in ever-increasing arcs until she had enough momentum to release her grip on the rope and slide through the open window and roll to her feet on the thick rug.

The slight thief turned around and pulled the shutters closed, making sure to leave her excess rope in a loose coil on the floor, in case she needed to make a quick getaway. Turning her attention to the rest of the room, she froze as the scrape of a match echoed through the bedchamber.

Yellow light flared to life by the bed, bathing the room in a soft glow as a small man lit a lamp and walked toward her.

"Not bad, Kitten. Not bad at all. A bit slow, perhaps, but I didn't give you a deadline, now did I?" Remarin, self-proclaimed World's Greatest Thief, stood in front of her, that same infuriating grin on his face that he wore any time he thought he had bested her.

"How did you get here before me?" the girl asked, pulling off her hood and shaking her auburn hair free. The loose curls tumbled down around her shoulders and softened her boyish features, if not the scowl written across them.

"I came in with a delivery of fish for the party, then bribed the stable master to let me work as a groom for the night. When I had a livery, I wandered aimlessly until I happened to find the kitchen, where I developed a limp and spun a tale for the cook about a horse stepping on my foot and the stable master sending me to her for a poultice.

"When she left the kitchen for supplies, I tied my hair back and pulled a page's tabard out of a basket of laundry sitting in the hallway outside the kitchen. I tossed the groom's livery into the laundry, put on a hat, miraculously healed my limp, and went back into the kitchen, asking where my mistress's afternoon snack was. The kitchen girls are so terrified of any of these noble bitches that they dressed up a plate with several delicious tarts and cakes, along with a few different cordials to aid in digesting the rich desserts.

"I conveyed the tray of delicacies here, to my lady's chambers, when I knew good and well she was bathing with her cousins and would retire immediately to the chapel for prayer and her wedding, with no time to return to her chambers before the ceremony, and the unfortunate robbery that occurred afterward. Speaking of which, shouldn't you get on with that part?"

"Aren't you the one that always says 'the simplest plans are the best' and 'don't complicate things overmuch; it's a recipe for disaster'?" the girl, Princess-in-Exile Kitarina Rutvor of Veosia, now known simply as Kit, the apprentice thief, asked.

"I didn't complicate anything, Kitty-cat. My plan was very simple —get through the front gate and figure it out from there. I wouldn't suggest it for everyone, but it worked for me."

Leaving my contributions to the success of his plan completely unspoken, as usual, came the dry voice of Trand, Remarin's partner. Trand was just a soul now, trapped within the form of a magical dagger than Remarin carried on his belt. No one knew exactly what Trand's powers were, but they definitely extended past merely ridiculing Remarin for his impetuousness and generally poor decision-making.

"As usual," Kit agreed aloud. Only she and Remarin could "hear" the dagger, and they generally communicated with him aloud, but could speak mind-to-mind in emergencies.

"So where is it?" Kit asked.

"Where is what?' Remarin parroted.

"Where is the gem?"

"Oh, that? I have no idea." Remarin pulled a chair out from a round table and sat down. He picked up an apple from a fruit basket in the center of the table and began to peel it. He wisely used a smaller knife for this task, choosing not to enrage Trand by using him for flatware.

"You mean you got here early and didn't bother looking for it?" Kit shook her head.

"I was tired," Remarin protested. "I've had three jobs today!"

"All of which were fake!" Kit threw up her hands in frustration and began to rummage through the apartment. She started her search with the large wardrobe that dominated one entire wall of the room, opening drawers and digging through folded undergarments and frilly blouses.

Remarin, for his part, didn't just watch but moved to the dressing table and began rifling through the jewelry boxes that littered the surface.

"It's a shame our employer is so particular about *which* gem we bring her," Remarin said. "There are enough gems in this box alone to pay for..." His voice trailed off, then he was on his feet and headed for the door.

"Get out," he whispered, blowing out the lamp as he passed it. Kit stared at him in wonderment, then shoved everything back inside the drawer she was searching and started for the window.

"What's wrong?" she hissed across the room to Remarin. In the sudden gloom of the bedroom, she could barely make out his shadow pulling slender throwing knives from his boots and wedging them into the doorframe, effectively jamming the door shut. The girl opened the window and tied the loose end of the rope around her waist. This would allow her to climb back to the roof and pull the rope up after her.

"How much rope do you have?" Remarin asked, joining her at the window and looking down. The courtyard some thirty feet below teemed with celebrants dancing, drinking, and enjoying fantastical displays of gymnastics, fire-dancing, sword-swallowing, and other feats.

"Almost forty feet," Kit said.

"Twelve feet from the chimney to the edge of the roof, five feet from the edge to the window makes seventeen, so you've got about twenty-three, twenty-four feet left. Sound right?"

"That sounds right, but—"

Remarin held up a hand to stop her. "Figure two feet to loop around you and tie off and you'll have about a seven- or eight-foot drop at the bottom. Cut the rope on the downward part of your swing and try not to break anything," he said.

"What the—Remarin!" The last word was more a curse than anything as he bent at the knees and picked the slight girl up around her hips.

Remarin took one step forward and hefted her out the window, tossing her toward the stones below. He watched for a second to make sure she didn't swing back into the building and crack her skull on the way down, then he stepped out the window and grasped the rope. With one foot on the sill and the other wrapped around the thin line, Remarin reached back and closed the shutters just as a mighty crash sounded from the hall outside the mistress's bedchamber.

"Not fast enough, you bastards," Remarin said with a tight smile, and slid down the rope. He came to the dangling end of the line some eight feet from the ground and swung himself out from the wall. On the backswing, he let go of the rope and fell, hitting the wall with both feet about five feet from the ground. He flexed his knees to absorb the impact and spun in midair to land in a florid bow before a clutch of nobles who stood staring at Kit, who knelt on the ground looking in all directions for an exit.

Remarin came out of his bow with both hands to the sky and announced in a loud voice, "The Black Cat Acrobats, ladies and gentlemen! Here on a one-night engagement celebrate Her Grace's majority! Enjoy the rest of the night's entertainment!" He pulled Kit to her feet and into another grand bow, which the girl mimicked with none of her usual grace. Remarin snatched two mugs of ale off a passing server's tray, pressed one into Kit's hand, and steered her toward the main entrance.

"What in the seven hells are you doing, Remarin!" Kit hissed, falling into stride with the older thief and keeping her voice to a razor-edged whisper.

"Keeping us alive," Remarin replied, draining half his mug in one long pull as he nodded to the gate guard.

"You there, stop!" the guard called after them. Remarin froze, and his hand slid toward Trand, sheathed on his waist.

"Yes, my good sir?" Remarin replied in his haughtiest tone.

"Please leave the mugs, sir. Cook will have my ears if any of them wander off," the guard said, his voice sheepish. Remarin nodded to him and set both mugs on a tray by the guards. "Have a good night, sir."

"And you as well, young man," Remarin said. He turned back to the street, and in seconds the lights and sounds of the party were just more faint city noise.

After several twists and turns carried them from the richest residential section of town to the more working-class sections with fewer prying eyes, the pair finally paused in their quick walk. Remarin let out a pent-up breath and motioned Kit into an alley, pulling off his shirt and turning it inside out as he did. Reversed, the shirt of midnight black was a deep maroon with brown accents. With the pull of a tie at the neck, the skintight garment relaxed the neck and bottom hem, allowing the shirt to flow over the thief's hips and cover the plethora of knives hanging from his belt. In seconds, he looked less like a prowler of shadows than a down-on-his-luck merchant or day laborer. A few judicious scuffs of mud across the tops of his boots and a moment or two kneeling in the dirtier parts of the alley completed his disguise.

Kit underwent a similar transformation, pulling yards of fabric from under her shirt to transform her from lithe cat burglar to skinny barmaid, as she skinned out of her black silk overskirt to reveal a whitish shirt and false corset garment hidden underneath, looking for all the world like a constrictive garment, but in reality allowing her all the flexibility she needed to do her real job while appearing to hold down another, more innocent one. The shirt she twisted into a cord and looped around her hips to hide the hilts of her own blades, and the tops of her boots folded down to show brown leather and buckles instead of just midnight black.

"Fine, now that we look like layabout Remy who works when he runs out of money and little sister Kate, who scrubs the barter at Bertrand's, do you want to tell me what all that was about?"

"There have only been two times in my career where I was hired to steal one specific object and ordered to ignore anything else in the room, to the exclusion of a fortune in gems. One of those was tonight," Remarin said, looking to and fro like he was afraid they were being watched.

"And the other?" Kit asked.

"The night we met," Remarin said. "When you were supposed to be murdered so your uncle could take the throne and I was set up to take the fall for it."

CHAPTER 17

"I told you, Taryn, it should have been a simple heist!" Remarin grunted as he backpedaled.

"And I told you that any harm that befell my queen would befall you fivefold! She has cut her arm, so I will cut yours. Off." The dark-skinned woman came in low with a thrust that Remarin parried easily, but only Trand's magically-enhanced speed allowed him to reverse his stroke and block Taryn's counter. Remarin backed up into a wall of Taryn's office, exotic animal heads poking him in terribly uncomfortable places as he dodged and weaved and generally tried to avoid the diminutive assassin's attacks. Taryn stood barely fifteen spans high and weighed less than six stone, but what she lacked in size she made up for in speed and deadly focus.

Her rapier and dagger wove a deadly steel net in front of Remarin, just waiting to catch him in a misstep. He held Trand in his left hand to parry, a curved short sword in his right. He blocked, parried, riposted, ducked, jumped, and generally tried to avoid the little murderer's attacks, hoping she would eventually wear herself out from the futility of it all. Remarin had spent a life avoiding people who wanted to kill him, right or wrong, so he was only mildly concerned with Taryn, no matter her position as Enforcer of the Assassins' Guild.

His mild concern turned to annoyance as he stepped back a hair too slowly and the girl scored a hit on him, slicing through his favorite black shirt and drawing a line of blood across his stomach.

"Ow!" he yelled. "Dammit, Taryn, would you *stop* this nonsense?"

"I told you, thief," Taryn said through clenched teeth, "you got my mistress injured, you pay the price in blood."

"Oh, for the gods' sake, she has barely more than a hangnail! Kit, tell your psychotic guard dog that you're not permanently scarred." Remarin turned to Kit, who sat in a plush armchair by Taryn's large wooden desk. The young woman sat sipping chilled wine with a slight smirk on her face, though she had leaned forward in her seat at the sight of the thief's injury.

"Don't kill him, Taryn," Kit called.

"I shall not, your majesty," the smaller woman replied. "I shall merely—"

Her words cut off as Remarin sheathed his knife and sword, stepped inside Taryn's reach, and dropped her to one knee with a vicious head butt. He reached down and grabbed her child-sized wrists, feeling the whipcord muscles in her arms. She struggled, but her strength was no match for her older, and much larger, opponent.

Remarin pulled her to her feet and head butted her again. Her eyes crossed, and she sagged in his grip, but refused to fall. "Are we finished?" Remarin asked.

"When you bleed, thief." Taryn grinned at him through crossed eyes. She twisted her arm, and almost quicker than he could see, she wriggled from his grasp and drew another pair of knives from her belt. Remarin just sighed and flicked out a foot, catching Taryn on the tip of her chin with the lead-lined toe of his boot. Her eyes rolled back in her head, and the head of the Assassins' Guild of Gorix crumpled to the floor.

"Was that completely necessary?" Kit asked.

Remarin looked down at the semiconscious assassin struggling to her knees. "Yes, I am fairly certain that was completely necessary." He walked over to the desk and took a seat in front of it, picking up a glass of wine from the desk and crossing his legs.

"She's just trying to protect me," Kit continued.

"Yes, Kitten, but she's usually trying to protect you from *me*, which is a little contrary to everything in the world, since I'm the one who saved you from your usurping uncle, not to mention the assassin said usurping uncle sent after you, then took you under my wing and trained you to be one of the greatest thieves the Western Realms have ever seen. Or not seen, which is a much better state for a thief. We would always prefer to be unseen than seen."

"You're also the one that got us chased from Elorfina in the middle of the night because you refused to pay a whore for her services," Kit replied.

"The things I taught that inept strumpet, she should have paid me!" Remarin protested.

"There's an argument to be made that she did, given the jewelry you 'found' in your pockets when we finally stopped running. Where were we then, Franjila?"

"For about a minute, then your dear protector got in a fatal argument with a watchman and we were forced into the swamps for a year and the only refuge we could find was Shu-Haroth, and I'm not even sure that counts as refuge."

"But by the end of the year, we had enough money from your gambling winnings—"

"Very few of them requiring cheating," Remarin chimed in.

"To come here to Casterlane and set up shop. And this place has been pretty good for the past three years," Kit finished, sipping her wine.

"But now it looks like that is coming to an end, Queen Kitten," Remarin said.

"Are you sure?" Kit asked. "Isn't it possible that the fence you took this job from is very particular in what he was looking for? How has he been to work with in the past?"

Remarin raised an eyebrow at the girl. "Those are good points, Kitten. You've been paying attention to this whole 'criminal empire' thing."

"I try, Remarin. Now answer the questions."

"Fine. This was a new fence, a trial job, as it were. We were still in the feeling-out phase of our relationship, so I don't have enough history to know if she was always particular, or if it was something just for this job. But that's not how the job works. I get hired to steal one thing, but if I see something else that catches my eye, I can take it. Unless there's a very good reason for me not to take it."

"Like the person who hired you to steal the one thing also owned everything else in the house," Kit said.

"Exactly," Remarin replied. "And they, or she, rather, didn't want to go to the trouble of chasing down the rest of her belongings after her patsy had been disposed of."

"You and me," Kit said.

"Quite likely more 'you' than 'me,' given your relatives and their tendency toward bloodshed," Remarin replied.

"So now what do we do? I've grown accustomed to it here. I would hate to have to leave on such short notice."

"As would I, Kitten. That's why Taryn and I will be going to have a conversation with my employer tonight. After she takes some berrawyn tea for the pain in her jaw, of course."

"You'll need more than tea when I finish with you, thief," Taryn growled, on her feet but weaving from side to side a little.

"Oh sit down, Taryn," Kit said, motioning to the plush chair behind the desk. "You know you won't best him when he's paying attention."

"I know," the diminutive assassin said, hanging her sword belt on a hook beside her desk. "That's why I'll poison one of his meals tomorrow, then cut off his arm." She sat behind her desk and nodded to Remarin with a smile. "Which hand do you pleasure yourself with, thief? I want to make sure I leave you some joy in this life, since after tonight you'll never hold a woman again."

"So I can make sweet love to you whenever I like, is that what you're saying?" Remarin sent one of his crooked half-smiles Taryn's way, and the small woman shuddered.

"I'd rather mate with a goat," Taryn replied. "It would likely smell better. At least goats get clean when it rains."

"Oh now I'm going to discuss hygiene with a desert rat from

Gorix?" Remarin rolled his eyes and leaned his chair back, putting both feet on Taryn's desk as he did so. "At least men of Bravis know better than to think washing in water brings on harmful spirits, unlike your backwards, and smelly, sand-divers."

Taryn grinned across the desk at her foe, settling into the old rhythm of argument that they both knew so well.

How long do you think they'll be at it? Kit thought to Trand who, besides being trapped inside an enchanted dagger, was Remarin's best friend for many years and partner in more escapades than either of them could remember at this point.

They could go for days, or until one of them gets hungry, the dagger's dry "voice" came back at her.

"When you two are finished flirting, let's spend a little time making a plan to question your new employer this evening. In the meantime, I'm going to bed. It's been a long night, and the sun is rising." Kit finished off the glass of wine and walked across the room to the door. She closed it behind her to the sound of even more friendly bickering between her two best friends, the thief and the murderer. *Oh, how differently my life has turned out,* she thought as she headed down the hallway to her bedroom.

"Where is my gem?" the raven-haired woman asked the second Remarin stepped across the threshold into her "office," really the back room of a rug merchant specializing in Tarvian silks, the finest rugs in the known world.

"Probably still right where it was before you hired me," Remarin said, pulling out a chair and propping his feet up on the woman's desk. "But you knew that already, didn't you?"

The flashing anger in the woman's eyes faded, replaced by momentary confusion then wry amusement. "How did you figure it out?"

"You were very explicit that I take nothing else, just the gem. Usually if I'm hired to retrieve a specific object, like a priceless gem borrowed from the Temple of Lightning, I'm given free rein to fill my pockets with anything else I can carry. It's a bit of a bonus, you see, for a job well done, especially if the job entails robbing one of the richest houses in the city on an evening where it's sure to be full of revelers and guards."

"But since I made it very clear you were not to steal the other jewelry or items you may stumble across..." The woman's violet eyes sparkled in the candlelight as she watched Remarin.

"Then my instincts started to itch, and I got the hell out just before the guards arrived. And oddly enough, they did arrive, just as I was standing in a strange bedroom with my hands full of women's underthings. Very nice silk underthings, I might add. Wispy, soft underthings, might as well not be wearing anything at all." He cocked an eyebrow at the woman sitting across from him and watched as a slow blush appeared on her cheeks and crept across her face.

"Oh, pardon me," he said. "It must be warm in here." He reached across the desk and handed her a scrap of silk. She blotted her brow with it, then looked at the fabric. Her face flamed crimson, and she hastily tucked the garment out of sight under her desk.

"My apologies," Remarin said. "I just thought you might want those back. Silk and lace underthings are so expensive these days, after all."

"Now what?" the woman asked, her cheeks glowing with a flush that ran all the way down her neck to the tops of her breasts. Remarin noted with some interest that they seemed to be very well-formed breasts, and perhaps independent of the effects of gravity. But she was a young woman yet, and such is often the case with young women that they can support more upper structure for a longer time than one would expect.

Eyes on the prize, Remoron. Trand's dry voice pierced Remarin's reverie.

Oh, my eyes are definitely on the prizes, the thief thought back.

How have I kept you alive this long? Remarin could almost hear the blade sigh inside his head. *Pay attention, idiot. She tried to get you killed last night, and she'll do it again if you let her. Don't forget, there are two guards outside that door that are big enough to pick their teeth with your shinbones.*

Remarin tore his eyes away from his employer's décolletage and focused on her eyes. "So why exactly did you arrange to have me caught rummaging through your underpants last night? I never even laid eyes on this sapphire you wanted me to...oh." Remarin's eyes grew wide, and he stared at the woman.

"Yes, exactly. 'Oh.' I no longer have the gem in question. And explaining that would be very unpleasant to the Priestess of Storms, so I had to arrange for the stone to be stolen. Then I could deflect attention to you, the mysterious thief spotted in my bedchambers who got away with the Gem of Thunder. You'd be famous as the thief who stole the most valuable gem in Casterlane."

"Until someone decided to collect the inevitable bounty on my head. Then I'm famously dead." Remarin scowled at the woman.

"You're a thief," the woman said, no expression crossing her face. "It isn't a career choice known for long and healthy lives."

"True, but I've worked diligently at avoiding the odds for so long, it would be a shame to become just another cliché at this point. So what's your plan now? I'm sure you've already informed the Priestess of Storms that your bedchamber was violated last night, and in a most unpleasant fashion, although if I'd known the quality of your under-things beforehand, I'm sure I would have tried harder to make it more pleasant for you." Remarin walked over to a small table and poured himself a glass of wine, passing the lip of the glass by Trand's hilt gem before bringing the glass to his lips.

It's clean, the knife told him. *Local vintage, relatively fresh, nothing to write home about, but it won't kill you.*

I love living with a wine critic on my side, Remarin thought. He sipped from the crystal glass and looked at the woman, who glared at him from her chair. She truly was a striking woman, with high cheekbones and a body that belied her daughter's coming of age celebration the night before. Her hair hung loose in dark curls over her alabaster shoulders, and violet-tinged eyes flashed at Remarin as she stared back at him. He let his gaze linger again over her cleavage, then brought it back to her face in time to catch the hint of a smile flicker across her lips.

Good, she thinks I'm besotted by her charms, Remarin thought.

You mean to say you aren't? That would be a first, Trand shot back.

It will take a lot more than a lovely pair of breasts bound in a silken corset to make me forget that she tried to have me killed last night. Now perhaps if they were unbound... Remarin gave himself a mental shake and focused on the task at hand.

"Well?" he asked.

"Well, what, thief?" she replied.

"Well, what are you going to do now, Your Grace? You don't have the gem, you don't have a thief to hand over to the Priestess of Storms, and you don't have a good excuse as to why you're meeting with me at all."

"Well, thief, that's where you're wrong," the woman said. "I don't have the gem, that much is true, because I sold it to cover an unexpected medical expense and the magical procedures I needed to endure afterward. But I do have a thief, as you are right here in front of me, and this note provides me with all the reason I ever need to be here, meeting with you." She pulled a folded piece of paper out of her corset, and Remarin sighed.

I suppose I'm going to have to kill a fair number of people to get out of here, he thought to Trand.

I sense the thoughts of six soldiers and one priest outside the door. But if you're going to start killing people, I'd start with her. She's the most dangerous person in the building, Trand informed him.

Remarin drew his rapier and Trand and leveled the sword at the woman's midsection. "Now Your Grace, what exactly would be worth all this trouble? It can't be just mere magical enhancement because that isn't that expensive, and besides, you don't need much."

"Thank you," the woman said, her eyes never wavering from the tip of the rapier.

Remarin's eyes followed her gaze to the tip of his blade, then to her stomach. "Ah, I understand now. An unwelcome visitor in the Duchess's womb. Someone's soldiers marched across your beachhead and it's been a while since your husband has been into the breech, so you needed to hide the evidence. And I get to pay the price for your indiscretions. Lovely."

The Duchess lowered her gaze. "I am sorry, if that means anything. I didn't want to have you killed, but when I heard who you were…"

"Wait, what?" Remarin's head snapped up. "What do you mean, who I am?"

"A messenger came through the Duke's audience chamber a few weeks ago looking for you, Remarin of Torin, son of Baron Jameson of Torin, the first son and abdicated heir who fled his responsibilities and his lands some twenty years ago to live the life of a common man. The description was uncanny, and the painting they replicated bore an amazing likeness to the scruffy wastrel currently holding down a corner of the bar down at the Blind Boar. Since it was rumored that you were not above taking on a risky endeavor for the right price, and since the messenger made it sound imperative that you be found and returned home at once, I decided to have you take the fall for stealing the gem. Your wealthy father could pay the gem's price as a ransom, and none would be the wiser. But then you had to go and get nervous, and start thinking, and now you'll have to die. I will, of course, apologize to your father for the misunderstanding." She stood and walked past Remarin to the door. The thief stood there, gaping, as she threw back the bolt and flung open the door, pointing at him.

"Take him," she declared, then ducked out past the first guardsman into the now-abandoned rug shop.

That went about as well as most of your interactions with women, Trand's "voice" sounded in his head.

Remarin snapped out of his shock barely fast enough to bring his rapier up to parry the guardsman's sword stroke. Unfortunately for the thief, the guard's heavier blade snapped the rapier off at the hilt, leaving Remarin holding about three inches of steel protruding from a hand guard. The soldier grinned at Remarin, showing a mouth full of bad hygiene, and Remarin punched forward with the remains of his sword. The three inches of blade was more than enough to pierce the bigger man's eyeball and skewer his brain, dropping the guard like a sack of potatoes. Remarin drew Trand and flicked him at the next guard's face. The dagger flew truer than an arrow, catching the man right in the nock between his chest plate and his throat guard. He went down in a gurgle of blood, and Remarin knelt to retrieve the first man's short sword.

Remarin stood up and stepped closer to the door, trying to keep the number of opponents to one at a time. He blocked, parried, and riposted the best he could with the shorter blade, but the guard on the other side of the door was equally handicapped by not being able to swing his long sword effectively. Remarin held out his hand, sent a quick mental command to Trand, and his dagger appeared in his palm. He dropped to one knee, thrust his sword up over his head in a crosswise block, and lunged forward with the dagger. A pair of quick slashes, and the deep cuts on the inside of the guard's thighs bloomed red on his black pants.

Remarin stepped back, allowing the bleeding guardsman to stagger forward. The man raised his sword once, but flailed impotently at the air instead of striking anywhere close to Remarin. His life's blood poured from the sliced arteries in his legs, and he collapsed onto the expensive rug. The panting thief looked at the two remaining guards standing in the doorway. They gawked at the blood-spattered little man, dressed in street clothes, clutching a dagger in one hand and a stolen short sword in the other. In front of him lay three highly-trained, well-equipped corpses that moments ago had been their friends. Doubt and confusion flickered across their faces as Remarin leaned against the large desk that dominated much of the room.

"Do you surrender?" he asked the stunned men. "It's okay, there's no shame in it. If you like, I'll even punch you a few times so it looks good for the Duchess."

At the mention of their demanding, and borderline insane, mistress, the men's faces hardened and their shoulders squared.

That might not have been the best thing to bring up right now, Trand said.

"Not the first time I've put my foot in my mouth," Remarin said. He took a deep breath, pushed off of the desk behind him, and charged the men. The guardsmen, stunned by the sudden attack from a man they wholly expected to be dead already, stepped back and to the sides, giving the slight thief just enough room to pass between them. Remarin's blades flicked out to each side as he ducked under the guards' arms, and their sliced sword belts clattered to the floor.

The first guard stood staring, his mouth open as Remarin slid Trand between his fourth and fifth ribs, twisting just a touch as the blade pierced his lung, deflating the organ, and stealing the man's last breath as he drew the knife out. The guard, his lifeblood pouring from his chest, clutched his hands to the wound and stared as his last few heartbeats were wasted on the floor of a rug shop at the hands of a master thief and his magical dagger.

The second man was quicker to react, dropping to a knee and snatching his blade from the scabbard, then bringing it up to knock away Remarin's thrusting short sword. Steel rang on steel, and the guard brought his greater strength to bear on Remarin, leveling deadly slashes at his neck and chest. Remarin backed up and ducked around towers of rugs and stacked carpets, keeping his eyes locked on the steel-gray orbs of the last of the Duchess's men, at least as far as he knew. He caught one sword stroke on his blade down by the hilt and twisted his wrist to lock blades with the guard. He lowered a shoulder and reversed his footing, shoving forward instead of ducking back. He drove the locked blades off to one side and pressed his shoulder into the guard's chest.

"Do you surrender yet?" Remarin asked, sweat dripping from his hair and onto the man's armored chest.

"Why would I do that? Your sword is over there." The guard jerked his chin at the locked swords by his right ear.

"True enough, but my knife is right here." Remarin smiled into the man's face and gave a little twist of his dagger. Trand made his presence known below the guard's waistline, just to the side of his armor's codpiece.

"One slip from me and you'll not need this bulging bit the next time you're fitted for armor," Remarin said. "Now drop the sword."

The guard, his face pale, did as he was instructed. Remarin stepped back, his sword trained on the guard's throat, then in the blink of an eye, he reversed grip on his stolen sword, rapped the guard sharply on the temple with the hilt, and dropped the blade on the wooden floor beside the unconscious man.

He slid Trand into his sheath and walked to the front of the store. Dariz, the store owner, hid behind the counter as Remarin approached.

"Please don't kill me," the portly bald man whimpered. Remarin reached over the counter and dragged the fat man to his feet. A wave of stench hit his nostrils, and it became apparent that Dariz had lost control of his bladder during the fight.

"I'm not going to kill you, Dariz. I just need you to do two things. One, I need you to empty the strongbox under the loose floorboard back there and hand me that money. Only the gold, not the paper money, and any gems you've squirreled away back there."

"I don't know what box you're talking about, Remy, and why were those men trying to hurt you?"

"They weren't trying to hurt me; they were trying to kill me. And you know why, or at least you know who they were working for, and you know that I can't stay in this city very long now that I've run afoul of her. So you keep the money box everyone knows about and you get out of here before she starts cleaning up witnesses, and I get the money from your 'extra' carpets and the drugs. Then we both leave Casterlane in opposite directions, and we both live a good long time. How does that sound?"

Dariz opened his mouth, protest writ huge on his face, but Remarin held up one finger. "Or I will gut you where you stand, take all the money, and set this place to burn in the largest blaze this commercial district has ever seen. Which will it be?"

Dariz looked at the man across the counter from him. This was not the wastrel Remy he'd come to know around the city's taverns and dancing hall. This was a powerful and lethal man, someone who was not to be trifled with. He stared at this bizarre not-Remy for a moment, then nodded and knelt behind the counter. He emerged a few moments later with a pair of bags. He handed the first one to Remarin, then stuck the other in his belt.

"We never see each other again?" the shopkeeper asked Remarin.

"Never," Remarin agreed. He watched as Dariz walked out the front door of his shop, turned right and vanished into the world.

"Now let's go find out who wants me to go home, and if I have to kill them," the thief mused, counting his money and stepping out into the afternoon sun.

CHAPTER 19

The man sat alone in the darkest corner of the bar, far from the fire, the small minstrel's stage where a geriatric bard plucked folks songs, and the door, yet with a clear line of sight to all three. The only blind spot for the table where the man sat was a chair tucked away under the stairs leading up to the rooms where Madame Xina's girls took their men up for a quick tumble. Usually the chair was occupied by Thod, Xina's "security chief," but tonight a smaller man sat there, paying no attention to the giggles and moans coming from above him. All his attention was focused on the man at the table, the man who had been there since mid-afternoon, ordering ale after ale and never standing to relieve himself.

He's pouring out his beer, Remarin thought to Trand.

If I still had legs, I'd kick him in the arse for such a crime, the knife replied.

No great loss, Bertrand's beer is half water and half horsepiss, Remarin said.

Says the one who can still drink. Even terrible beer is better than life without beer.

I said I'd find a way to get your body back.

For now, just concentrate on keeping yours alive. His heartbeat just sped up. He saw something.

"Dammit," Remarin muttered, twisting himself around in his chair to get a glimpse of the door. His cubbyhole provided a perfect view of the stranger, but the tables scattered throughout the room cut off his view of the door, and the piano by the stairs blocked his view of the bar area. He was blind to two-thirds of the room, and now that was coming back to haunt him.

Remarin finally let out a sigh and stood up, motioning for a serving girl to come to him. She bustled over, but Remarin wasn't interested in food.

"What is it?" Kit asked, her bubbly demeanor dropping away the second she was out of sight of the rest of the customers.

"Who just came in?"

"A couple of guardsmen. Private, not city. What did you do?"

"Whose guards?"

"What did you do?"

"I might have killed a few of Duchess Newlan's guards this afternoon."

"You might have or you did?"

"Well, I didn't exactly count their heartbeats, but they certainly looked dead when I was finished with them."

"When were you going to tell me this?" Kit's eyes flashed in the shadowy corner.

"Soon," Remarin said, looking past Kit to the table in the corner. "Shit!" he hissed.

"What now?" Kit asked.

"He's gone," Remarin said, pushing past Kit to get a better look into the room. He stopped cold when a dark cloak filled his vision.

Remarin looked up into the grizzled face of Jacob of Laren, the man who, until moments before, had occupied a seat in the corner of Bertrand's pub. The face was much the same as Remarin remembered from his childhood, kind eyes deep-set beneath bushy dark eyebrows, now shot through with gray. The beard Remarin remembered dripping water from the rain on his first hunt as a child was now more salt than pepper, but the jaw it covered still set firm in his trim face.

Steel-blue eyes stared down at Remarin, and he was once again a child of twelve, holding a knife above the still-beating heart of a deer he felled in his father's forests. He touched the arrow protruding from the majestic animal's side, and the deer kicked feebly, still running in its mind although its body lay bleeding out onto the carpet of autumn leaves. Tears welled up in Remarin's eyes as he pressed the knife to the deer's throat, then Jacob's hand wrapped around his own and steadied his grasp as he sliced the animal's throat and ended its suffering.

Those same eyes stared down at Remarin as Jacob's body hemmed him into the corner. The slight thief took in the old Huntmaster's build, still trim with long arms and legs that could cover forty miles in a day without rest, then decided not to push the issue. He picked up his empty mug from the floor beside his chair and slid it along the bar to the watching Bertrand.

"It's fine, Bertie. If he wanted to kill me, I would have been dead two days ago. We'll be in Xina's office for a bit, then the place is yours. And Kate's done for the night." Bertrand's eyes widened, but he nodded to Remarin.

Kit raised an eyebrow at the thief.

He looked back at her and said, "May as well lose the apron, Kitten. We're pretty much done for here. Let's take this party some place more private, shall we?" Remarin's shoulders were square and his jaw set, every vestige of the lighthearted rogue vanished in an instant staring at the older man. He stepped forward, and the bigger man blocked his path.

"It's all right, you old bear. I know better than to try to outrun you when you've got the scent, even now. Follow me upstairs, then you can tell me why you're here and we can decide if there's going to be an argument or a real fight."

The big man chuckled, but stepped aside. Remarin led the others past Thod, who sat on the bottom step. The guard stood as Remarin approached, but the thief waved him off with a slight gesture. Thod's eyes went wide, and he headed for the door as Remarin, Kit, and the newcomer climbed the stairs. There were a few scattered glances their way from the regulars who had never seen "Remy" or "Kate" climb the stairs to the pleasure rooms, but a hasty round of refills from Bertrand diverted their attention back to their mugs.

Remarin led the pair down the hallway, past a series of closed doors with various sounds coming from the other side. He stopped before the last door on the left, knocked three times quickly, knocked twice, then three times slowly. He waited a moment, then opened the door and motioned for the others to follow.

The trio stepped into a well-appointed office, dominated by a large wooden desk facing the door. Two chairs faced the desk, with one high-backed leather chair behind it. In the leather chair was buxom forty-something woman with auburn hair piled high atop her head. A few stray ringlets lay scattered across her olive skin and teased down along her décolletage, contained within a green and crimson corset.

"Hello, Xina," Remarin said as he closed the door behind them, then shot the bolt and dropped a heavy wooden beam across the opening.

"That bad?" the madame asked, sipping dark red liquid from a thin crystal wine glass.

"My time here seems to be at an end, my dear. So, too must be our relationship. I'll be needing our stash, and an uninterrupted hour or so with my old friend here."

Xina nodded and withdrew a slender key from within her corset. "All this time, Remy, I thought you'd come looking for this," she said. She reached below the surface of the desk to unlock a drawer. She pulled out the drawer with a screech of wood on wood.

"As much fun as it would have been to look for it, what would I have done once I had it? Steal from myself? Seems not only counterintuitive, but downright silly."

"But we could have had such fun playing hide and seek with the key," Xina said, and her smile told tales of a younger woman with a younger woman's appetites.

"Or some other things, I'm sure. But alas, that ship has sailed, my dear, and I need the money, and the room," Remarin replied with a gentle smile. Xina handed him a bulging sack and a smaller pouch that rattled like gemstones.

"Here you go, Remy. You've been a good partner. Bert and I would have been out of business a dozen times over if it hadn't been for you." Xina came around the front of the desk and hugged the thief, who blushed to the roots of his hair.

"I hope you've learned a trick or two because you're on your own now, love." Remarin returned the hug, then gave the madame a pat on the rear as she headed toward the door. The woman giggled like a girl of twenty again and stepped out into the hall. Remarin replaced the bar across the door and pulled a chair out from against the wall to sit near the others. He sat, then motioned for the other two to do the same.

"I'd offer drinks, but I know that Jacob never drinks while on a hunt, and you won't call this hunt over until I walk back into my father's keep, will you, Jacob?"

"Not the slightest chance, Your Grace. I was given a task by your brother, a task that I intend to see to its end. Only then can I hang up my bow."

"Once I'm safely stuffed and mounted over Steven's fireplace?" Remarin asked, a wry half-smile not reaching his eyes.

"You know I wouldn't be here if it wasn't important. I know exactly how much you're interested in the responsibilities of your birthright," the older man said.

"That would be not interested at all," Remarin replied.

"Could we pause for a moment and bring me up to speed on a few things?" Kit leaned forward. "Like Remarin having a birthright and you addressing him as 'Your Grace'?"

"That's how we address nobility in our land, girl. We all don't speak unless spoken to when in the company of our betters, so why don't you sit there and look pretty, and if I need someone to fetch me another ale, I'll let you know." The bigger man's tone spoke volumes, and Remarin covered his mouth with his hand as Kit's face grew more and more flushed.

She took a deep breath and stood. The girl walked over to the small bar set into the wall, poured herself a healthy glass of red wine, and downed it in one quick gulp. When she turned back to the men, the slightly timid serving girl was gone. In her place was a young woman who, while dressed in the rags common to a tavern girl who offered no services more than a mug of ale or bowl of thin stew, still exuded an air of propriety, as though she would be more comfortable directing a staff of servants than scrubbing bar tops, or more properly placed doing needlepoint in the parlor of a great house than discussing her upcoming flight from a whorehouse.

"Mr...Jacob, is it?" The big man nodded, his face showing just a hint of the confusion he undoubtedly felt. "Jacob," Kit went on, "My name is Kitarina Rutvor, and I am Queen-in-Exile of Veosia. Remarin has, for the last number of years, worked to keep me safe and help me begin my efforts to reclaim my throne from my usurper uncle, Alexander Rutvor, who now styles himself King Alexander I of Veosia. I assure you, sir, that he is no more the King of Veosia than I am a tavern wench, and if you need another ale, I would certainly suggest you get it yourself, unless you fancy wearing your mug for a hat!"

Jacob looked at Remarin, who sat grinning at the exchange. "Once again, Your Grace, you have found yourself in the company of an amazing woman," said the big man.

"That is a true statement, Jacob," Remarin replied.

"Now, will you choose to answer my questions, or shall we discuss this once my Lady-at-Arms arrives?" Kit asked.

"I address Remarin as 'Your Grace' because he is the ancestral Guardian of the Gate, a pair of small island nations—"

"I know where it is," Kit cut the big huntsman off. "And you...work for the Duke? For Remarin?"

"Not for Remarin, exactly. More his brother, now."

"His brother?" Kit asked.

"Steven," Remarin added. "He was the dukely type. Tall, fair-haired, built like a man who you would expect to find riding a horse at the vanguard of a cavalry charge and swinging a sword in glorious battle."

"For all the glorious cavalry battles that take place on a five-mile square hunk of rock that has no more than fifty feet of flat ground in a straight line anywhere on the island," Jacob said with a grin.

"Fair point, but you can't argue that I was never the type to be a leader of men," Remarin replied.

"I never argued that fact, Your Grace. Not once."

"And can we skip the 'Your Grace' nonsense? I left all that a long time ago."

"Left is a generous term for it, Your—sorry." Jacob stopped himself.

"Sounds like there's a story here, Remarin. And is that even your name, or are you going to be something dull, like Robert?" Kit asked.

"Oh no, Remarin is my given name. It was my eighteenth great-grandfather's name, or something appropriately heir-like. Steven was the one that got to have the normal name. The normal life. He could bed who he liked, wed who he liked, live how he liked, whatever he wanted. I had to marry whoever was politically expedient, do the right things in public, pretend to care about things like currents and eddies and wakes and lighthouse defenses."

"You're from Pallas!" Kit exclaimed, sloshing the last of her wine out onto the rug.

"Close," Remarin replied. "I'm supposed to be Duke Remarin of Torin, slightly larger of the Twin Isles of Pallas-Torin, the Gateway to Savos and all the Eastern Realms."

"Your island, or the two of them, are among the most important military and shipping points in the world," Kit added.

"Yes, because the two islands sit at the end of a pair of archipelago that form a natural choke point leading into the Sea of Savos, which leads to the great Port City and the Niching River, which is the only water route inland to the Eastern Realms."

"But that country is vital to the survival of the East, both militarily and economically," Kit said. "The Dukes of the Twin Isles have histori-cally wielded great power and wealth both in the East and with Western traders. Why would you want to leave?"

"Have you ever been to Torin, Kitten?" Remarin asked.

"No, I've just read about it in books."

"That explains the question, then. Yes, my realm is incredibly important because you can't get to the rich Eastern Realms without passing within range of our catapults and arbalests. And our siege engineers have become very good shots over the years, so no one bothers trying to pass without paying the appropriate tribute. So there's plenty of wealth to spread around. And no one to spread it around to."

"I don't understand," Kit said.

"There are only about six hundred people on Torin, Your Majesty," Jacob cut in. "His Grace bores easily, as you may have noticed. By the time he was eleven, he knew every person on the island by name and had managed to irritate almost every single one of them to the point of near-rebellion. By the time he was sixteen, he was slated to take over operation of the great arbalests on the Point of Torin."

"By the time I was twelve, I had figured out the calculations to fire said arbalests completely over the Straits of Adral and onto the engineers manning the catapults on Pallas. It was decided that I should never, under any circumstances, be allowed to take over the siege engines."

"Or the lighthouses," Jacob said.

"Or the lighthouses," Remarin agreed. "Due to an unhealthy tendency to change the 'all clear' signals to 'dangerous reefs' signals."

"And vice versa," Jacob added.

"True enough," Remarin replied. "So by the time I was sixteen, I had eliminated myself from anything fun on the whole island except hunting, and as there was already a Huntmaster who showed no inclination toward death or retirement, and as hunting wasn't deemed a suitable occupation for a young Duke, I abdicated."

"You ran away," Jacob corrected.

"I abdicated, then ran away," Remarin expanded. "I did leave a note, along with my mantle of office. I left it on Steven's bed. It said, in very well-taught script, 'I abdicate.' Then I signed it and dove off the cliffs into the Straits."

"At sixteen?" Kit gasped.

"I made arrangements with a passing merchant to pick me up and smuggle me into the Western Realms. I had a few gold from my birthday and figured I could trust in my wits to keep me alive. Not long after I got off the ship in Dulvise, I met Trand, and the rest is history. I've been living by my wit and charm ever since then."

And he remains alive, to the shock of us all, Trand said to their minds.

CHAPTER 20

"And that's my story, or at least the very dull beginnings of what turned out to be a very interesting life. And a fairly pleasant one, at least until this afternoon. So Jacob, what brings you to Casterlane?" Remarin asked.

"You, of course. But you knew that already. Just as I'm sure you knew that your father died some five years ago. He caught a chill while fishing and never recovered."

"I heard," Remarin said, his voice soft and sober.

"He spoke of you on his deathbed. He said—"

"Later," Remarin cut him off. "I doubt you've been looking for me for the past five years to give me the message, so let's move along to what brings you chasing me."

Jacob raised an eyebrow, but nodded. "Your brother is ill, and his son is too young to rule. Someone must sit the throne until Steven recovers or until his son, Gareth, reaches majority."

"Why not the Duchess? Surely Steven married some imminently sensible woman from a powerful political family, so their marriage could be a partnership both expedient and profitable."

"The people would never accept her, Your Grace. She is of Pallas. The royal family of Pallas, actually." The older man fixed Remarin with a steady gaze, his eyes speaking of many things under the surface.

Remarin let out a long breath and sagged back in his chair. "Genevieve of Pallas is my brother's wife."

"Yes, Your—" The big man stopped himself at a glare from Remarin. "Yes, she is."

"Well, bugger me. I suppose I have to go home after all. Who's looking after things while you're gone?" Remarin stood and walked over to a small wardrobe in the corner and opened it. He reached inside and pulled out a pair of packs and two dark, hooded cloaks. He passed a pack and a cloak to Kit, who took them with a questioning look.

"The Seneschal has been managing most of the affairs of state since your brother's illness left him bedridden," Jacob said.

"Then what do you need me for? Old Bartlemas has a deeper understanding of the island's affairs than anyone and commands more respect than any should other than my brother."

"True, Your Grace, but Bartlemas died three years past. Also of a chill that he couldn't be rid of. Bartlemas was old, yes, but he was a hearty bastard. He should have had no trouble shaking a chill."

"You suspect something?" Remarin paused while rummaging in the wardrobe to peer at Jacob.

"Not at first, but when your brother fell ill with the same symptoms, I decided to find someone to sit the throne that I could trust. When I couldn't find anyone like that, I started looking for you."

Kit laughed, and both men stared at her. "What?" she asked. "It was funny!"

"I would be amused as well, except I know Jacob has no sense of humor. So someone killed the old Seneschal and made my brother sick. I assume you suspect the new Seneschal?"

"It does make a certain amount of sense, don't you agree? He has access, opportunity, and the knowledge."

"It makes sense," Remarin replied, "but only if he gains something from it. Without Pallas…"

"Now you see why the citizens would never trust Genevieve."

"Because she's obviously a Pallasian spy sent across the Straits to take over Torin and steal our... what does Torin have to steal, Jacob? I've forgotten."

"Sheep, Your Grace. They could steal our sheep. That would be unfortunate."

"Especially for the sheep, I suppose. Fine, let's go." He shouldered a pack from the wardrobe and strapped on a sword belt holding a new rapier to replace the one he broke the night before.

"Wait just a moment, Remarin," Kit said. "Why are we in such a rush? And why are there packed bags in Xina's closet? And what were you saying to Xina and Bertrand? What the hells is going on here?"

"Calm down, Kitten," Remarin said. "We're in a rush because Jacob thinks he's been followed, and I've never known his instincts to be wrong about anything. It's annoying, frankly. There are packs in Xina's closet because I knew from the day we arrived that our departure may be unexpected and under rushed circumstances. That's why I bought this place."

"Why you what?" the young princess gaped at him.

"One of the first things I did when we got here was to buy out all of Berty and Xina's business shares. Then I installed them as managers and taught them how to make money. All the while, I made sure that we could use this place a refuge and a meet-up point if things ever went pear-shaped. And I would definitely call needing to take over my brother's throne pear-shaped. And that's before we get to the Duchess Newlan's guards, who want to arrest me then make me disappear for something I didn't steal, or the fact that I still think our cover here is in jeopardy."

"What makes you say that?" Kit asked. "If this guy works for your brother, then that explains why he was sitting there drinking through his beard all night."

"But he's alone, so that doesn't explain the man enjoying Tone-Deaf Tremond's lute stylings beyond all reason at the back of the room. Or the weaselly-looking twit at the end of the bar who didn't bother to change his Veosian coins when he took the assignment to hunt you down."

"And you know this how?" Kit asked.

"Oh that? I stole his purse." Remarin reached inside his shirt and pulled a small coin purse out of a pocket hidden there.

"Was he like this when he lived on Torin?" Kit asked Jacob.

"No, ma'am. He was irrepressible, but he never went out of his way to get killed. That has developed since he left the Islands," Jacob replied.

"Har-har," Remarin fake-laughed as he walked toward the door. A set of rapid footsteps echoed from the other side, and Remarin threw open the door to admit a glaring Taryn.

"What do you want, thief? I was in the middle of a very important meeting when this great slab of humanity barged in and demanded that I return here with him. If this cost me—"

"Shut up, Taryn," Remarin said, and tossed her a pack. "Did anyone take undue notice of you coming up here?"

"What?" The baffled assassin looked back and forth between Remarin and Kit. "What do you mean, thief? And how dare you—"

"Listen, cutthroat." Remarin closed on the stunned woman in a flash, his jaw set and his eyes chips of ice set deep in a scowling face. "You claim to be a trained assassin, so why not act like it for a moment instead of just bitching about everything? Did anyone take note of you climbing the stairs?"

"The man at the bar, the one whose mug held water. He watched me. There may have been another by the stairs, but Xina's goon got in my way and I couldn't get a good look at the entire room. But the skinny bugger with the rat face definitely perked up when I walked in. What's happening?" Gone was the tempestuous young woman full of bile and thunder, and in her place was a calm professional. Taryn slipped the pack on her back and tightened the straps to hold it in place while giving her maximum motion of her arms.

Remarin tossed a belt with a set of long daggers to Taryn, then passed one to Kit holding half a dozen throwing knives. When she had it secured, he handed her a short, recurved bow and a quiver of arrows. He strapped a pair of bracers onto his arms with several small daggers tucked inside, then walked to the opposite wall and pulled on a bookcase. Nothing happened. Remarin looked confused, then pulled on the head-height bookcase again. After several seconds of tugging, the shelving unit pulled away from the wall and books began to tumble down onto the confused thief's head.

"Dammit, I knew better than to trust a whore," Remarin spat.

"What's wrong?" Kit asked.

"That was supposed to be a door," Remarin said, pointing at the bookcase. "In the next room is a trapdoor leading down behind the stairs into the sewers with another stash of supplies hidden in a niche in the wall. From there we could have walked unseen out of town to a small farm where I have half a dozen horses stored."

"You really did plan this out quite well, thief." Taryn's voice held more than a little awe. "I always knew you couldn't possibly be as stupid as you appeared, but I had no idea you were actually intelligent."

"Thanks, I think," Remarin replied. "But Xina decided that she had better ways to spend the money I gave her to pay for those renovations, so now we have to find a way out the front of the pub. Hopefully without killing too many people." He looked directly at Taryn when he said the last, as if to make sure she, in particular, heard and understood him.

"What about the window?" Jacob asked. "We're only on the second floor. We should be able to drop a rope down that far without much trouble."

"Good idea," Remarin said. "Kit, get the rope from your pack and secure it to the desk. Taryn will go first, then Jacob, then you, then me. Hopefully we can get out of here before—" His words were cut off by a pounding on the office door. "Before that," he sighed, drawing his rapier.

"Open this door in the name of Duchess Newlan!" a deep voice bellowed through the door, pounding in time with his words.

"Go to hell!" Taryn shrieked. "Ain't the Duchess got nothing better to do than bother a working woman trying to earn a living? What the hells does she want with me anyhow?" The lithe assassin tossed her pack into a corner and started stripping out of her clothes. She motioned to Remarin to do the same, and after a brief second, he followed her lead. Waving frantically for Kit to keep working the rope, he turned to the sofa situated along one wall. Pulling it away from the wall, he released two levers on the sides and it folded flat into a bed. Remarin reached under the sofa and pulled out a flowered coverlet, then slipped underneath it. He threw a blanket to Taryn, who now stood topless before the door.

She motioned for Jacob and Kit to drop to the floor, and she pulled the door open, rage written all over her face. Four or five guardsmen in full armor stood in the doorway, all faced with a trim woman half-covered in a blanket. Taryn stood on tiptoes and pulled down the chin strap of the lead man's helmet until they were eye to eye.

"What do you think you're doing, pounding on the door like that? You got me man all off his rhythm and almost put his willie in the out portal, if you know what I mean! And you!" She pointed at a guard farther back in the queue. "What the bloody hells do ye think ye're looking at? Are ye staring at me tits? Ye wanna see me tits, ye bloody wanker?" She lowered the sheet to just below her breasts and gave them a shake.

"There ye go, there's a good look at some tits for ye, ye great stupid fucks! Now get out of here before I cut off all your wee little willies and send you home with them hanging out yer earholes!" She slammed the door in their faces, catching the lead man solidly on the nose, and dropped the bar back across the metal cradles.

Keeping her voice unnaturally loud, she turned to Remarin. "There, there, sweetie, the bad men are gone now. Let's see if we can wake that little fella back up. There you go, luv, Mommy's here, he can come back out to play." After a few seconds of cooing and moaning from beside the door, Remarin heard the shuffle of five pairs of very confused feet walk back down the stairs with much less enthusiasm than they ran up.

Taryn collapsed to her knees, tears streaming down her face as she convulsed with strangled laughter. She rolled on the floor for long seconds before she controlled herself enough to stand and get dressed.

"Oh, that was fun!" she whispered as she and Remarin, both fully dressed again, joined Kit and Jacob at the window.

"Street seems clear," Jacob said. Taryn nodded, hopped the windowsill, and nimbly scampered down the rope. Kit followed, quick as her namesake feline, and Jacob looked at the two women safely on the ground below them.

"I'm the only one that hates this idea, aren't I?" the big man asked Remarin.

"You're the only one who doesn't climb into and out of places you're not wanted every night. The rest of us, it's our life. So out you go." Remarin gave him a gentle shove, and the massive Huntmaster put one leg over the sill and grabbed the rope with both hands. He threw his other leg over with a groan, and long moments later, he was on the ground, massaging his sore palms from the rope burn.

Remarin looked around the office, said a mental goodbye to Casterlane and the life he'd built for himself, then hopped out the window and scampered down the rope like a circus monkey.

He looked at his companions and said, "Well, here's something I never thought I'd say. Let's go home to Torin and save my brother's life."

CHAPTER 21

Remarin stepped off the gangplank and walked along the dock, his fingers trailing along the ropes strung from ship to shore and vice versa. His face was solemn and his eyes roving, even as his feet led him along to the rear of the small ferry they had taken from the mainland to Torin. Jacob and Taryn stood at the rear of the ferry awaiting the little luggage they had taken from Casterlane, a pack and bedroll for each of them and a pair of saddle-bags for Jacob.

Once the luggage was collected, Kit joined them and looked around the dock with an appraising eye. "Looks like a dock," she said. "Wet, boats, smells of fish, smells of people who smell of fish…yep, Remy, I'd definitely say it's a dock."

"Keep it down, Kitten," Remarin said, his face half-hidden within the deep folds of his cloak.

"Shall we proceed to the—" Jacob started, but Remarin cut him off with a sharp look and a wave of his hand.

"Yes, Harlan," he said, laying heavy emphasis on the false name. "We should go immediately to the inn and secure lodging for the night. What did you say was the name of the larger place?"

"There's only the one inn with rooms to let, sir," Jacob replied.

"The other places are just taverns and singing halls. It's called the Sea Pony, and old Luka has run that place since the dawn of time, but his mind is still sharp as a razor."

Remarin nodded, hearing the unspoken message of "the innkeeper will certainly recognize me and might even remember you, especially if his shoulder still hurts when it rains." Remarin reflected on a wild ride through town and sending old Luka, then just "Luka" flying headfirst over his horse's head to fetch up against a large rock in a field after a merry chase and a disagreement over the cost of several mugs of ale.

"So we might cut the dust from our throats at one of the smaller pubs and see about a room to let over a shop in town or something after that fashion?" Remarin replied.

Jacob nodded, and the thief waved an arm as he said, "Lead on, oh overgrown one!" He nodded to Taryn, who split off from the group and lagged behind, pretending to peruse the offerings at a fishmonger's stall. Remarin and Kit followed Jacob up the street from the docks, and Taryn hung back long enough to tuck in behind and follow the man in the dark red cloak who followed the trio.

Jacob led them through the crowded streets of Torin, turning this way and that seemingly at random, finally ending up down a narrow alley standing in front of a battered wooden door. Jacob tried the door, found it locked, and proceeded to pound on the door with his fist.

"What will he do if someone opens the door?" Kit asked Remarin.

"Probably kill them," he replied. "That door leads into Jacob's own kitchen, and he only stays in this house when the winter sets in deep. So anyone in there now shouldn't be too surprised to wake up with several feet of steel protruding from their ribs."

Remarin gave Kit a little shove farther down into the alley and said, "Find something to hide behind; our boy should be here any second now." As Kit moved past Jacob's bulk into the shadows, the man in the red cloak stepped into the mouth of the alley.

Surprise ran through the man's posture as he saw his quarry standing in front of the door, arms crossed and staring at him. He stiffened further when Taryn stepped in close behind him and pressed a dagger to his back, just to the right of his spine.

"With just the slightest pressure, I will puncture your liver and sever your spine. One of these injuries is universally fatal; the other prevents you from running for help to perhaps thwart my plans for leaving you gasping for life in a spreading pool of your own blood. After I deal the fatal blow, I'll cut your throat. Not deep enough to kill you, just enough so you can't scream. Then I'll gently sit you down against the wall of that building right there and leave this alley with my friends. We'll go on about our merry way, unimpeded by whatever ill you planned to have befall us, while you sit here, trousers filling with your own blood. It will take several minutes to die, so I suggest you use that time to make right with whatever gods you worship, since you'll see them in very short order."

"Unless you answer all our questions, of course," Remarin added.

"Yes, that," Taryn agreed in a disappointed hiss. "If you answer all our questions truthfully, I'll have no choice but to let you live, no matter how it offends my sensibilities."

The man stepped farther into the alley and lowered his hood.

"Donavan?" Jacob said, dropping his hand from his sword hilt.

"You know this man?" Remarin asked.

"As do you, Your Gr—"

"It's fine, Jacob. I know who he is, even if he doesn't remember me. And you don't, do you, Remarin? I don't blame you. I was young when you left, just a little tag-along always right where you didn't want me to be, always knocking over the fireplace tools and getting us caught in your mother's bedchambers stealing candy from her maids."

"Donny!" Remarin burst forward into the alley and embraced the man. "Gods, you've grown! You're a full man now, aren't you?"

"I've seen thirty-five winters, Remarin. Remember, I'm barely younger than yourself."

"Well, there's a secret loosed," Kit murmured.

"What's that, miss?" Donavan turned his attention to Kit, and she took a moment to evaluate the newcomer. He was a handsome man with a broad, cheerful face and a light beard, close-trimmed. His sandy hair was cropped short, and his clothes and smooth hands spoke of someone who worked indoors, in gentle conditions. Tiny ink spots on his cuffs and a permanent stain on his fingers told the story of a scholar, or scribe perhaps. Certainly someone who wrote a great deal.

"Remarin has been very close with his precise age, at least for the few years I've known him. So now I see he's not yet forty, not quite so much the wise old man as he may have hinted at."

Certainly not wise, Trand interjected. Kit brought her hand to her face and faked a cough to hide the laugh that escaped.

"What are you doing here, Donny? Taryn almost skewered you. She wasn't joking, you know," Remarin asked.

"I was sent to make sure that you and Jacob made it back to the keep unmolested," the young man said. "There are some within the household who wonder just how welcome you will be."

"I'm sure there are plenty within the household who are more likely to welcome me home with a clenched fist than with open arms. Has Swordmaster Eleric ever gotten all the blades out of the ceiling of the training hall?"

Donavan's face went sober. "Eleric died in a hunting accident a month ago. He went out hunting stag and came back draped across his saddle with a broken neck."

Jacob flushed crimson. "Dammit. I knew I shouldn't have left. Eleric was one of the few men who knew what I was doing and who I was looking for. I thought he could handle himself, but it seems I was wrong."

"What kind of inquiry was made into his death?" Remarin asked.

"The Seneschal ruled it death from a fall, and no inquiry was made," Donavan said, his face grim.

"So what, he just accidentally fell onto his horse and broke his neck?" Remarin asked. "Or did he fall off his horse, die from the fall, then his corpse got up and climbed back onto the horse and headed home? That's the stupidest thing I've ever heard, and I've negotiated whorehouse pricing in Elorfina! Where is my brother? I'm obviously going to have to beat some sense into that boy." Remarin started for the mouth of the alley, but Jacob and Donavan blocked his way.

"Get out of my way," Remarin said.

"No," Jacob said. "I didn't spend the last half year away from my home searching for you just to let you run headlong into a trap now."

"Listen to him, Remarin. The big one is much smarter than he looks," Taryn said from the end of the alleyway. "Besides, I think we should find someplace else to be, unless we want to meet with a number of armored men wearing bright blue tabards over their breastplates."

"Shit," Donavan muttered. "Those are the Private Guard, a group of so-called elite troops supposedly dedicated to protecting the Duke's person and property. Everything I've seen makes them out to be more mercenaries hired by the Seneschal to silence anyone who disagrees with him. They're probably looking for me."

"Why are the Seneschal's men looking for you, Donny?" Jacob asked.

"Probably because I mentioned in a tavern last night that I felt the Seneschal had carnal knowledge of goats, and perhaps his own mother as well." Donavan had the good grace to blush, at least.

"Oh, good gods, Donny. Do you have to try to keep *all* of Remarin's memories alive?" Jacob groaned, then pushed his way back to the door he'd funded on so mercilessly. He withdrew a key from his belt, opened the door, and motioned for the others to precede him indoors.

Jacob's small house had all the trappings of a bachelor's home that only saw use in the coldest of months, which is to say nothing at all. A solitary plate and cup sat on a small round table with two chairs that sat in the middle of the room near a round-bellied wood stove with a pipe leading up and at a right angle out the wall. A pile of hides made up a pallet in one corner of the room, all from different animals. One small door in the far wall led to an indoor water closet, the sole concession to comfort in the room.

"Good lord, Jacob, you live even more like a monk than I remember!" Remarin exclaimed, running his finger through the thick coating of dust that clung to every surface. "I think you'd be more comfortable sleeping in the forest."

"I've always been more comfortable sleeping in the forest, Remarin, you know that," the big man replied.

Taryn walked through the room, inspecting every floorboard and tapping on every wall. "This place seems secure. I like the small windows. No furniture makes for easy fighting, too."

"Only one exit," Kit added. "That makes things a little difficult."

"But also only one place for attackers to come from. And the narrow alley outside means they have to funnel in awkwardly, making them easier to take care of one at a time. If only there was a back way out…" Remarin said.

"There is," Jacob said with a smile. "I was worried that one of you would find it, but it looks like my carpentry is still pretty good." He knelt by the table and put his finger into a knothole in one of the floor boards and pulled up. The board came up, along with several others in a square just large enough for Jacob to get his shoulders through.

Remarin walked to the trapdoor and peered down. "Nice," he said, nodding. "Looks like a solid enough ladder, but the drop won't kill anybody, either, in case you need to make a quick exit."

"Which is the story of your life, Remarin," Kit said with a grin. "Not to be the whiny princess—"

"But if the shoe fits…" Remarin said from the window.

"Go to the hells, Remarin. Some of the places you've dragged me since we left Veosia make this look like my bedrooms back at the palace," Kit went on. "As I was saying, how long do you expect us to stay here? If it's more than one night, we'll need a few things to make it livable. At least a blanket or two, if nothing else."

Remarin looked around the sparse room. The stack of hides would provide a reasonable sleeping surface for one or two people, and one of them would always be on watch. Donovan would have to stay with them thanks to insulting the Seneschal, but Jacob could return to the palace if he needed to. *No.* Remarin shook his head. Better for them to stay together until he could sort out the situation at the palace.

"I think we only need to be here for a few hours. We may as well get right to work, especially if things are as precarious as Jacob believes." He turned to the big man. "How many of my back doors did you seal up after I was gone?"

"All I could find save two. There's still the loose stone in the back corner of the stables and the passage connecting the palace moat and the city sewer is still accessible if you're small enough. You've grown a bit since sixteen, but not much. You and the girls should be fine, but Donny and I don't stand a chance."

"Not to mention trying to swim in armor is a good way to end up trying to walk across the bottom of a moat. We three will break into the palace while you haul Donny back in your custody. Meet us in my brother's chambers two hours after midnight."

"Will you remember how to get in?" Jacob asked.

Remarin looked at him, eyes narrowed. "I started sneaking out of that castle when I was eight years old. It may be two decades past, but I still remember the way to get back in."

CHAPTER 22

"You don't remember how to get inside, do you?" Taryn hissed, her whisper echoing off the sewer walls like a shout in an alleyway.

"Of course I remember how to get inside," Remarin whispered back, his own voice almost a breath floating on the rancid air. "We just need to get to the overflow valves for the moat, then swim across the overflow on the castle side, move the bricks I loosened when I was a child, and slip right inside." He was currently passing the beam of his hooded thieves' lantern along the stones of a narrow side tunnel, barely ten feet from the main thoroughfare of the city sewers. They had slipped into the damp tunnels beneath Jacob's hideout an hour before and were moving generally northward when Remarin held up his hand to stop them, then stepped into this side tunnel where he had spent the past ten minutes looking for something.

"Why are there overflow valves in a moat?" Kit asked. She leaned against the mouth of the side tunnel, occasionally scanning the main tunnel for pursuit, or for the creatures that were rumored to live in sewers. She wasn't precisely sure which she was more afraid of finding.

"Because Torin is a very compact island, Kitten. The keep is built atop the tallest hill in town, and if the rains get too heavy, the moat can overflow the banks and spill out into the street. Since the moat is a part of the castle's sewer system, that leads to unpleasant things rolling down the street into the nobility's houses. So they added the overflow valves when I was very young to let the water and other things flow into the sewer in the rainy season. I saw an opportunity for mischief and took it." His eyes brightened as though a thought struck him suddenly, and he stooped slightly, aiming his light lower.

"I have learned more about sewers since I began my association with you than perhaps any other princess in history has known."

"You say that like it's a bad thing. Ah, here we are. I was looking too high." He aimed his hooded lantern at a point low on the wall and illuminated an odd sigil carved into the damp stone. The carving was faded with age and slime, but it was still discernible as a man-made marking, and Remarin grinned like a schoolboy as he pressed on the adjoining squares. After several fruitless seconds, one of the stones depressed slightly, and a stone several feet away popped out from its surroundings. Remarin hurried over to the protruding block and wiggled it free. He turned slightly and set the brick down gently on the narrow walkway beside him, then reached into the hole left in the wall.

The thief pulled back his hand and grinned at his compatriots. "Got it!"

"Got what, thief?" Taryn whispered.

Remarin held out his hand to display a small leather pouch, moldy from being stored in the damp for so long. He tugged at the drawstrings, finally drawing Trand to slice the knotted cord around the neck of the bag.

Typically I'd slice open your thumb for daring to use me for such a mundane task, not to mention getting that muck on my edge. But I want to know what's in the bag, the dagger "said" to Remarin over their mystical link.

"Hold this," Remarin said, passing the lantern to Kit. She took the lantern and aimed it at his outstretched palm as he opened the bag and shook three items out into his hand. First was a heavy key, made of what had likely once been polished brass but now had turned alternating brown and green with years.

"The key to the castle, literally. This is a skeleton key I made when I was eleven. It should open any door in the building, unless it's magically warded or has a particularly sensitive lock. You hold onto that," he said, passing the key to Taryn. "Guard it with your life. I left it stashed here because it was the most dangerous thing I owned at the time. With this, an enemy could go anywhere they liked inside the Keep of Torin. They could assassinate anyone, steal anything, generally destroy the kingdom. No matter how much Father and I disagreed, I didn't want that to happen."

"So why leave the key here?" Kit asked.

"I didn't exactly trust the captain I'd booked passage with, and if he was going to kill me and toss my body overboard, I wanted to make sure I hadn't given him free reign of the castle as well. So I hid it here, where no one but me would ever find it."

And even that was a near thing, Trand remarked. Kit smiled, Remarin scowled, and Taryn as usual looked nonplussed at being left out of the conversation. No one knew why Kit could hear the enchanted blade's thoughts, but she could communicate with the trapped thief as easily as Remarin.

Remarin turned his attention back to the pouch and gave it another shake. A sparkling gold necklace tumbled out, with a gold locket attached. It was a delicate piece of work, a spider-silk thin chain holding a locket the shape of a heart, with delicate scrollwork all over the outside surface. Remarin drew in a sharp breath, then tucked the locket away into an inside pocket.

"And what do we have here?" Taryn asked, her voice taking on a mocking lilt. "A memento from a childhood love? A picture of an old girlfriend? Let us see the girl, Remarin. Let us see the beauty that could hold your heart for all these years."

Remarin turned to Taryn slowly, and when he looked at her, his eyes were chips of ice. "Do not ever ask me about that locket again, if you value your tongue."

Taryn looked up, expecting to see the normal jaunty, teasing thief. The face that met hers was nothing like that. Remarin's jaw was set in a tight line, and there was nothing of a smile anywhere about him. Taryn gulped and nodded.

"What else is in there?" Kit asked, to break the heavy silence.

"Should be one thing only," Remarin said. He gave the bag a final shake, and a gold ring fell into his palm. It was a large, heavy chunk of metal, far too large for a child's hand. Emblazoned on the face was a crest, and fabric was wrapped around the back of the ring to make it small enough for a teenager to wear. Remarin's face was a mask as he drew Trand.

Don't give me any crap, please, he "said" to the dagger.

Wouldn't dream of it. I can feel how important this is to you was the muted reply.

Remarin cut the strips of fabric from the band of the ring, dropping the scraps into the sewer to float soundlessly away. His work done, he sheathed the blade and slipped the ring onto the next to last finger of his right hand. It fit perfectly, the gold gleaming in the dim illumination from the lantern. He flexed his fist, opening and closing it several times, then shaking his hand as if trying to become accustomed to the weight.

"How does it feel?" Kit said, her voice barely above a whisper.

"Strange," Remarin replied. "I never thought I would set foot on this isle again, much less feel this ring on my finger."

"Is it heavy?" the girl asked.

"Heavier than I remember, and I was a very small boy of thirteen when last I wore it."

"Now you know what comes with it," Kit said.

"And that has a weight all its own," Remarin agreed.

"Quiet!" Taryn hissed, slamming her hand down over the lantern's shutters and plunging them into the purest darkness. "Thomone cometh," the assassin lisped intentionally, knowing how far "s" sound carries in a quiet environment. All three pulled black hoods up and over their faces, then slipped into the shadows and stood motionless.

Taryn and Kit pressed their backs to one side of the tunnel. Remarin turned the face of his lantern to the wall and took up a position opposite them. They didn't have to wait long before a narrow beam of light pierced the black and two men stepped past the tunnel's mouth.

The glow from the lantern did little to illuminate the men, only giving enough glow to show one was small, in robes, and one was large, with mail armor glinting here and there. The large one held a huge hand-and-a-half sword in one hand, while the smaller man seemed unarmed save for the lantern. They were silhouetted by the dim glow of the lantern, but Remarin and the women cloaked themselves in shadow as though they were born of them.

"Do we need to go down there?" the big one asked, gesturing off to the side tunnel where the trio waited.

"No," the smaller one said. "That goes down to the tanneries, then empties out into the marshes beyond the Western side of the moat. You think it stinks here, try wading through that shit. Even if he is trying to slip in through his favorite back door, he won't go down there. Prissy little prince Remy never did like the common folk, so he's got no friends to call on down that part of town."

"Sounds like you didn't like him very much," the larger one said. "What did he ever do to you?"

"He was a brat," the small man replied with a disdainful grunt. "Always strutting around like he owned the place, ignoring his lessons, distracting the teachers, making things difficult for those of us who wanted to learn."

"So now you're hunting him through the sewers?" There was a hint of mockery in the big one's voice, and the little one bristled.

"I'm doing the same thing you are—following orders. If the Master wants him found, we find him. If the Master wants him dead, we make him dead. If the Master wants him dressed up like a May festival tart in a frilly dress, then we shave his cheeks and put some bloomers on him."

"It might take a little more effort than that, Chalvis," Remarin said, stepping into the main passage behind the two men and pulling the hood from two sides of his lantern. The men covered their eyes from the sudden light, but the hood cut just enough light on the back side of the lantern for him to avoid being blinded, while still letting him see his hunters.

The big man was a mercenary, Tarvian by the look of him, his chain mail hauberk covered with a heavy leather cuirass. Leather gauntlets and bracers covered his arms, and his legs were covered by the long tail of his shirt, split on the sides for easier movement. A helmet capped his head, with an open face split by a thin nose guard. He was well over six feet tall and near two hundred fifty pounds, and he slid one foot back into a defensive stance and set the point of his huge sword low and toward Remarin.

The smaller man had the look of a scribe or librarian, sporting brown robes and a deep hood cast back on his neck and shoulders. His bald pate gleamed in the lantern's flicker, and he squinted momentarily, then recovered.

"Remarin!" the little man shouted, recognition lighting up his eyes. "How convenient. Now we can bring you before our Master and get out of these stinking sewers."

"That's funny, Chalvis," Remarin said, his eyes never leaving the big mercenary. "I would have thought the sewers would be a perfect home for a rat like you."

"You know the hunted?" the mercenary asked.

"Chalvis and I go way back, oh muscled one. We went to school together. Chalvis was one of the rare city children with the aptitude to be schooled with the royal family. Unfortunately for him, aptitude was the only thing his parents could give him, and Chalvis always resented that a little."

"Resented how you and the other nobles treated me like trash beneath your custom-made boots," the little man snarled. His hand flashed into his cloak and back out with a throwing dagger. He flung the weapon at Remarin, who sidestepped the clumsy throw without even seeming to look at his would-be assailant.

"Twenty years is a long time to hold a grudge, Chalvis," Remarin said. "Now why don't you tell me who your Master is before I beat you all the way back to Elorfina?"

Chalvis cocked his head to one side. "What in all the hells are you talking about, idiot. I've never been to Elorfina."

"No, but I have. And 'Elorfina' means 'subdue, but don't kill him,'" Taryn said from behind the man. Chalvis whirled about, meeting Taryn's fist with his oncoming jaw. He collapsed like a sack of potatoes, and Remarin grinned at the big Tarvian.

"Let's dance, big fella."

CHAPTER 23

The mercenary stepped forward, thrusting with his sword. Remarin slid his rapier free from its scabbard with his right hand and drew a basket-hilted sword breaker in his left. He knocked the bastard sword aside with the sword breaker, then sliced a line across his opponent's left leg with his rapier. Remarin glided past his foe, then slid back inside the big man's guard, blocking the sword up and slamming his elbow into the big man's solar plexus. His right arm went numb as his elbow slammed into the hardened leather cuirass, and it took all his strength to hold onto his rapier.

The big man wrapped his arms around Remarin and started to squeeze. He shifted his sword to one hand and clasped the other hand around the wrist on his sword arm, pulling in and pressing his knuckles deep into Remarin's ribcage. The nimble thief looked around frantically for some way out, lashing out with his head trying to head-butt the bigger man, trying to break free before all the air was crushed from his lungs. Spots started to appear in his vision, and he struggled even harder, kicking and thrashing for all he was worth. The mercenary was unfazed, squeezing ever harder. Remarin focused all his remaining strength on one more strike, concentrating all his energy into a back kick intended to take out the huge man's knee. He lashed out, and as both heels connected with the Tarvian's kneecap, the mercenary let out an *"Oooooffff"* in Remarin's ear, and he dropped to both knees in the sewer.

Remarin's feet hit the ground, and the big man's grip loosened. Remarin sprang forward two steps, then pivoted, his rapier ready for a killing thrust. His would-be strangler knelt in the sewer water, looking at Remarin with very confused eyes. Standing behind him was Kit, a bloodied dagger in her right hand and her hood still lowered over her face. The girl grabbed the mercenary's hair with her left hand, then drew the blade across his throat with her right. She then released to big man's body, which collapsed to one side with a low splash.

Remarin looked at Kit. "I had that under control," he said, his voice nothing more than a strangled croak.

"I'm sure you did," she whispered back. "But the rest of us didn't need the extra attention your splashing around was going to draw. Besides, you have the little one to interrogate. You didn't need both of them."

"You've spent far too much time around Taryn, Kitten. It's made you cold."

"I prefer the term practical. Aren't you going to steal his purse?" She pointed to the dead swordsman.

"I don't need to do that now. I'm home, and I'm fairly important here, so people are usually pretty good about giving me money."

"Oh really?" she asked.

"Yes," Remarin replied. "It's called taxes."

He walked over to where Taryn had Chalvis trussed up like a Christmas goose. The little man knelt on the floor on a raised walkway that ran along the sides of the sewer. Remarin leaned down and pulled the man's hood all the way back, exposed his balding pate.

"Lost something, Chalvis? Like that beautiful hair you were always so proud of? Or just your standards, cavorting about in the sewers with a mercenary? The Chalvis I went to school with would never have been found in the company of a lowborn, and a Tarvian at that. What happened, Chalvis?"

The little man glared up at Remarin, but said nothing. The thief leaned down and dropped his voice. "Then let's ask a simpler question, shall we? Who is this Master you spoke of?"

Chalvis's eyes went wide, but he clamped his lips shut tight and shook his head.

"Oh, yes you will, Chalvis. You'll tell me, it just depends on you how quickly you tell me, and how much Taryn gets to hurt you before you do. Remarin jerked a thumb over his shoulder at the trim assassin. Taryn cracked her knuckles and grinned.

"I can't, Remarin," the little man said, his voice quavering. "I simply can't. Couldn't you just forget we ever met, for old time's sake?"

"I could, Chalvis, but we hated each other in the old times, remember? You were always the sniveling little teacher's pet, quick to report on anyone who might have been skipping sword practice to go fishing or who might not have been quite as ill as he convinced his mother's lady-in-waiting that he was. So why in the world would I do you, of all sneaky little bastards, any favors?" Remarin's face was cold, his eyes cold chips glaring out at the balding prisoner.

Chalvis sneered up at Remarin, and some of the bully he had been as a child surfaced. "I can't tell you anything about the Master, Remarin, so go ahead and let your bitch beat me to within an inch of my life. It doesn't matter, you'll learn nothing from me."

Taryn stepped forward, her knife raised, but Remarin raised a hand. "No, Taryn, don't kill him. That's what he wants. See the muscle under his left eye? See how it twitches? That's Chalvis's tell. His eye twitches when he's about to piss himself from fear. And trust me, if I were on my knees covered in shit in a sewer looking up at a ghost and an assassin, I'd be terrified, and I'm a much braver man than Chalvis."

"You know nothing about me, you traitor! You deserted your kingdom when she needed you the most. You left us in the hands of a cripple!" Spittle flew from Chalvis's lips as he shouted up at his captors. "Now you come back? Now, when everything is set in motion? No, Remarin, you don't get to spoil everything again. HELP! He's here! Help me!" Chalvis's voice echoed off the tunnel walls as he screamed. Taryn and Remarin exchanged quick glances, the Taryn stepped forward and opened the small man's throat from ear to ear.

His shouts turned to one long gurgle as his lifeblood cascaded down the front of his once-fine tunic.

Chalvis turned to Remarin as the light faded from his eyes and said nothing. The little man fell to his side, a vindictive smile on his face. He slipped off the walkway into the water with barely a splash, quickly vanishing beneath the surface.

Remarin reached down to hood the lantern, plunging them into darkness. "We've got to move, and quickly now. If Chalvis had any friends, which I find doubtful, they'll have heard the ruckus. They won't be able to just follow the sound because of the tunnels and the echoes, but they know someone's down here now, and we'd rather they not find us."

"I'm blind as a bat down here now, Remarin," Kit whispered. "My night vision is completely gone."

"It'll come back in a few minutes," Taryn hissed. "But we'd be better served by not being here when that happens. Anyone who heard your little rat squeak will be working their way here."

"Don't worry, I can maneuver through these tunnels blindfolded, much less night blind," Remarin said. "Kit, walk behind me with your hand on my belt. Taryn, you follow Kit the same way. I'll go slow, and make sure you don't lose your grip." The girl nodded, and Remarin took her hand and placed it at his hip on his belt.

The trio started moving through the sewers again, slow and silent as water running across glass. True to his word, Remarin navigated the twists and turns of the tunnels without hesitation, and by the time Kit's eyes had adapted to the near-impenetrable darkness, they were standing at the mouth of a tunnel where it opened up into a junction of several other tunnels feeding into a large reservoir with a water level a few inches below the tunnel they were in. The reservoir opened up several feet above the mouth of the tunnel, and as Kit looked up, she saw the overflow ports Remarin mentioned.

"So the moat is right there?" she asked, pointing across the reservoir to the stone wall.

"Yes, and across the moat is the castle."

"How wide is the moat?" Taryn asked. "And how long have we been in these gods-cursed sewers?"

"The moat is fifty yards wide, just a little too far to swim across underwater without needing to come up for air, at least not if you haven't been training for that exact thing," Remarin said.

That sounds like the voice of experience talking, Trand said to Remarin and Kit, his dry "voice" floating in their minds.

You've been quiet since we got here, Remarin sent back to his friend.

I've been doing some thinking, Trand replied. *I knew you were something different when we met, Remarin. Apparently I didn't know the half of it.*

Sorry about that. It was pretty important to me that no one know my past, or my station.

Not even those of us who opened our homes to you?

It wasn't my finest moment, but by the time I made it to you, I was in a bad place, if you recall.

Oh, I recall. You were half-starved and vicious as a wolf with a haunch of deer. At the time I was amazed we were able to civilize you at all, even a little, but now I understand we were just reminding you what it was like to be a human being, not completely teaching you.

You taught me plenty, my friend. You taught me plenty. And I swear, some day, some way, I'll get you back into your body.

"If you're done talking to your silverware, could we return to the task at hand?" Taryn asked. "How exactly are we going to get up to the ports? They're at least ten feet up a wall slick with I don't even want to think about what."

"I'm pretty sure that's my job," Kit replied. "Remarin may be the best thief in seven countries, even though one of them is Shu-Haroth, and there's nothing to steal there, but I'm the best cat burglar anywhere."

"Confident much?" Remarin crossed his arms and cocked an eyebrow at his protégé.

"I learned all my modesty from you, teacher," Kit said. While Remarin stifled a laugh, Kit reached into a small pouch at her waist and withdrew and small set of metal spikes and leather straps that she slipped onto the toes of her boots. Once the spikes were secured in place with the leather, she withdrew a pair of gloves from the pouch and slipped them on. The gloves were covered with small metal studs sharpened to keen points. Kit flexed her hands, testing the combination of leather and metal against the air, then withdrew a coil of thin rope from her pack and slipped the coil over her head and one shoulder. She looked down at the pool below her, suppressed a shudder, and wrapped a long scarf around her face. Then she took a deep breath and stepped off the ledge into the water.

She vanished beneath the surface of the murky water for a few long seconds, then reappeared halfway across the pool. She swam to the far wall, just below the overflow ports, and pulled herself along by way of a narrow stone ledge. Holding herself in place with one hand, she pressed her other hand against the wall and pushed, wiggling her fingers to set her spikes into the cracks between bricks. Grip secured, she did the same with the opposite hand, then pulled her body up until it was bent almost double as she locked her toes onto the inch-wide shelf of stone.

"That's the part I could never do," Remarin said to Taryn, the admiration evident in his voice even at a whisper. "She's more limber than most circus acrobats, and braver than a lion tamer."

"You care for her quite a bit, don't you, Remarin?" Taryn turned to look at him.

"She's like a little sister to me," the thief answered, his eyes never leaving Kit's form as she began to scale the muck-slick wall.

"Of course she is," Taryn murmured, a tiny smile playing across her lips. They watched in silence as the trim young woman moved up the wall, testing each hand- and foot-hold as she climbed, never rushing, holding most of her weight with her legs and using her hands to guide her way up. Ten breathless minutes later, she reached up to the overflow port and froze.

"What's wrong?" Remarin called in a low voice.

"There are bars. Even I can't fit through them," Kit's voice floated down.

"I know. It's okay. The middle ones aren't secure," Remarin called back.

"They feel pretty solid to me," Kit replied after reaching up and wiggling the two center bars.

"You have to know the trick. Tie off and send the rope down," Remarin said.

Kit nodded once, then turned back to the wall. She repositioned herself until one hand was wrapped tight around the end bar and slid the rope off her shoulder. With one hand, she peeled off a pre-tied loop and dropped that back over her shoulder. She then reached into her belt pouch and pulled out a small metal clip. She clipped the loop of rope around a bar, then slipped her other arm through and hung there, both hands and feet free. She set another loop on the far side of the port, then tied off one end of the rope to the bars and tossed the rope down and across to Taryn. The assassin caught it, then turned to stare at Remarin.

The thief looked back at her. "Don't tell me this is the first time you've ever climbed a rope."

"No, but it is the first time no one died because of it."

"Well, maybe you'll get lucky and we'll find somebody for you to kill." Remarin grinned at her. "Now climb."

Taryn wrapped the rope around her waist and leapt out over the water, gripping the rope high enough to keep from swinging into the pool, then planted her feet wide on the opposite wall and walked up the wall, pulling herself hand-over-hand. Less than a minute later, she slipped into the waiting loop of rope and threw the rope back to Remarin.

Don't screw this up, came Trand's "voice." *I don't want any of that muck touching me.*

I know the feeling, Remarin sent back. He made a loose loop around his waist, then jumped out and up, grabbing the rope high above his head and swinging his legs forward for added speed. Heavier than Taryn and Kit, he knew he couldn't pull himself up as smoothly, so when his feet met the far wall, he dug a toe into the nearest crack and pushed off, scaling the wall and pulling himself up at almost a dead run. Bare seconds after his jump, he dangled from the rope between Taryn and Kit, wrapping the rope around his right leg so he wouldn't slide down into the water some ten or more feet below.

"Ladies," he said with a nod. Remarin pulled himself up so his face was level with the overflow port and reached out to test the center bars. The portal was a half-moon, about two feet high at the tallest point of the curve, with five bars mounted into the stones surrounding it. Remarin wiggled the three innermost bars, grunting with effort. Nothing moved at first, but then after a few choice words muttered under his breath, the centermost bar slid up into the wall a few inches.

"Got it," Remarin said. He slid the bar up three inches, just enough for the bottom to clear the lip of the portal, then he wiggled the bar free and slid it into his belt. He repeated the process with the two bars next on either side of it, leaving the outside bars in place and making an opening just large enough for the thief to slip through.

"Here's the situation," he said, dropping down to whisper to Kit and Taryn. "The moat is several feet below the portal. Apparently it hasn't been a very wet summer. So you two will slip through the hole and swim to the left. Get across the moat as quietly as possible and wait for me under the drawbridge. I'll meet you there and we'll make our way into the keep. Taryn, you first."

The woman nodded, then reached up and pulled herself through the opening, sliding up and across the stone portal like an otter, all lithe dark muscle. There was barely a splash, then Remarin turned to Kit.

"Ready, Princess?"

"You haven't called me that in a long time," the girl said with a grin.

"I thought since we were going to be hobnobbing with royalty, it might not hurt to remind you that you belong here, too."

"Just not the very specific 'here,' of course," Kit said with a smile and the wave of a hand at the expanse of sewer around them.

"No, not here, but... oh, get out there, you know what I meant." Remarin grinned at her, then held out a hand for her to step into. Kit placed her foot into his palm and pushed off, sliding up and through the arched portal almost as soundlessly as Taryn. Remarin heard the light splash and set to work.

CHAPTER 24

Remarin detached the rope loops from the outer bars, slid through the opening out into the moat feet-first, and spun himself around until his belly was pressed flat to the stone wall. He stayed there for several long moments, listening through the darkness at the jingle of guards' mail atop the battlements. Hearing no change in the rhythm of the guards' pacing, he quickly slipped the center bars back into place and untied Kit's rope. He coiled it around himself the best he could while clinging to a water-soaked stone wall in the middle of the night, then let go of the bars and dropped into the water. He pressed his feet into the wall and shot halfway across the moat before his burning lungs forced him to resurface.

The slender thief allowed himself to float to the surface and rolled over onto his back to listen for any alarms. The keep lay silent ahead of him, and the guards continued their watch high above, their boot heels clicking along the stones in a familiar rhythm. Remarin drew another deep breath, rolled under the surface of the moat, and kicked his way across to the stone wall of the castle's lower levels and dungeon. He surfaced just enough to catch a breath and his bearings, saw the drawbridge with two slim forms barely discernible from the shadows that surrounded them, then dove back under the surface and swam the rest of the way to where his companions awaited him.

"Here's where it gets a little tricky," Remarin said.

"Because trudging through miles of sewer in the pitch black and swimming across a moat was the easy part," Kit said.

"Glad you agree," Remarin shot back. "Because I'm not sure I can still fit through the passage I used to use to sneak in and out of the castle. We can give it a shot, but I might be too broad in the shoulders to fit through the hole."

Taryn gave the slight thief an appraising glance. "This would have to be the first time those words were ever uttered."

"So what do we do then?" Kit asked.

"Well, we find the passage first, then we get it open after two decades. Then we see if it's as small as I remember, then if I can't fit, we work on figuring out a Plan B."

"We work on making a Plan B while we freeze our asses off in this disgusting water," Taryn said, her eyebrow climbing to the sky.

"You say that like it's the stupidest thing we've ever done," Remarin replied with a grin.

"No, but it does make the top ten," Taryn said with a scowl. "Where is this passage?"

"We need to circle around to the left, to the back side of the keep. There used to be a false stone in the bottom corner of the back wall of the stables."

"Remarin, why was there a false stone in the stables?" Kit asked.

"Because I paid a stone mason to chisel out the real stone and replace it with a false one," Remarin said. "I wanted to go exploring, and my father wanted me to stay inside where it was safe. So I would go off to the stables and 'sulk.' Little did he know I just made sure that the stable master and my nurse were very well acquainted, so whenever she followed me to the stables, there was a guarantee that my movements would be unnoticed for several hours at least."

"You really were born like this, weren't you?" Kit said.

"Now you see why I left, don't you? Could you imagine the terrible trouble that could befall any kingdom that I led? It would be worse than asking Taryn to negotiate a peace treaty with the Sons of Armot."

"The followers of the war god that think women exist only to bear children? Yeah, that would go over well," Kit agreed. "Fine, let's go see if you can get back in through your childhood hidey-hole or if you've gotten too fat in your old age."

"Fat? No one said anything about getting fat. I said I might be too broad in the shoulders. Did you hear anyone say anything about fat?" Remarin turned to Taryn, who just shrugged her shoulders and swam away after Kit. Remarin reached down with one hand and poked himself in the belly, feeling very little give. "Nobody said anything about getting fat!" he hissed, then dove under the water and swam away around the keep toward the stables at the rear corner of the massive building.

Remarin surfaced alongside the two women several minutes later and pressed himself to the wall of the moat. "This is the back of the stable," he said, voice low.

"We know," Kit replied. Remarin gave her a questioning look.

The young woman sniffed the air. "There's a certain fragrance in the air, Remarin, and while it smells slightly better than we do, it's a near thing."

Remarin huffed a laugh under his breath, then turned serious. "The space between the back wall of the stable and the edge of the water will be our most exposed. Stay as low as possible and try to keep the splashing to a minimum as we climb out. There's only about forty feet, but we'll be completely exposed to anyone passing by on the opposite shore, and a supremely easy shot for anyone on the battlements."

He looked each woman in the eye, then nodded at them and pulled himself from the moat. He slithered onto the grass before the castle and lay motionless for several heartbeats. Finally, satisfied that he remained unnoticed, he snake-crawled through the high grass to the outer wall of the keep. As Kit and Taryn followed his path across the small patch of grass, Remarin began tapping at stones in the wall. "If memory serves, and it usually does, the false stone should be right about...here!" He grinned as his tapping echoed back at him with a hollow *thud* as his questing fingers met wood instead of stone.

"Kit, if you would do the honor of removing said stone." Remarin gestured to the false rock.

"Why don't you want to do it?" Kit eyed Remarin, suspicion built on years of "thieving lessons" that invariably got her thumped on the head, dropped on her behind, or simply bruised and battered, came flooding back to her in a second.

"Because you're still wearing your cat's claws, and you can get a good hold on the thing. It's been more than twenty years, remember? The wood is swollen in place by now."

"Oh," she said, a slight blush creeping across her cheeks.

"What, you thought I had it rigged so a huge spider would jump out? That would be brilliant, but I don't have that kind of time."

The girl reached up with her spiked gloves and wiggled her fingertips into the cracks around the edge of the "block" Remarin indicated. She pulled once, twice, and then with a *crack* that split the air, the aged wood gave free and split in half. Kit tumbled backward, landing on her tailbone with an almost-silent "*whoof*," and Remarin's arm flashed out to keep her from tumbling all the way back down into the water.

"Who goes there?" shouted a voice from above, and Remarin shoved Kit back toward the wall. She dove into the hole in the wall and scrabbled out of sight as the thief and Taryn pressed themselves tight to the outer walls of the keep. Light from a lantern above flashed around them, but after a few seconds, Remarin heard the guard mutter something about "stupid horses" and the light vanished. Taryn slipped into the hole behind Kit, and Remarin knelt at the dark opening.

Here we go again, back where I never thought I'd go.

We've been a lot of places we never thought we'd go, Trand sent back to him.

Yeah, but I never owned any of those places, nor did I have quite as many people who wanted to kill me.

You obviously forget the exact number of angry husbands and fathers you've left behind in some of those desert towns.

Remarin chuckled, then slid into the narrow passage. He threaded his right foot through a handle on the backside of the lightly mangled false stone, and as he crawled into the blackness, he twisted the cover back into place.

"Nice one, thief," Taryn said a few feet ahead of him. "Now where are we going?"

"This passage should go about fifteen feet and then turn straight up. There will be another false stone that lifts straight up and lets out into one of the back stalls of the stable. Take care not to spook the horse. That's a good way to get trampled."

"Great," Kit's voice drifted back to him. Remarin heard the soft scratch of her clawed gloves and shoes moving away as she proceeded down the tunnel. Several moments later a muffled "Uh oh" floated back.

"Uh oh?" Remarin asked, hurrying along the tunnel but coming to a sharp stop when he ran into Taryn's backside. Without enough room in the tunnel for more than one person at a time, it made for an awkward position. "What uh oh?" Remarin asked. "There shouldn't be any uh oh." The thief's voice was going shrill.

"Give me a minute, you big baby. It's locked is all. I'll have the bar tripped in…there it is! Kit's triumphant voice came back just as a shaft of warm yellow light shot into the tunnel. Remarin took a moment to admire the shapeliness of Taryn's curves, as they were right in front of him, then she followed Kit out of the tunnel and Remarin joined them in an empty stall at the back of the stables. Taryn pressed her finger to her lips and pantomimed looking around. Remarin nodded, then dropped his pack and sword belt onto a pile of hay and began to remove his clothes.

Kit's eyes went wide, and she spun around as Remarin stripped to the skin. He pitched his sewer-drenched clothing into the tunnel and pulled a new set wrapped in wax paper from his pack.

"It's a good thing I went to see if there was anyone about before you started rattling that paper, Remarin. Nice butt," Taryn said as she slipped back into the stall and gave him a *whack* on one cheek as she dropped her pack and started to strip as well.

"You going to get changed, Kit, or you going to meet Remarin's only living relative reeking of the sewer?"

The girl blushed, then her eyes flashed. "No one told me to bring a change of clothes, so I suppose I'm going to be the smelliest girl at the ball tonight."

"Doubtful, Kitten. There are clothes in the bottom of your pack; Taryn just wanted to torture you for a little while," Remarin said.

"Fine," Kit said, dropping her pack. "But no peeking." Remarin kept his back turned as she changed from one set of thieves' blacks to another, then passed her a full skin of water.

"Well, we're inside, now what?" Taryn said, looking at Remarin.

"If my guess is right, we have about an hour to get to my brother's chambers and meet Jacob and Donovan. Then we should be able to see just how sick he is and figure out a plan from there."

"Do any of these plans include you staying here and ruling in your brother's stead?" Kit asked.

Remarin turned to the girl and took note of her wide eyes and the tension in her shoulders. She looked like she was ready to cry, fight, or run away, and he stepped closer to her. "No," the thief said softly. "I promised you we would get you back your throne and avenge your father's murder, and we will. I didn't want to rule here before I knew there were real options, and I sure as all the hells don't want to spend my life trapped on this rock now that I've seen what the world out there is like. So we'll do our duty here, then we'll head back to Veosia and have a nice little chat with the man sitting on your throne. Sound good?"

"Sounds very good," Kit said with a feral grin. "I've got a few things I want to say to my uncle."

"And say them you will, Kitten. But first, let's go try to save my brother's kingdom, and his life."

CHAPTER 25

The trio stepped out of the empty stall into the deserted stable, the quiet whickering of horses the only sound disturbing the still night air. Remarin led them to the front of the stable, then instead of opening the door, he turned right and climbed the ladder into the hayloft. Kit and Taryn shared a look, then shrugged and followed Remarin up.

Cool blue moonlight streamed into the hayloft through large hay loading bays in the front of the stable. Remarin pressed his back to the wall beside one of these bays and motioned the women to him.

"What are we doing up here?" Kit asked.

"We're taking the high road to my brother's chambers," Remarin replied. "There's no way we make it through the halls undiscovered, so we're going to climb on top of the stables, run across the rooftop, hopefully without being noticed, jump across a small gap to the battlements, climb one floor up to Steven's chambers, and hope that my brother's reflexes are no faster than they were when we were children."

"And if we're seen or captured?" Taryn asked.

"Please don't kill any of my brother's guards. They're just doing their jobs. Besides, the dungeon only has two cells, and they're dry and pretty nice, as far as cells go."

"And Gods know you're seen your fair share of cells," the assassin shot back.

"That I have, that I have." With that, Remarin stepped into the opening, sprang straight up and caught the nearest beam with his fingertips, then kicked his feet twice and swung himself straight up and out of sight. Kit and Taryn heard just the slightest sound from the roof as Remarin landed, then began making his way toward the far wall. Taryn followed suit, then Kit, who barely got enough height on her initial jump to catch the beam, but her light weight allowed the lithe young woman to flip herself high into the air before coming back down on the rooftop.

Kit spun in place on the ridge beam of the stable, taking in her surroundings. The keep sat high above the city, and she could see the business district sprawled out in front of the castle like a river delta, just across the moat and the raised drawbridge. The half-full moon provided ample light for her to count the eight guards along the battlements, all of them facing outward, the most logical place for a threat to appear. She kept herself low to the ridge and walked to the end of the stable, where Taryn and Remarin waited for her. The two seemed embroiled in an argument, as usual, but managed to remain silent.

As she arrived, Kit realized what the root of the argument likely was—her. Her safety, more to the point, which was something Taryn took very seriously, and Remarin…somewhat less so. The "small gap" between the battlements and the stable roof was more in the neighborhood of ten feet, with nothing to break a fall but the cobblestones some twenty feet below.

"She is not trying that jump, you idiot," Taryn hissed.

"You just watched her fly through the air like a squirrel hopping up onto the roof. This is nothing!" Remarin argued. "I was making this leap when I was ten years old; she could do this in her sleep!"

"In your dreams is the only place Kit will be jumping over that ridiculous distance—" Taryn's mouth hung open as she watched Kit sprint past her and vault the gap, landing in a roll atop the battlements and kneeling in the shadow of the far wall.

Remarin grinned and took three running steps, then launched himself from the roof. He landed in the center of the wall on both feet, rolled forward to disperse his momentum, and turned back to look at Taryn with an insolent grin. The assassin made a rude gesture at him, then followed across in a fluid leap that made her look more like a floating dark shadow than a human.

"That is the window to Steven's rooms." Remarin pointed up one floor above their heads. "I need you to go up ahead and anchor the rope, then I'll climb the rope and swing in the window."

"Why don't we just go into the tower here and use the door?" Kit asked, pointing at the heavy wooden door less than ten feet in front of them.

"There will be guards," Remarin said.

"I don't think so," Kit disagreed. "Two of these towers seem to have guard barracks in them, but this one and the one directly across from it don't. At least, I haven't seen any guards come out of them, and there has been a steady stream from the other towers."

"The other tower belongs to the Seneschal, so that's likely where our poisoner is dozing, if Jacob's wild tales are to be believed," Remarin said.

"You still haven't said why we can't just use the door," Taryn said.

"Fine," Remarin grumbled. "I wanted to show off, make a grand entrance. But you're right, no point climbing the tower and getting a crossbow bolt between the shoulders for our troubles. Let's use the door."

The trio walked in a crouch below the level of the battlements to the tower door, and Remarin reached for the knob. It turned in his hand, and the door swung outward. Remarin slipped into the tower stairwell, followed by Kit, then Taryn.

The thief pulled the door closed without so much as a whisper, then turned to start up the stairs and froze. Taryn had a maid pinned to the wall, her arm against the plump woman's throat and her stiletto pressed to the skin just below the woman's eye.

"So much as a breath out of you and I'll shove this blade through your eye into your brain. You'll be dead before I even drop you. Do you understand me?" The terrified maid nodded, reddish-gray curls shaking loose under her white cap.

"Is Lord Steven in his chambers?" Remarin asked. The woman nodded.

"Is anyone with him?" She nodded again.

"His wife?" Another nod.

"Here's what's going to happen," Remarin whispered to the woman. "You're going to go back up those stairs, knock, and walk in just like always. When they ask, you'll say you forgot to pick up His Grace's socks that need to be darned. As soon as you're inside, move to the side and get out of our way. Otherwise you may end up between me and my...and what I need to do, and that would be bad for you. Do you understand me?"

The terrified woman nodded, then her eyes rolled up into her head and she fainted dead away.

Remarin looked at Taryn, who shrugged. "I only choked her a little," the assassin protested.

"Whatever," Remarin said. "Tuck her away somewhere and let's get this over with." He slid sideways past Taryn and knelt at the door atop the stairwell. He slowly turned the knob, finding it locked. Remarin knelt before the lock, withdrew a small set of picks from a wrist sheath and set to work. Seconds later, he turned the knob ever so gently and stood, motioning the others to stand behind him.

With a nod to his cohorts, Remarin threw the door open and barged into the room, charging directly toward a sitting area in the center of the chambers. Taryn spun off to the right, sword in hand, looking for guards to engage. Kit followed suit to the left, but neither woman met with any resistance. Remarin drew himself up short as he saw the room was empty save one woman sitting in a high-backed chair, a silver tea service on the table beside her chair. She wore a dark green gown set off with pearls that accented her alabaster skin and flaming red hair. A light dusting of freckles danced across her cheeks and décolletage, and one loose curl dangled in front of her ear. She held a needle and a sock in her hands, and its mate lay across her lap.

Guess that bit about the maid darning socks was doomed from the jump, Trand "said."

Remarin sheathed his sword and sketched a rough bow. "Milady, please pardon the intrusion. We're looking for His Grace."

The woman looked up at Remarin, her features as bland as if three armed ruffians charged into her private chambers every night. Remarin froze as he got a good look at her and dropped to one knee, bowing his head with a formality Kit had never seen in him, even masquerading as the highest of nobility.

"Your Grace," he said, his voice low. Kit and Taryn exchanged glances, then both women dropped to one knee, mimicking Remarin's pose of deference.

"Oh get up, Remarin," the woman said with a smile. "We've been waiting for you." Something in her voice said that she had waited far longer than she was saying. Kit filed that piece of information away for future reference and took a good look at the Duchess. She was a youngish woman, a few years younger than Remarin, but when her eyes landed on the thief, it was as if she turned into the preteen girl she must have been when he left, a blushing maiden awestruck by the daring young Duke.

That explains a lot, Kit mused.

It does indeed, Kitty-cat, but what are you going to do about it? Trand's "voice" broke into her thoughts.

I'm not going to "do" anything, butter knife. It's none of my business. Or yours, she fired back mentally.

Keep telling yourself that, Kitten. Say it often enough and you might even believe it. Kit felt the imprisoned thief's presence withdraw from her mind, and she turned back to look at Duchess Genevieve. She was a lovely woman, curvaceous and soft where Kit and Taryn were all lean muscle and sharp edges. Kit reckoned that she had not a single callous on her hands, nor a single scar from a dagger anywhere on her person, then paused for a moment in wonder. *That's what my life would have been like if not for dear Uncle Alex.*

Had her uncle Alexander not murdered her father and framed Remarin for the crime, she would have grown up much as this woman did—attending balls and parties, with feasts in her honor and men competing for the right to wear her favor in a joust. *She* could have been the soft, well-fed girl with curves everywhere and a pearl-brocaded gown cut just right to emphasize all her charms, with long hair carefully coiffed and hot tea steeping on the table…

Kit rose and stepped up beside the Duchess, drawing her short sword and laying it against the other woman's throat in a smooth motion. "Who else is here?" she asked, her voice cold.

"Kit." Remarin sprang to his feet, reaching for her. "What in the hells are you…"

"There are two cups, Remarin. Both steeping. Who belongs to the other cup? Who is the real reason Her Grace here is fully dressed for a formal appearance in the middle of the night? It takes three ladies-in-waiting to get into one of those gowns. I know, I've done it."

"This is a smart one, big brother. You should keep her around." The newcomer's voice came from the doorway off to the right of the sitting room. A broad-shouldered blond man stepped into the room, and Kit fought the instinctive urge to kneel. Taryn didn't, dropping her head at the entrance of Duke Steven of Torin.

"Hello, brother," Duke Steven said with a wan smile at Remarin. "Did you come to reclaim your throne? Because I fear I won't be needing it much longer." The large man chuckled, which turned into a hacking cough and left him wheezing and sagging against the door frame for support. Genevieve sprang to her feet and ducked under her husband's shoulder, walking him over to a chair near hers. Kit stepped forward and took the Duke's other arm, helping Genevieve lower him gently into a sitting position. The Duchess gave Kit a grateful look, and a wealth of information passed between the two women in that briefest of glances.

Kit stepped back, tears springing unbidden to her eyes, and she quickly turned away from the Duke and Remarin, dashing unshed tears away with the back of one hand.

"Are you alright, Steven?" Remarin asked from where he still stood, stunned by his brother's sudden appearance and by how frail he looked. The Duke's once-lustrous blond hair now lay lank across his scalp in wispy hanks. Gone was the powerful young man who had taken over the rule of Torin when his father died, and in his place was a man old before his time, a withered shell of a man who a casual observer would guess closer to eighty than thirty.

Just as they had the Duke settled into his chair, the door across the sitting room burst open and Jacob and Donavan spilled in, jostling each other through the door and finally charging across the room to stand before the Duke and his brother.

"Dammit, Remarin, what did you do?" Jacob asked.

"What did I do? What the hell did you two do? You were supposed to meet me here and explain everything to Steven, but I get here and you're hiding in Genevieve's bedchambers?" Remarin turned to the Duchess. "And you're sitting out here sipping tea? While your husband does what? Stages a grand entrance by collapsing into my arms?"

"Her arms, actually," Kit said, her cool voice cutting through Remarin's hysterics. All eyes swung to the young woman, who raised an eyebrow at the Duchess and smiled. "Which is apropos, I suppose, since this whole farce was her idea."

CHAPTER 26

The silence in the room was deafening as everyone stared at Kit. Remarin's mouth shut with an audible *click*, and Duke Steven reached over and took the second teacup from the table. Genevieve smiled at Kit and motioned for her to continue.

"Well, it was obvious, wasn't it?" Kit asked. "Only a member of the royal house could give the Huntmaster leave to be gone from the grounds for the length of time that Jacob has been looking for Remarin, so that narrowed the field to the people in this room, the young Duke, and the Seneschal. As the young Duke has, I presume, been insulated from all the suspicious occurrences," she looked at Genevieve with this, and received a nod in return, "and since the Seneschal is one of the more likely suspects, neither of them would have sent for a backup Duke. That leaves the people in this room, and from what Remain has told us of his brother, he's nowhere near conniving enough to make this plan. That leaves Duchess Genevieve."

"Guilty," the Duchess said. "I knew that Remarin had certain skills in getting into places where he wasn't technically supposed to be, so I thought if I could find him, he could be persuaded to set aside old grudges and help save his brother's life."

"But how did you find me?" Remarin asked.

"You never changed your name, boy," Jacob replied with a snort. "Not after you got what you thought was far enough away. But you didn't count on traveling merchants remembering the singing barkeep from Casterlane."

"You always were the best hunter I ever saw," Remarin said. "Well, Your Grace," he turned to Genevieve with a bow, "now that we're here, what do you intend to do with us? I'm fairly certain the statute of limitations has expired on any crimes I committed here."

"Are you blind, Remarin?" Genevieve looked up at him with tears in her eyes. "Something is killing your brother. Your baby brother, and only you can stop it."

Remarin stepped forward and knelt between her chair and Steven's. "I know, Gen. I know. And I will. I promise. Now, Stevie, what can you tell us about the illness?" Remarin asked his brother.

"At first it was just a general malaise. I never felt well, never had much appetite, not much energy," the Duke replied.

"I can see why you were worried," Remarin said to Genevieve. He turned to Kit. "Stevie's always had the appetite of a bear and the energy of a stallion. When we were teenagers, he could ride for hours, then practice sword for two hours more, then be ready for a fine night of—" He stopped himself, a blush spreading across his cheeks.

"I remember, Remarin. I knew you both then. I knew exactly what I was getting when I married Steven. An honest, stalwart, steadfast man with a pure heart and an unwavering dedication to his family and his duty."

There was no accusation in the Duchess's words, but Kit saw Remarin flinch nonetheless. He gave his head a little shake and asked Steven, "When did you first notice you were more tired than usual?"

"I only began to see it in myself after Father died." He closed his eyes for a moment, then focused on his brother. "It never made sense to me that he died of a chill. He was stronger than me, than any of us. For him to fall ill like that, and then to waste away to nothing was... It was terrible to watch."

"I'm sure it was," Remarin said. "But then what happened? You became Duke, then you took on this wasting disease, too?"

"No, nothing like that," Steven said. "Well, now that you mention it, after three years, that's exactly what happened. I sat the throne for a year before I felt any illness whatsoever. Not even so much as a sniffle. Then one morning last fall, I woke up feeling stiff in the knees. Then it progressed to my shoulders, and my back, and now it's so bad in the mornings I can barely move. Some days I barely make it to my citizens' audiences, and the past two weeks I've missed court more times than I've held it."

"So it's progressing. This disease, I mean," Remarin said.

"Yes. And it's beginning to move faster. Last week I could stand on my own; this week I can barely walk holding the Staff of Thunder, and you know what its regenerative properties are like," the Duke said with a lopsided grin.

Remarin turned his head to look up at Kit. "Whenever Father would punish us, which in my case was often, I would sneak into the armory and lean against the wall with the Staff of Thunder in one hand, and no matter how hard Father whipped me, ten minutes in the armory with the Staff and I was ready for more mischief."

"He told me before he died that he always knew when you would sneak into the armory; that's why he never felt bad about hitting you," the Duke said.

"And here I just thought he liked beating me bloody," Remarin said with a wry smile.

"I think it was more that he knew he was going to have to keep beating you bloody, so he might as well make it easier for you to recover." The Duke grinned back at him, and the years and pain melted away for an instant. Kit watched as the Duke sat up a little straighter as he shared a moment with his brother. Remarin no longer looked like the ruffian and burglar he had been for years. His carriage was straight, his bearing that of someone accustomed to his words carrying weight, and his rocklike jaw set in a sharp line, the only physical resemblance the two men shared.

Remarin's eyes narrowed as he looked at his brother's eyes. "Steven, can you see me?"

The Duke started, then shook his head, his jaw working as he struggled to contain his emotions. "I never could hide anything from you. How did you know?"

"Your eyes never focused on mine. You're looking at me, but I'm less than two feet away and you haven't looked me in the eye once. That's not like you."

"I liken it to living in perpetual dusk or fog," Steven said. "I can see shapes and colors, but everything is muted, like I'm looking through a cloudy lens."

"I've heard of this," Taryn said. Everyone turned to stare at the assassin where she stood apart from the rest of the group. "What? I wasn't always an assassin. I had a family, once. My father's brother got the cloudy eyes when he got old. He described it just as you did. The town physician could do nothing for him, but a wizard passing through town was able to remove the haze from his eyes with a spell. He said the eye has a lens, and sometimes it must be cleaned. I don't know what he was talking about, but my uncle saw perfectly for several years."

"Then what happened?" Genevieve asked. "Did the spell wear off?"

"I don't know," Taryn said. "He got drunk and fell off his wagon while driving. A cart full of turnips crushed him flat. But as far as we know, he could see perfectly when he wasn't blind drunk."

"Well, that's hopeful, I suppose. Now we just need to find a wizard to fix Stevie's eyes," Remarin said.

"And keep me away from turnips, apparently," Steven added.

"I'm glad to see you've kept a sense of humor, brother," Remarin said. "Because whatever is happening to you is quite likely to get worse before it gets better."

"What do you mean?" the Duchess asked. "You're here now, and you'll get to the bottom of whatever's happening, and you'll stop it, right?" Kit saw the hope shining in the woman's face, and the shine of unshed tears in her eyes.

Oh hells, Kit thought.

And now you see it, Trand replied in her head.

She's in love with him.

Both of them, it seems. She certainly dotes on her husband.

But she worships Remarin. And if that isn't love, I don't know what is.

You'd know, wouldn't you? Trand's dry voice rang through her mind.

We're not talking about me.

Are we ever going to?

Not if we don't have to. And we certainly don't have to when we have a Duke being slowly murdered before our eyes.

"Is there anyone new in court?" Kit asked. "Not even really new, but someone who has been added to the household or the family's inner circle since Remarin left?"

"The entire household staff, almost, is new since then. Plus, the Swordmaster, the Seneschal, and the tutors. It seems Remarin was enough for most of them, and they moved on to less stressful careers than education."

"Like infantrymen, or testing hangman's nooses," Steven said. "Remarin and I were… challenging pupils, to say the least."

"Speak for yourself, woolen-head," Remarin said with a smile. "I was a perfect student."

"If by perfect you mean a perfect monster," Steven fired back. "You remember that poor languages teacher that you made resign her post in three days?"

"A remarkable effort, even for me," Remarin said with a grin. "I spoke only backwards from the moment we met until she ran screaming from the classroom. She was to teach us five separate languages, but I was already fluent in nine by the time she came to us. So I spoke backwards in every language she tried to teach us. Steven, for his part, went along with it."

"I wasn't as good at languages as Remarin, but I could get by, and when in doubt, he's not a bad guy to follow."

"So I've noticed," Kit said. Genevieve's head snapped up, and she fixed the younger woman with a piercing gaze, then nodded.

"So after three days of trying to get us to conjugate Franjillan verbs, she finally threw down her tablet in the middle of the floor and stormed out of the room. Seconds later, we heard a commotion at the stables, our Horsemaster arguing with a woman, her voice getting more and more shrill. Finally, Father stormed out of the throne room, shouted at the Horsemaster to give her a damned horse, threw a purse of money at her, and the sobbing woman rode through the gates, never to be heard from again."

"That one was a personal record," Remarin said. "It usually took me at least a week to get rid of a tutor."

"So most of the staff is new," Kit said. "That makes things a little more difficult."

"Not really," Taryn chimed in. All eyes turned to the trim woman in head to toe black. "Ugh, stop looking at me. I'm neither pretty nor interesting."

"That may be true, my homely darling, which it certainly is not, but it's also irrelevant. How is this task less difficult than we think?" Remarin said. "And for the record, you're wrong, I find you very… interesting." He finished with a grin.

"You walk a fine line, thief, royal family or not. Had you said you found me attractive, I would have been forced to gut you, and this looks like a very expensive carpet."

"Very," Steven agreed. "But you were saying?"

"Yes." Taryn nodded. "We don't need to look at anyone who has arrived since Steven has taken the throne."

"And why not, exactly?" Jacob asked from where he stood by the door.

"Because the same thing that's killing Steven is what killed Father," Remarin said with a glance at Taryn. At her nod, he continued. "So if we assume this is some type of poison or spell, then it was placed on Father first, then either recast, or moved to Steven somehow after he took the throne."

"Well, that does narrow the pool somewhat," Genevieve agreed. "Unfortunately, most of the new staff that came on between the time you left and the time Steven took the throne…"

"Came with you when you came here to marry," Kit said.

"This child understands much about life at court, Remarin. Something tells me she is more than she appears at first glance," Genevieve said.

"Aren't we all, Gen?" Remarin asked, a gentle tinge to his voice and a sad half-smile on his lips.

"I assume that you can vouch for the people that you brought with you, Your Grace?" Taryn asked.

"I would trust every one of those women with my life. I do, actually. They have unfettered access to my rooms, my food, my drink—everything. If one of them wished me ill, they would find it a simple matter to hurt or even kill me."

"But they wouldn't," the Duke chimed in. "Those women have all been with Gen since she was a child. They practically raised her. No, I refuse to believe that any of your ladies-in-waiting have anything to do with this." There was a strength in his voice that left no doubt to the strength of his mind, no matter the condition of his body.

"Alright, we'll exclude them from the investigation for the time being, but understand that there may come a time when we need them to answer some questions—" Remarin's words cut off as he spun to the door. "Defend my brother!" he hissed to Taryn.

The assassin never hesitated, just drew her knives and placed herself between the Duke and the door. Kit and Remarin both drew rapiers and stood before the chamber door as heavy footsteps clanked to a stop outside.

"Jacob, we'll want you to open the door," Remarin said.

"Why's that?" the Huntmaster asked.

"They're less likely to skewer you on sight than any of the rest of us," Remarin said. "Donny, get in front of the Duchess. We don't need any accidental crossbow fire emptying one of Torin's thrones prematurely." The man drew a short sword and stood before Genevieve. A pounding on the door called their attention back to the front of the room, and Jacob hurried to open the door.

"Who calls?" he asked, his face pressed to the wood.

"Open in the name of the Duke!" came a loud voice from the other side.

Jacob pulled the door open and glared at the cadre of armed guards in the hall. "What in the hells are you idiots doing, banging on doors at this hour? Have you no understanding of what it means to be ill?"

The front most guard stammered something unintelligible, then a small man in robes of the richest velvet swept into the room, brushing past Jacob as though the brawny forester was some underling beneath his notice.

"Pardon the interruption, Your Grace," the little man said, his voice oozing with oily charm and affected concern. "We had reports from one of the maids that there was an assassination attempt upon your life. The poor girl said that a dozen devils all clad in black accosted her on the stairs and bludgeoned her to unconsciousness."

The guards had by now filed into the room, six solid, unsmiling men in full chain with long swords and heavy shields. They spread out in a line on either side of the door, glowering at the inhabitants of the room.

"Remarin, please let me introduce you to my Seneschal, Durbin Temfosst. He handles all the day-to-day operations of the island since I have fallen ill. Durbin, please meet my brother, Remarin. He's here—"

"Just passing through, Seneschal Temfosst," Remarin said, a goofy grin plastered across his face. "My girls and I are on the way through Savoy, planning on exploring the pleasure houses of the East. We seem to have exhausted the capacities of Western amusements, if you get my meaning." The transformed thief leered at the little man like the two of them shared some secret bawdy joke.

The Seneschal looked at Remarin, then turned to Kit and Taryn, who both still stood with weapons at the ready. "You're taking *these* two to a pleasure house? I'd be afraid either of them would cut my throat while I slept. Especially that one," he said, gesturing to Taryn. "Are you sure she's a woman?"

"Oh, I assure you, my friend, she is every inch a woman, and some nights more woman than I can handle. But my tastes have never been what one would call commonplace. That's why Father sent me away in the first place. Right, Stevie?" Remarin cast a leering grin at his brother and waggled his eyebrow suggestively. Kit put a hand over her mouth and coughed, smothering her smile behind her palm.

"Whatever you say, brother," the Duke replied, obviously confused.

Genevieve stepped in, rising and offering her seat to the Seneschal. "Gentlemen, I must retire. It is long past time for me to retire. Ladies, would you mind assisting me? I fear my own handmaidens are long abed. Gentlemen." She nodded to the men and headed to her bedroom, followed closely by Taryn and Kit.

If he needs me, you call to me, Kit sent to Trand.

Don't worry, Kitten, he thinks he's already outwitted this guy.

Keep him alive, Trand, Kit said.

I will, Kitten. Now go keep an eye on Genevieve. She's in at least as much danger as anyone out here.

The women left the room, and the Seneschal turned to Remarin. "Now that your girl toys are out of the room, would you like to tell us why you're really here? And make it good. We have reason to believe that Torin is under attack by spies and assassins, and who better to sneak into the castle and murder the Duke than his long-lost brother?" The little man locked eyes with Remarin and grinned.

"Guards! Arrest these men!"

CHAPTER 27

Steven shouted "No!" but the guards ignored him. It was obvious where their loyalties lay. Remarin sprang into action, his years living on the streets and above the law leaving him with knife-edge reflexes.

"Jacob, guard the Duke! Can't have any 'accidents' in the fray, can we?" the thief yelled as he ran his rapier through the thigh of the nearest guard and left it there. The man went down in a heap of shiny mail and red blood, and Remarin plucked the longsword from his hand. The heavier blade had none of the finesse of his finely balanced rapier but had the benefit of being able to block the other guards' weapons without shattering. Remarin parried a thrust from one guard, stepped inside, and with his off hand, slammed the butt of his dagger into the man's head.

Oh, hello, Trand, Remarin "said" to the enchanted blade, which had been on Kit's hip the last time he saw it.

Hello, Remarin. What did you do to make these *men want to kill you?*

Nothing, I swear! I think the Seneschal might be in on the plan to kill Steven and take the throne.

That's my Remoron, always thinking two steps behind the rest of us. Behind you!

Remarin dropped to a knee and spun around, just as a sword whirled over his head. Remarin stabbed the man in the foot, then stood up abruptly and tagged the guard on the point of his chin with his sword hilt. The man's eyes rolled back in his head, and he dropped to the floor in a crash of metal.

You're working very hard to keep these men alive, Trand remarked.

They're guards. They pick up a sword and try to stick it in whoever they're told to. It's not their fault the Seneschal is a traitor. Remarin shouted over the din toward the Duchess's bedchamber. "Kit! Hold the room! Keep Gen—the Duchess safe!"

He turned back to the fray without waiting for a response. Two guards down, four to go, plus the Seneschal, wherever he might be. Remarin took in the rest of the room. Jacob struggled against two guards, but was holding his own, barely. Donavan was a veteran of more barroom brawls than Remarin could count, and he was having no difficulty fending off the lone guard facing him.

That leaves one, Remarin thought as he heard the scrape of boots on stone behind him. He threw himself forward into a roll and spun around, suddenly six feet away from the stunned solider who apparently thought he'd scored an easy kill.

"Stabbing a man in the back? That's not sporting at all," Remarin said, then hurled Trand through the air to ring off the man's helmet hilt-first and bounce high into the air. The dagger winked out of existence at the apex of its flight and reappeared sheathed at Remarin's hip. The guard took one step back, then another, then his eyes rolled back in his head, and he toppled over backward like a felled oak.

"Stevie, if you've got anything left, now's the time to use it!" Remarin called to his brother, who pushed himself from his chair just as a sword blade pierced the chair from behind. The room fell silent as the guards and Remarin's friends saw the Seneschal, Durbin Temfosst, standing behind the Duke's chair holding the hilt of a longsword.

"Traitor! Seize that man!" Duke Steven bellowed, and the guards responded instantly. No longer concerned with Jacob or Donovan, they almost stumbled over themselves getting to the small black-clad man. But the Seneschal was too fast, and he reached the door before anyone laid a hand on him.

"We aren't finished, Your Grace." The little man turned and gestured at the Duke before he yanked the door open. He turned to run down the stairs but flew back into the room and landed on his back instead. A black-clad foot hung in the air for a second, then Taryn stepped through behind it. She closed the door and stalked the semiconscious Seneschal as he scrambled backward on his hands and rump. After long seconds, Temfosst clambered to his feet and ran to the Duke's bedchamber door.

Remarin cut him off, longsword at the ready. "Not this way, friend."

The little man turned and ran to the Duchess's door, turned the knob, and flung it open. He then backed away from the door with Kit's blade at his throat. The young princess looked nothing less than a stone killer as she glared at the traitorous courtier.

Desperation beading on his forehead, the Seneschal took one last look at Steven, wavering beside his chair but standing unaided. "Another week and you'd be dead, you great buffoon!"

"Call my brother names again, and you won't see another sunrise, much less a week," Remarin said, his voice like ice.

Temfosst laughed, a high, reedy laugh that was shot through with fear. "A week? I should dream of living a week! I won't last a day when he learns I've failed. And if I betray him, everyone I've ever known will be massacred." The little man reached out and slapped Kit's blade away from his throat, leaving a bloody scratch as he stepped back. He turned to the window and crossed the ten feet at a dead run. Kit lunged for him, but she was a hair's breadth too slow. Glass and old wood splintered on impact, and the Seneschal plummeted to his death on the rocks below. Remarin ran to the window, but all the remained of Durbin Temfosst was a pile of broken pieces and black robes.

Remarin pulled the short sword from the back of Steven's chair and let it clatter to the floor. "Sorry about your chair, brother."

Steven lowered himself into his seat and leaned back. "Thank you, Remarin. I'd likely be dead if it weren't for you."

"You're my brother, what else would I do?" the thief answered, sitting in the other chair.

"Many would have run," Steven said, his voice weak.

"I've run from this castle once, Stevie. Once is enough," Remarin replied.

"So you'll stay?"

"For a while. There's a lot to uncover about this Temfosst and his plot."

"Not to mention who was pulling his strings," Genevieve added, entering the room in her nightgown. The guards covered their eyes or conspicuously looked elsewhere, but the pretty Duchess just laughed. "Calm down, boys. I'm covered head-to-toe; you don't have to fear for my modesty." And indeed, she wore a heavy burgundy robe over her gown, exposing only the occasional hint of arm or scandalous ankle. Remarin stood as she came into the room, but she waved a hand at him.

"Sit down, Remarin. I'm sure one of these gentlemen will bring me a chair from the Duke's chambers, won't you?" She waved a hand at one of the guards, who scurried into the other room and returned seconds later with a large armchair. He placed the chair at Steven's right hand, and Genevieve sat. Remarin retrieved his rapier from the floor as Kit sheathed her blade and Taryn returned her knives to various hiding spots on her person.

Jacob and Donavan relieved the guards of their weapons and armor and sat them against a wall in the main chamber. Jacob paced back and forth in front of them, glaring at the battered and bloodied men and muttering under his breath. After several long minutes of this, he stopped and spoke.

"Who is the ranking officer here?"

A young guard second from the end raised his hand.

Jacob moved to stand right in front of him. "Who are you, boy?"

"Lieutenant Singet, sir," the man said. His voice was thin and shaky, but he looked Jacob in the eye and didn't flinch.

"Why were you following the Seneschal, Singet?"

"He told us the Duke had gone mad and was going to murder his wife and the heir," the young man said.

"The Duke," Steven said.

"Yes, sir," Singet replied. "Seneschal Temfosst said you were going to murder your wife and son."

"No, lad," Steven corrected kindly. "I meant that my son should be referred to as 'the Duke' from here onward." He smiled at the guard, then turned to Genevieve. "I know I was never the Duke you wanted, but I loved you with all my heart, and I hope that you came to love me, at least a little."

Genevieve looked at her husband, her mouth hanging open, and sprang to her feet. Kit looked around the room for a threat, then her eyes locked on the Duke as he pulled a tiny dart from his upper arm.

"It seems our little traitor had one last surprise for me. Brother, please remember…" he said, then collapsed forward and lay in a crumpled heap on the stone floor. Genevieve cried out and dropped to her knees by the Duke's still form, and Remarin crossed the distance between them in seconds, kneeling beside the Duchess and pulling her back slightly.

The slight thief took his brother's body and rolled it over, stretching Steven out so it looked like he was in peaceful repose. He took a pair of black leather gloves from his belt and slid them on, then removed the dart from Steven's fingers.

"Taryn," Remarin called, and the black-clad woman stepped to his side. He handed her the dart and said, "Find out what kind of poison was used, then see if that narrows down who might have sent Temfosst."

"Of course," Taryn said, slipping on gloves of her own before handling the poisoned dart.

"And Taryn?" Remarin called from the floor.

"Yes?"

"If any of the guards seem reluctant to answer questions, kill them. Slowly."

Taryn grinned down at the thief. "Absolutely."

Remarin reached down and pressed his fingers to Steven's neck for a moment, then drew his hand back. He passed his hand over his brother's face, closing his now-vacant eyes. Genevieve collapsed then, sobbing, onto her late husband's chest. Remarin stood and looked around the room.

"Donny, go to the young Duke's bedroom. Wake him, but keep him in his chambers. Tell him his father is ill, and he must be strong for his mother. Take several men that you trust beyond all others. You and one or two others stay in the room with…" He looked at Donavan with questioning eyes.

"Gareth," the large man replied.

"Gareth," Remarin repeated, rolling the name around in his mouth like he was tasting an unfamiliar fruit. "Stay in the room with Gareth and protect him at all costs. My nephew is the Duke now, and there is no heir. If any ill befalls him, Torin will be thrown into turmoil the like it's never seen before."

"I'll take care of it, Your—" Donavan cut himself off at a sharp glance from Remarin, then nodded and headed out the door.

"Kit, take Trand and guard Genevieve. Jacob will stay here with you. If anyone comes through that door that isn't me or a priest, kill them. Do not hesitate. You know what's at stake here."

The young woman nodded and drew her rapier. She waved the slender blade at the seated guards. "What about them?"

"I think they're probably loyal, but stupid," Remarin replied. "Stick them in the Duchess's chambers and blockade the door. If there is anything to point us in the direction of my brother's killer, it will be in Steven's rooms, so no one goes in there until I return."

"And where are you going this time, Remarin?" Genevieve said from the floor. She looked up, tears pouring down her face. "Do you have another ship to catch?"

The pain was evident in Remarin's face as he replied, "No, Gen, I'm going to get the priest to give my baby brother last rites, and then I'm going to call the Privy Council to session. They are the only ones with the authority to enthrone Duke Gareth in an emergency, and that needs to be done before he addresses the city at dawn."

"At dawn? Remarin, have you taken leave of your senses? He's only a boy of twelve, and he just lost his father!" Genevieve protested. "He cannot possibly—"

"He must," Remarin said, his voice flat and emotionless as cold iron. "If he wants to hold that throne, he has to lay claim to it now, before anyone can raise the specter of doubt as to his readiness, especially with another heir suddenly returned."

"You don't think?" Kit asked, her eyes wide.

"Jacob somehow found us just in time to get us here before my brother died," Remarin replied. "Name change or no, we'd escaped notice for a dozen years until very recently. No, there's no coincidence here—Temfosst had something to do with our being discovered. I'd wager that he learned of Jacob's mission and planted someone in a tavern to casually 'remember' me. And I can almost guarantee that if Gareth isn't sitting that throne in audience tomorrow, you're going to hear rumblings in the taverns all over Torin that Steven was never meant to hold the crown in the first place, and that rightful Duke Remarin has returned to take control."

"And has he?" Genevieve asked. "Is that why you came back?"

"If I wanted that throne, it would have been mine already, Gen. I came back to save my brother's life and kingdom. I've failed him once tonight. It won't happen again." He turned and strode to the door. "Remember, no one enters but me or a priest. And that priest had better have me hot on his heels. And Gen?"

The Duchess looked up, her cheeks awash in tears. "What is it, Remarin?"

"I'm sorry," the thief said, his own eyes threatening to spill over. "For everything." And with that, he stepped through the door and was gone.

CHAPTER 28

The evening of the next day saw a weary Remarin collapse into a chair across the table from Duchess Genevieve. She was beautiful, even dressed in deepest mourning black, but her eyes were dry and her expression severe.

"What is the plan, Remarin? We've installed Gareth on the throne, and the Privy Council seems content for now to operate with him as titular ruler while I operate as his regent until he comes of age, but we still must uncover who is behind his father's murder." Her jaw was set, and Kit watched her carefully.

Taking notes, Kitten? Trand spoke in her mind.

After a fashion, Kit replied. *She's a strong woman, and now she'll rule this kingdom for half a decade until her son comes of age. There's a fair bit I could learn from her.*

And she loves Remarin.

Just had to twist the knife, didn't you, Trand? Kit thought at him crossly.

Pun completely intended, I'm sure, came the smug reply.

Remarin straightened in his chair and waved Taryn to the table. They were gathered around a large table in the sitting area of the Duke's chambers. Duke Gareth was asleep in his room, and Remarin,

179

Kit, Taryn, Genevieve, Jacob, and Donavan sat behind the remnants of a large meal. Donavan still gnawed on the leg bone of a turkey, but the others were finished with their food.

"I don't have much of a plan, Your Grace."

"Really, Remarin? You're going to get formal on me now? Everyone in this room knows that we were involved before I married Steven. Hells, everyone on the island probably knows. I think you can forego the titles when we're among friends." Genevieve's eyes sparkled a little as she teased the weary thief.

"Fine," Remarin said with a grunt. "I don't have much of a plan, *Gen*. Better?"

"Much," the Duchess replied, her hands folded primly on the table.

Remarin continued. "We searched Temfosst's body, but all his clothing was made here in Torin. There was nothing in his chambers to indicate where he originally came from, and not even Trand could glean his birthplace from the few words we heard him speak."

"Who is this Trand? You've mentioned him a few times," Donavan asked.

"He's my best friend," Remarin replied.

"He's the dagger," Kit said at the exact same moment.

"They're both right," Taryn said in response to the confused looks from the Torin natives.

"My best friend is trapped inside my magical dagger," Remarin said. "But it hasn't managed to shut him up, or improve his sense of humor."

My sense of humor is sharper than your rapier, Trand said. Kit snorted a laugh. Remarin looked grumpy.

"He talks inside my head. Kit's too. It's a long story, best left untold. Forever," Remarin said.

"Your searching may have been fruitless, but mine was not," Taryn chimed in, holding up a small vial with the dart that killed Duke Steven inside. "There was a very tiny amount of poison still on the tip of the dart. I diluted it in water, then dripped the water solution onto a piece of paper. After it dried, I burned the paper, and it turned the flame green."

"Viper's Kiss," Remarin said, blowing out a long breath. "That complicates things, doesn't it?"

"It does indeed," Taryn replied.

"What is Viper's Kiss, and why does it complicate things?" Genevieve asked.

"Viper's Kiss is a poison chosen by professionals across the globe. It is tasteless, odorless, completely safe to handle with bare skin, so long as you don't get any into your blood, and fatal within minutes. There is no known cure, and nothing save powerful magic will counter its effects," Taryn explained.

"So it's a powerful poison. We knew that already. What makes things more complicated?" Kit asked, leaning forward onto her elbows.

"Viper's Kiss is made from one very specific mushroom that is only known to grow in one forest," Remarin said.

"Well, that's great," Kit said. "Now we've narrowed down our search for who sent the assassin. Where is this forest?"

"That's the problem, Kitten," Remarin replied. "It's right outside the city of Bravis, a city we both know all too well."

The young exiled monarch leaned back in her chair, a worried look on her face. "Shit."

"Exactly, my dear Queen-on-the-run," Remarin said. "This poison came from the forest outside the walls of the capital city of Veosia. You remember Veosia, don't you? The country you're supposed to be the ruler of except for your usurping uncle who murdered your father and tried to kill you?"

"I remember," the young woman said.

"So do I," Remarin went on. "I remember how he framed me for that murder, tried to have me killed, and forced us both into exile. And now it seems like no small coincidence that the man who murdered my baby brother used a poison from Veosia."

"You think Uncle Alexander had something to do with this?" Kit asked.

"You said it yourself, Torin is very important to trade with the East. Whoever controls Torin is halfway to controlling the Gates. And if your dear Uncle Alex controlled the Gates, he would very quickly have more money and power than any man in the Eastern Realms," Remarin said.

"No matter who he had to slaughter to get it," Taryn added.

"Exactly," Remarin agreed. "Gear up, Kitten. Tomorrow, we ride for home. I've got a usurper to kill, and you've got a throne to claim. Get plenty of rest because the revolution starts at dawn."

PART III
REVOLUTION

"Remarin, am I ever going to go anywhere with you that doesn't involve a sewer?" Kit asked as her foot slipped in the muck and she wobbled a little before pressing herself against the curved wall of the huge tunnel.

"That depends, Kitten. Am I ever going to go anywhere with you that there won't be dozens of armed men wishing desperately to see the color and shape of my spleen?" Remarin whispered back without looking.

The pair navigated the tunnels beneath Veosia by feel and memory, plus the very rare glint of light coming through the grates in the streets above their heads. By Remarin's reckoning, they were nearing the main thoroughfare of the market, which should mean that a side tunnel was...right there!

"This way," he hissed, turning the right. Kit followed, a hand wrapped around the back of his belt.

"Taryn?" Kit asked into the shadows.

"Here," came a faceless voice in the darkness, the sure-footed assassin needing no aid in traversing the treacherous sewers, nor any assistance in following Remarin, no matter how little light was available.

Not going to ask about me? Trand said from Remarin's belt, his ruby pommel stone winking at Kit momentarily.

No, cheese-cutter. I know you'll always find your way home. I'm less confident in our fearless leader, Kit replied silently. The mental link she shared with the ensorcelled blade grew stronger by the week, until she could now speak to Trand from a distance of many city blocks.

I've called Remoron many things over the years, but somehow I must have left "fearless" off my list.

"You two know I can hear you, right?" Remarin's voice, even tinged with irritation, still barely floated over the still air in the sewer. "We're almost to Mara's back entrance. She should remember me, and once we're inside, we can get cleaned up and find a place to stay while we get the lay of the land."

"When you say that she should remember you, does that mean she will remember you fondly?" Taryn's whisper was barely louder than the whisper of the water moving alongside them, yet the woman managed to leave no doubt as to her thoughts on the matter.

"Everyone's a comedian when they don't have to lead," Remarin muttered. "You know, I abdicated one throne already. I'm not afraid to leave you two down here to blunder about lost and go on my merry way."

I'll cut off parts of you that you are inordinately proud of if you ever seriously consider such a thing, Trand "said" before either of the others had a chance to respond.

Remarin glared down at the dagger on his hip, sparkling with a mirthful crimson light as if his old friend were laughing at him. He opened his mouth to speak, then his hand passed over a depression in the wall, and he froze. "Stop," he whispered. He pronounced his "s" sounds like "th" to cut down on the sibilance in the quiet tunnels, but no one mocked his caution. Their journey home to Veosia had been dangerous enough, traveling at night and close to the major roads but never on them, dodging bandits and legitimate traders alike to keep their profile as low as possible. But now, back in the land that Kit was rightful ruler of, the very real danger they were in pressed down on all of them like a boulder.

Remarin's delicate fingers trailed across a wooden door set into the tunnel wall, an obvious addition that the city architects never intended. He pressed his body to the door, feeling around the edges for traps or tripwires. He disabled a small wire strung across at knee height and another right at the level of a person's ankles. *I remember Mara being more trusting.*

Maybe she learned a lesson from dealing with you, Trand replied. *But in all seriousness, Remarin, it's been eight years. Mara may not even own this brothel any longer, or even be alive.*

Come on, Trand. Mara was the toughest madame in Veosia. I don't want to even think how bad it would have gotten if someone was wicked enough to remove her. Remarin felt for the small panel in the center of the door, pushed it in, then reached into the void and twisted the handle inside the opening. The door swung inward silently, and Remarin stepped through, Kit and Taryn close behind.

They stepped into a darkened room, and Taryn closed the door, which latched into place with an almost imperceptible *click.* "Trand, you want to shed a little light on things?" Remarin asked, holding the dagger overhead. The ruby-red pommel stone flared into a brilliant light, bathing the small room in crimson. They stood on the edge of a small storage room, crammed with blankets, bedding, and furniture. One wall was stacked head-high with trunks, wisps of fabric leaking from the seams like overfull water basins. Stairs led up to a door set into the ceiling, and a short three-legged round table sat on a small rug near the center of the room.

A lantern sat on the table, so Remarin walked over and lit it. Trand extinguished his glow, and the more natural lantern light filled the room. Remarin reached up above the table and hung the lamp on a ring that seemed to be there for that purpose.

"There's a note on the table," Kit said.

Remarin picked it up and read it aloud. "Hail, traveler. If you have found your way into this room, we are either friends, or you are here to rob me. Whichever the case, there is nothing in this room save clothes and used bedroom furnishing. Please help yourself to either, particularly the clothing if you plan to visit my more public areas. There should be something in the trunks to fit all but the most extreme of sizes. I apologize, but footwear is expensive, and my patrons are far less likely to leave that behind if they leave my establishment in a rush. But be assured that my floors are kept clean and free of splinters, so please avail yourself of the clothing and do not be concerned about walking my floors barefoot. Signed with an M, so I guess Mara is still running the roost," Remarin said, looking at the stack of trunks.

Taryn was already at the wall of leftover clothing. "There are sizes written on these," she said. She tapped a high trunk. "Slight women, small-breasted. That describes both of us, Kit." She reached up without waiting or asking for help and hauled the trunk down. She and Kit set to rummaging through it, with Kit holding up various shirts and pants against her body to model them. Taryn pawed through the box until she came up with black clothing that met with her approval.

Remarin found a box that described his slight build and moved boxes around until he could get into it. The clothes were generally solid, if unspectacular, and had the added bonus of not being worn through a sewer after two weeks straight on the road, so moments later, it was a significantly better-smelling trio that emerged from the portal in the floor, each holding their boots in one hand.

Remarin poked his head up into a storeroom behind the brothel's kitchen, his head instantly wreathed in the warm air and appetizing smells from the next room. The pantry was deserted, just a small room with shelves stacked high with containers of spices, flour, and dry goods. Remarin scampered up from the hole in the floor, then moved aside so Kit could ascend. Taryn followed immediately after and dropped the door back into place. It fitted into the floor without even a seam, and no visible handle.

"Looks like somebody built that door with quick escape in mind," Taryn said with an approving nod.

"Can't imagine why anyone would want to install a bolthole in a whorehouse," Remarin said, then pulled open the door into the kitchen.

The bustle of the kitchen came to an immediate halt at the sight of the trio, then a silver-haired woman dressed in cook's whites hurried over to them, a cleaver waving in her right hand and a headless chicken hanging from the other. "You! I know you! You trouble! Last time you were here, big fight! You get out, you get out now!"

"Looks like she really does know you, Remarin," Kit said, the corners of her mouth twitching up despite the stout woman brandishing a cleaver at them.

"Larelle!" Remarin exclaimed. "How good to see you again. You look as lovely as ever. You haven't aged a moment in all the time I've been gone!" The thief opened his arms wide, threatening to envelop the cook in an expansive hug.

Larelle, for her part, was having none of Remarin's good cheer. She waggled the cleaver under his nose with a scowl. "You poking at Larelle. You always poke, poke, poke, little thief. One day, Larelle cut off your little poker. What will you do then, little thief?"

"Well, my dear, perhaps I should show you what I can do with my little poker before you decide to cut it off. How does that sound?" Remarin gave the older woman a leer, and Kit braced for the bloodshed to commence.

Instead, the hefty cook roared with laughter and hugged Remarin, lifting him clean off the floor in her exuberance. "I have missed you, little thief! Where have you been? Chasing other whores? There are prettier whores in Veosia, to be sure, but no better food in any brothel this side of Gorix, and those whores all witches. You know Larelle speak truth!"

"Yes, Larelle, you speak truth. You also break ribs, dear, so put me down."

She did as he asked, then turned to Taryn and Kit. "Who are girls, little thief? You bring them to Larelle for fattening up before you sell them to Mara? The tall one is ugly, but the little one would bring a good price for a night. No tits, though. Good you brought them to me first. Leave them here for a month. I give them huge bosoms, Mara pay you better fee."

Remarin just closed his eyes, waiting for the fireworks to start. When Taryn didn't eviscerate the cook on the spot, he opened first one eye, then the other, to find all three women staring at him, waiting for an answer.

"Um…I'm not her to sell them to Mara, love. But we do need to see her. I need her help, and so does my friend Kit here." He gestured to her, then to Taryn. "Taryn, um, she…"

"Doesn't need anything," the assassin said. "I'm not here to be a whore."

"You don't like whores?" Larelle asked, and her tone told anyone listening they were venturing into dangerous territory.

"I don't have any opinion on whores," Taryn said. "I just wouldn't be a very good one. Too many knives in my underclothes."

Larelle stared at the gaunt woman hard for a long moment, then roared with laughter. "I like you, skinny girl! You funny as Remarin thinks he is! You sit, all three of you. Sit, eat, and I send for Mara." With a snap of her fingers and a wave of her hand, a butcher's block was cleared off to one side of the kitchen and a cloth tossed over it. A plate of bread, cheese, and sliced cured meats was set in the center of the impromptu table, and a jug of wine with four mugs appeared from somewhere.

Larelle took a seat on a stool, gestured for the table, and poured four mugs of wine. The trio sat around the table, piling cheese and meat onto bread, then slathering it with mustard and other spreads brought forth by kitchen helpers.

Kit had just taken her first bite when Larelle looked around, and seeing the kitchen momentarily deserted, said, "We alone now, Remarin. So you tell me why you bring dead heir to Veosian throne into my kitchen through sewers?"

CHAPTER 30

Remarin froze, then relaxed as the cook let out a full-bodied laugh that shook every part of her. "Look at you, little thief! You tighten up so much your butt waterproof! You think I not recognize my princess? What you take me for, idiot?"

Remarin just sat still, his mouth opening and closing like a fish flapping around in the bottom of a boat. He had recovered almost enough to form a sentence when Mara swept into the room in a billow of silks and perfumes. Remarin and the others scrambled to their feet as the force of nature known as Mara entered.

"Remarin! So good of you to come visit me," the madame said. She didn't so much walk as she glided, but she glided in a wake of color and fragrance, her voluptuous form wrapped in what appeared to be nothing more than gauzy handkerchiefs of varying sizes and colors, all carefully tucked and pulled to reveal some aspects of her glorious form and conceal others depending on how she moved.

Mara sailed through the kitchen, somehow making a grand progression out of crossing twelve feet of floor, to fetch up before the poleaxed thief with a smile stretching wide across her rouged cheeks. She drew back a perfectly manicured hand and sent it sailing through the air to land alongside Remarin's cheek with a slap like the crack of a whip. "That was for leaving town without telling me," the stout woman said, a prim smile on her round little face.

She drew back her other hand and laid another resounding slap across Remarin's cheek, turning the gaping thief's head almost completely around. "That was for leaving town whilst owing me money."

Mara stepped forward, grasped the front of Remarin's borrowed shirt in both hands, pulled his face down to hers, and pressed her crimson lips to his. She kissed the stunned man for nearly a full minute before she released him, gasping, to step back and straighten up. "That was for coming back. It's good to see you, Remarin." She turned to Kit. "Your Majesty, welcome to The Devil's Doorbell, the finest brothel in all of Veosia." Mara swept down into a low bow, then hastily stood, rearranging several silks that threatened to lose their structural integrity under the onslaught of gravity and the precipitous shifting of her bosom.

The proprietress cast an appraising eye over Taryn. "You are welcome, my lady. I only ask that if you feel it absolutely necessary to slit throats while you are under my roof, that you do so on a carpet or in a bed. It is so difficult to remove blood from a wooden floor."

Taryn gave the blowsy woman a tight nod. "I have found that it is often simplest to sand the floor and refinish it after a killing. But I shall endeavor to keep my mess to a minimum."

"I thank you," Mara replied. She made her way around the table to sit by the cook, patting the stern woman on the knee. "Now, Remarin, why have you brought this magnet for trouble and bloodshed to my doorstep? You must know that the price on her head, and yours, is high enough to make even me consider handing you over to the Royal Guard."

"That's why we're here, Mara. You may have considered turning us in, but most everyone else in this godsforsaken city would have just rapped us on the head and bundled us off to the castle," Remarin said, sitting down at the table and gesturing for his companions to join him.

Taryn shook her head, standing by the door, but Kit took a seat and leaned forward onto her elbows. "If you know who I am, then you know what my presence here means."

"Absolutely, my love," Mara said. "It means you're completely daft."

"What?"

"It means that you're idiot enough to think you can overthrow your uncle and take your throne back. I assure you, that is impossible."

"I'm not an idiot," Kit said, standing. Remarin put a hand on her shoulder, but she shrugged it off, color rising in her cheeks. "I am the rightful ruler of Veosia, and I will no longer stand by while that murdering usurper sits on my father's throne."

Mara looked the young woman up and down, her gaze appraising. "Not bad. What do you think, Larelle?" she asked the cook.

"Not bad," the gruff woman said. "Almost believed her myself. Needs a sword in hand, maybe. But good for a child. Still insane, but almost believable."

Kit looked from Mara to the cook, then back. She turned to Remarin, who completely failed to hide his grin behind a hand. "You are mocking me. All three of you. I will not be mocked! I am the—"

"You are nothing, child." Mara's voice snapped out cold as an icicle, and Kit froze in mid-rant to gape at the previously flighty-seeming madame. What sat before her now wasn't the gauzy, ephemeral woman who breezed into the room and flitted around like a multi-hued butterfly. Where that woman had sat now was Mara the Flower, the shrewd businesswoman who owned her own pleasure house, owing nothing to any man for three decades, who whored her way to wealth, then set herself up in competition with the male-run brothels and drove half of them into bankruptcy after they underestimated her.

"You are nothing because no one knows you live. Your uncle Alexander did a fine job of painting Remarin as a ruthless killer to the general populace, and regardless of what those of us in the Guild knew as fact, to the average Veosian you have been dead these eight years. Dead queens can't rule, love, no matter how great a bastard the man they depose may be." Mara folded her jewel-toned arms and stared at the girl.

For her part, Kit recovered quickly. Years of traveling with

Remarin had sharpened her wits, and her tongue. "Dead queens can't rule, but I've watched dead princes come back to life." She pointedly did not glance at Remarin, who she felt stiffen at her side at the mention of their sojourn to Torin. "First we let the people know that I live, then we rally them to my banner."

"Not quite, Kitten," Remarin said.

"I've told you…oh, never mind," Kit started to correct him for the thousandth time, then sighed and shook her head. "What do you mean?"

"We do exactly what you suggested, just in the reverse order." The thief smiled at her, and Kit's stomach did a tiny flutter at his green eyes and the dimple in his chin.

"I don't understand," she admitted.

"First we get them to want to rebel, then we build a mysterious figure for them to rally around. Finally, once we have their sense of justice frothing for revolution—"

"And their romantic souls throbbing for a leader out of legend…" Mara chimed in.

"Then we reveal that it's you behind it all, and we storm the gates of your father's castle, thrown Uncle Alex over the battlements to his death, and install your delightful little derrière on the throne," Remarin finished with a little seated half-bow. "It's the stuff bards sing about for decades, if not legends. That reminds me, we need a bard. Do you still have that foppish little blond fellow drinking his way through your wine cellar?"

"He went off a few years ago with a brutish Northman, a shady half-elf, a nudist, and some idiot street preacher," Mara replied. "Too bad. He was brutally stupid but played a good tune."

"That's not all he played well," the cook said with a leer. "He knew how to ring Devil's Doorbell." She let out a full belly laugh and slapped Mara on the back.

"As terrifying as that imagery is," Remarin said. "It doesn't get us any further toward our goal."

"Oh?" Mara said. "Then we can reopen the trapdoor. Because the only goal we can help you with here is getting the hells out of town and vanishing to some other city where Her Majesty's likeness isn't stamped on currency."

"Come on, Mara," Remarin protested. "There's no way a despot like Alexander is good for business."

"Oh, he's terribly inconvenient," Mara agreed. "He's thrown in his lot with the Priests of the Rod, and you know they are no friend to the pleasure houses. He taxes all business relentlessly, and his Guard is more corrupt than old King Rutvor ever dreamed of being." She waved a hand at Kit, who looked aghast. "Oh don't look so shocked, dearie. All City Guards are corrupt to one degree or another, but your father's men were reasonable. We fuck a few of them for free every month and they walk on by."

"But not these new guards," Larelle, the cook, growled. She spat on the floor in disgust. "They fuck all they want for free and want protection money on top of that. Fuck them." She spat again.

"So you should want to help us," Kit protested. "We can make it better. We just need to get the word out that I'm alive, then—"

"Have you heard nothing we've said, child?" Mara asked, her voice needle-sharp. "You go rushing around town bleating about the return of the queen, and we'll all be on pikes at the city gates by dawn."

"My uncle is putting heads on pikes? That's abominable," Kit said.

"Oh sweetie," Mara said, the pity in her voice evident. "If only it were that kind. No, his men skewer the entire body on the pike, then they stand the body up, pike and all, right outside the city gates. They bury the end of the pike in the ground, so the person's feet only start off a few feet off the ground. They're usually dead before they slide all the way down to the ground. Usually."

Kit swallowed hard at the mental image. "That's..."

"That's the kind of man who would murder his brother, try to kill his sister, and take out a contract on the life of a perfectly innocent thief," Remarin said. "Which is why we need to get this bastard out of power as quickly as possible."

"We can't, Remarin," Mara protested. "I have a lot of girls here, some of them are barely eighteen summers. They've all seen too much as it is. I can't risk bringing down the wrath of the Guard on my head. Not again."

"Again?" Remarin asked.

"Fuckers killed Cestine," Larelle growled. "She wouldn't open her legs for a guard who wanted her and didn't want to pay, so they flogged Mara, took three of the youngest girls and sold them to slavers, and put Cestine up on a pike at the gate. This time they nailed a crosspiece to the pike so they could tie her feet to it. They wouldn't even let her slide down the pike to die."

"I can't put my girls through that again," Mara said. "I won't. Not even for you."

"Okay," Kit said with a nod. "But can you at least get us to someone who can help? There must be someone working against my uncle, some kind of opposition."

"There is," Mara said, reluctance etched in every dimple on her round face. "But you won't like it, Remarin."

"Why's that? Did I sleep with his wife before I left town?"

"No," Mara said, her face solemn. "You slept with her, and got her brother killed."

"What are you talking about? Remarin asked. "I don't know anyone with a brother, except for…no. That's impossible."

"It's not just possible, it's the truth. The guard took Gaither for fencing stolen goods, and Inelle moved underground. Literally. She's led the Guild of Thieves and the Guild of Shadows for the past four years. If there is anyone in Veosia with as much reason to want to see your uncle twist at the end of a rope as you, Majesty, it's her."

"Fuck," Remarin said.

No fucking kidding, Trand agreed.

"Well," Remarin said. "I suppose there's nothing else for it. Set up a meeting, Mara. It's time to go see the Queen of Knives."

CHAPTER 31

Even in the pitch dark of the sewers, Remarin knew the way from Mara's basement escape hatch to the Thieves' Guild Hall without a misstep. Eight years was not near enough to dull his memory of the route to the place he once considered home.

Penny for them, Trand "said."

She hates me.

But she loves me, so she sees some point in keeping you alive.

She did when she needed me, but it may well be that with her improved state among the underworld of Veosia, that she no longer feels that way.

She won't kill you out of hand, Remarin. That's not how Inelle operates. She may kill you, but she'll make you suffer almost unimaginable pain first.

I have a very vivid imagination.

This is not a situation where that is a benefit.

Two torches blazed in the otherwise lightless sewer, blinding the trio the instant they turned a corner.

There are two men coming, Trand broadcast to both of them. *Keep Taryn from murdering them, please. That would not get your meeting off to a good start.*

"Let them disarm you, Taryn," Kit whispered. "They aren't going to harm us."

"Not you two, at least," a gruff voice sounded from Remarin's dazzled vision. Then a fist slammed into his gut, and another against the side of his head.

"Fuck, Klaus!" Remarin yelped. "That fucking hurt!"

"It was supposed to, you asshole. You left town owing me five rulls," the gruff voice replied. A hand grasped the collar of Remarin's jacket and hauled him to his feet. Thick hands expertly patted him down, removing his rapier and four throwing knives, but leaving Trand perched on his hip. "You can keep the jeweled knife. Inelle's orders. But I'll be taking this," the man said as thick sausage fingers relieved Remarin of his purse.

"Come on, Klaus! There's fifteen rulls in there!"

"Consider it interest, asshole. Next time, settle your debts before leaving town. The rest of them clean?" he asked. Remarin's vision began to clear, and he looked up into the face of Klaus Cooper, a stout bruiser often tasked with guarding things and people the Thieves' Guild didn't want going off on their own. Remarin was less surprised that the thug had been assigned to welcome him home than he was that Klaus was still alive at all.

"Didn't you have a bounty on your head big enough to buy an entire caravan? How are you still drawing breath?"

"Bounty got cashed in. Klaus Cooper is dead, his head delivered to the palace three years ago. Right about the time a useless cousin of mine with a predilection for little boys came to Veosia to visit."

"And that cousin's name was?" Remarin asked.

"I don't remember. I called him Baby-Fucker. But he looked enough like me to settle the warrant, especially since the Captain of the Guard was only a week into his promotion. Now we going to stand in piss all day, or you coming in to your meeting?"

"I'm honestly not sure which is preferable," Remarin said.

Piss, Trand said.

"Piss, for a certainty," Kit agreed.

"Yeah," Klaus said with a nod. "If you'd seen the look Inelle had on her face when she found out you were coming to visit, you'd definitely prefer standing in piss."

"Thanks, Klaus," Remarin said, his voice as dry as he wished his boots were. He glanced at Taryn and Kit, now weaponless and blinking the last of the dazzle from their eyes. "How did you keep the light from turning around the corner? I would have expected torches like that to be visible for half a mile down here."

"Magic," the big man said, scratching his chin through thick reddish whiskers. "Inelle hired a witch soon as she took over, cast masking spells down here so the light only goes where we want it to go. Lets us see people first and disarm them while they're still dazzle-blind."

"Not a bad trick," Kit said. "What if they object to being disarmed?"

"Then we disarm them," Klaus said, his voice flat. Kit stared at him for a moment, then the corner of his mouth turned up, and his pun became apparent. She feigned shock, having known all along exactly what he meant, and the big man bellowed laughter as her eyes went wide.

What was that about? Remarin asked Trand.

She wants him to think her näive and innocent, matching her looks. Classic ruse, making yourself look innocent so people underestimate you. You should try it some time.

I do that all the time. I let people think I'm an idiot, then when I kill them they're completely surprised. And dead.

That only counts as a ruse if you aren't an idiot. In your case, it's just honest advertising.

Shut up, butter knife.

Their escorts led them through the door, which opened to a complicated sequence of knocks from Klaus. He chuckled at Remarin's look of surprise. "What do I care if you hear the passcode, Remarin? In ten minutes you'll either be welcomed back into the fold with open arms, or you'll be dead. Either way, doesn't matter if you know the code."

Remarin didn't answer the big man, because he was right. The next few minutes would decide much more than just the success or failure of Kit's planned coup. It would decide if they ever walked out of this particular section of sewers.

Klaus led them into a small room, where he and his cohorts handed off their weapons to a skinny woman with a hatchet-shaped face and a scar running along the left side of her jaw. Her mouth opened slightly when she got a good look at Kit, and Remarin winced inwardly.

Looks like we haven't done such a good job disguising our Kitten after all, he thought to Trand.

I suppose a haircut and bad dye job isn't enough to fool anyone these days. But we should have known that after Mara twigged to the deception right away.

Mara's insanely perceptive. That's how she always gets rid of the troublesome girls before they get out of hand. I didn't expect it out of a door guard at the Guild Hall. Klaus doesn't seem to have noticed it, at any rate.

Klaus would be lucky to notice she was a woman if she had her hand down his pants, he's that oblivious.

Remarin turned his full attention back to the Hall as the skinny woman led them through a wooden door. Klaus and his bruisers stayed behind, so Remarin decided this woman was to be their escort. "Hi there," he said in as friendly a voice as he could manage. "Are you new to the Guild?"

"I've been a Shadow for twenty years, Remarin. I knew you when you first fled to Veosia as an idiot child and cleaned up many of your messes for Mistress Disonia before you left."

An assassin, then. That explained the tight-fitting black silk clothing, good for slipping into places without leaving so much as a thread behind. Remarin let his eyes wander along the woman's shape, looking for bulges of weapons. Sure enough, now that he was looking, the bracelet around her left wrist was studded with tiny darts, impossible to recognize unless you knew what you were looking for. That meant there was probably a blowgun strapped to an arm or thigh, folded over but able to snap to full length and fire a poisoned missile in seconds. The telltale bump of daggers protruded from the top of each boot, and the cord around her right wrist ended in two "decorative" orbs, perfect for pulling a garrote taut around a throat.

"Did you find them all?" the assassin asked.

"Almost certainly not," Taryn said from behind him. "He doesn't even know to look in the sole of your boot for a razor, or for the smoke capsules hidden in your hair."

"Don't give away all our secrets, sister," the hatchet-faced woman said with a narrow smile.

"I didn't," Taryn replied, making it clear that there was more she saw that she didn't mention.

Remarin felt like the mouse trapped between two very hungry cats, and he didn't enjoy the sensation. He cleared his throat, drawing the assassin's attention from Taryn and back to him. "Then it seems you have me at a disadvantage, my lady. Might I inquire as to your name?"

"You might. I wouldn't answer, though. So don't bother." She led them through the crowded storerooms in the rear of the Thieves' Hall, filled with racks of clothing and costumes for various cons and capers. Remarin recognized several uniforms he had worn, or ones just like them, in various escapades over the years. Past the racks of costumes were the training dummies, some for fencing, some targets for knife throwing, and the pair of pickpocket dummies laden with bells and tiny traps to snare unaware fingers if their target "caught" a thief being less than nimble.

As they continued along their circuitous path through the Guild Hall, Remarin began to suspect something was unusual about their route. "Do you need me to lead us to the Master's office? Because you've brought us through the dining hall twice now and out different doors, and unless you've rebuilt the Hall in the past half-dozen years, the stairs to the Master's office are in the opposite corner of the building."

The assassin spun, a dagger appearing in her hand and flashing toward Remarin's throat. "You'll follow me, or I'll gut you where you stand. You are no longer a member here, and you shall—"

"No." Kit's clear voice cut the woman off mid-sentence. "I am not a member here, and never have been, but you clearly know who I am, and likely know why I am here. I will not be led around like a puppy on a leash, paraded through the same room time and again like a confused buffoon for the rest of these men and women to laugh at. Now sheath that blade and take us to your Guildmistress immediately."

The woman stepped back from Remarin and turned her grim gaze on Kit. "Or what, little princess? What will you do to me if I don't? And more to the point, what will you do to them?" She gestured behind her, where a dozen thieves, ruffians, bruisers, and murderers stood glaring at them.

"I'll carve open your belly and strangle you to death with your own intestines. Then I don't suppose it will matter to you very much what I do with the rest of them, will it?" Kit stood resolute, her blue eyes flashing. She may have been standing in a thieves' lair surrounded by hundreds of criminals, but she showed no more fear than if she were at a petting zoo.

"Well said, young lady," came a voice from the clump of thieves. The crowd parted, and a stern-faced woman of some middle years stepped through. She wore pants, with a wide sash around the middle and a saber tucked into it. Her silver hair was tied back in a ponytail, and her blouse billowed over her pants as if it carried its own wind with it.

Trand, when did your sister become a pirate? Remarin asked.

I have no bleeding idea. For once, the blade carrying the soul of his best friend and former partner seemed as dumbstruck as Remarin.

"Good to see you again, Inelle. I wish it were under different circumstances," Remarin said.

"I don't know, Remarin. I sort of like these circumstances. After all, I decide if you live or die, and I've always rather wanted to make that decision."

"No, Inelle, you've wanted to kill me. There's a difference."

"Not really, but let's not quibble. Your Majesty Princess Kitarina, welcome to the Den, home of the greatest thieves, cutthroats, pickpockets, assassins, second-story men, robbers, bruisers, card cheats, and scoundrels in Veosia. What can we do for you today?" Inelle took off the huge plumed hat she wore and bowed deeply, crossing one polished boot in front of the other.

"You know why we're here, Mistress Inelle," Kit replied. "I want to kill my uncle and take back my throne, and you want to help me."

CHAPTER 32

"Pardon the theatrics," Inelle said fifteen minutes later when they were settled in her chambers. "There were a lot of rumors going around about Remarin's return and what it was going to mean to me and my reign. I needed to get that sorted before we moved on to the important things."

"What kind of rumors?" Remarin asked.

"Whether or not you had come back to be the King of Knives, of course." Inelle pulled the saber from her sash and hung it on a hook on the wall. She unwound the sash and hung it on a separate hook below the sword.

"Why the hell would I want to do that?" Remarin asked.

Inelle turned to look at Remarin, her round face betraying her surprise. "Why? Hell, Remarin, why wouldn't you? Everyone knows it's better to be atop the heap than at the bottom, where all the shit rolls!"

Remarin rose from his chair and walked over to a small bar set along the wall. He poured himself a brandy, swishing it around in his glass as he thought about how best to proceed.

Inelle, a dangerously perceptive woman even before she took over as Mistress of the Thieves' Guild, watched him in silence, her arms folded across her chest. "What are you not telling me, Remarin?"

"I might not have been completely honest with you and Gaither about who I am."

"You're a modestly handsome thief with shite impulse control and far too much faith in his ability to talk himself out of trouble. You're a horrible influence on young people, a world-class philanderer with a string of broken hearts trailing you across three continents, and despite being one of the single most mendacious human beings I have ever had the extreme displeasure to encounter, you do have a small, nay, minuscule shred of loyalty in your soul. Just the barest hint of goodness, not enough to count for anything among the gods, but just enough to seduce a lovely and dim-witted young princess into thinking she can redeem you. Did I miss anything?"

Remarin, struck to silence by the expansiveness of Inelle's degradation of his character, barely managed to say, "You left out irresistible."

"And you're too skinny, with a flat ass," Inelle replied.

This was the last straw for Kit and Taryn. Trying desperately to remain stone-faced, they made the mistake of looking at one another when Inelle said "flat ass," and their resolve broke. Taryn let out a bellowing horse-laugh while Kit slid from her chair to the floor, clutching her stomach in a paroxysm of giggles, crescendoing to peals of laughter that descended to hiccups in seconds.

Remarin just stood by the bar, his brandy forgotten, staring as the three women laughed this discomfiture. After almost a full minute of belly laughs from the women, he cleared his throat. "Are you quite finished?"

"Not even close, but I can take a break." Inelle extended a hand to Kit, helping her off the floor and pounding her on the back to help her hiccups. Then she walked over and sat behind her desk, a massive thing of dark wood that Remarin remembered from Gaither's jewelry shop. It had always looked out of place there, just a simple hunk of wood, massive and plain, sitting in the middle of an ornate shop. Inelle followed his gaze, then nodded.

"This is the only thing that remains from our shop. The crown," she spat on the floor, "took everything else. Didn't even take things, just declared the entire building 'confiscated' and threw me out in the street. That cockweasel Trudeau from Hightown moved right in and installed his inbred moron of a nephew in my shop. I stood there on the street, staring in the window, until finally a pair of Trudeau's men dragged out a trunk with my clothes and this desk. Lucky for me, Klaus was nearby. He gave me a place to sleep while I charted a new course for myself."

"How did you end up here, running the Guild?" Taryn asked.

"That's a long story, love. Longer than we have time for, and I'm not sure how I feel about telling it to strangers, besides." Inelle turned her attention back to Remarin. "But now, Remarin, my old friend, you said you might have—gasp—lied to me and Gaither about something?"

"Well, I did give you my real name, that much at least is true. But I'm not a thief. Well, I am a thief, but not out of necessity."

Kit interrupted. "What His Grace is trying to tell you is that he is actually Remarin of Torin, a Duke by birthright, albeit renounced, and that he never needed to steal to survive, and he never wanted to lead a Guild of Thieves because he never wanted to lead anything more strenuous than the pursuit of a tavern girl's virtue."

Remarin's face reddened, and he looked at his boots. "While I expect I would have phrased it differently, she got all the high points."

Inelle leaned back in her chair with a smile, folding her arms under her generous bosom. "Well, well, well, that does alter the situation somewhat, doesn't it? Not only do I have the supposedly deceased Princess Kitarina, but I also have a ducal prince in my Hall. That changes the ransom available significantly…"

Her next words were cut off by the *thunk* of a dagger burying itself into the wooden back of her seat, quivering an inch from the side of her neck. "Choose your next words carefully, Guildmistress, or they shall be your last." Taryn held a second knife poised to throw in her right hand, and two more in her left.

Inelle's voice never rose, nor did her glance even flicker to the blade protruding by her face. "You'll be dead ten seconds after I shout."

"You won't live long enough to shout. I'll pierce your throat before you can draw breath."

The moment stretched into eternity, then Inelle reached up beside her neck, pulled the blade free, and pitched it underhand to the assassin. "Relax, child. If I wanted to turn Remarin over to the guards, I would have done it years ago. He, and your lady, are safe with me. But I feel somewhat less so with you. It seems I need to re-evaluate my security personnel, and perhaps teach them how to disarm my guests."

Taryn caught the knife in her left hand without dropping the other two. She only relaxed her throwing arm when Remarin gave her a tiny nod. "If I am unable to sneak a few small knives into a meeting, I am unworthy to call myself a Sister."

Inelle's eyebrows rose. "A Shadowed Sister? Remarin, you have stepped up in the world quite a bit. I mean, traveling with the Heir of Veosia is one thing, but the Sisters are legendary."

Remarin allowed a split second of confusion to wash over his face, but quickly got his features under control and nodded. "Taryn is quite good at what she does."

"If ever there was an understatement, that was it," Inelle said. "But no matter. So you're a prince."

"Renounced."

"So you're a renounced prince. That's about as useful as tits on a rooster. Why does that matter to us here?"

"I believe that Alexander was behind the murder of my father, my brother, and the attempted murder of my nephew. I think he is trying to take over the Gates to control sea trade."

"I hate to seem thick, Remarin, but who gives a shit? What does that have to do with this, here?" She waved her arms around to indicate all of Veosia.

"Very little, except that I have two thousand of my nephew's Mountain Men and thirty of his fastest ships descending on this city at my command. We aren't here just to attack Alexander and drown in our own blood, Inelle. We're here to depose the son of a bitch."

"And then kill him," Kit added. "Very publicly, and very painfully. I'm thinking something with tar and feathers."

"Are we back on that?" Taryn asked. "I thought you decided against the messy stuff."

"I go back and forth. But I have a strong desire to see my cowardly uncle covered in chicken feathers," the princess said.

Inelle let out a small chuckle at the pair. "Well, Princess, do you have any plans on exactly *how* to get your uncle covered in chicken feathers?"

"I don't suppose he's a client, is he?"

"No, love. That self-righteous bastard doesn't come down here where the real working folk live."

"That would have been too easy, I suppose," Remarin said. "I guess we're just going to have to do it the way we planned."

"Which is?" Inelle asked.

"If we tell you, you're a conspirator. That's death if they catch us," Kit said.

"Love, I committed three capital offenses just by not calling the Guard the second I saw you. Not to mention actually speaking with you. I'm hip-deep in this mess, child, as is every rogue and cutthroat out there. Remarin has a price on his head and a death sentence for anyone that aids him, too. No, Majesty, we're with you, until the last bell tolls."

Kit nodded. "That's what we hoped, but had to be sure. We have men coming, but they're three weeks out, and not enough to take the Keep by main force. They can put down a small uprising of loyalists and keep peace in the city while we transition, but they aren't numerous enough to overthrow a castle."

"Still not hearing a plan," Inelle said.

"We infiltrate the Keep through the servants," Remarin said. "The Keep uses a lot of scullions, stablemen, and the like. We can use your thieves and assassins to replace the normal men and women as they go to work. That gets our people in while getting as many innocents out of harm's way as possible."

"Perhaps we can infiltrate some of the Guard as well," Inelle said.

"How do you plan to do that?" Kit asked. "The Guard are a stiff-necked lot, and I doubt many of them come in here on any given night."

"They don't," Inelle agreed, "but I have a way to get men into the Keep in Guard uniforms."

"Undetected? I doubt that," the princess scoffed.

"Trust me," Inelle said. "You dear," she motioned to Taryn, "open that door and tell the guards I need to speak to the Master of Arms."

Taryn did as the woman asked, then returned to stand by Kit's side. Remarin opened his mouth to speak but fell silent at the Guild-mistress's upraised hand. A moment or two later, a steady knock came at the door.

"Come," Inelle called.

The door opened, and a stocky man in a chain shirt came in. His bald head was bare, and his round face had the flush and reddened nose of a man who liked his ale, but his bearing was stiffly military, and his slate-gray eyes were sharp. He wore a long handlebar mustache, and he snapped his heels together as he saluted the Queen of Knives. "You called, ma'am?"

At his voice, Kit's eyes widened, and she turned to look at the man. "Uncle Drew?"

The old soldier spun on his heel and looked at the woman standing to his left. "Kitarina? My Kitten, is that you?" A huge smile split his face, and he rushed forward, knocking Taryn aside. He picked Kit up in a fierce hug and spun her around. "I thought that bastard uncle of yours killed you! I thought you were lost to me like my…like your father." He broke apart from the young princess, took a step back, and knelt at Kit's feet.

He drew the sword from his belt and held it out in his hands. "Your Majesty, Queen Kitarina Rutvor, I pledge you my sword, my life, and my honor. I will defend you with my life and pledge myself to your service. I am yours to command."

Kit straightened, and her expression grew solemn. She took the sword from the kneeling man and tapped it to each shoulder. Then she put it back across his hands and said, "From here and forever forward, you are Sir Andrew Rutvor, my man, and my blood. You are as deserving of our family name as any to ever bear it, and no man shall take it from you."

Sir Andrew looked up at Kit, and tears ran freely down his cheeks. "I'm sorry, Your Majesty. I couldn't save him. I tried, but…"

Kit knelt before the man and pressed her forehead to his. "Had you died with him, our land would truly be destroyed. For it is by your arm that we shall overthrow this vile usurper and reclaim my throne. My father is gone, but I yet live. And as long as there is breath in my body, I swear that I will not rest until Alexander Rutvor decorates the front walls of my castle with a pike up his treacherous ass!"

Remarin looked over at Inelle, who beamed at the reunion, her own eyes damp. "Yeah," the thief remarked. "I think having the old king's Master of Arms in our pocket makes it a little easier to get inside."

CHAPTER 33

Three days later, Remarin meandered through the Bravis Marketplace, known far and wide as a place where anything was for sale, as long as you possessed the coin and the looseness of morals to acquire it. Remarin found that nothing had changed in his near decade-long absence. There were still shops and stalls filled to bursting with fruits, meats, spices, and fabrics alongside other merchants boasting an unparalleled variety of weapons, ammunition, armors of the mundane and purportedly enchanted varieties, not to mention potions and poisons for any ulterior motive.

Remarin slipped through the throngs of people picking through cheap trinkets and haggling over the price of a pound of beets, wondering not for the first time why anyone cared enough about beets to argue the price of them. For himself, he always considered beets more of a thing that appeared on a plate to be slipped under the table to the dog, rather than something consciously purchased and prepared.

The slender thief passed a row of silk merchants, trailing his fingers along the bolts of brightly colored fabric before moving on. He stopped for several moments and rifled through a jeweler's display, picking up and casually discarding random rings and earrings for several moments before finally passing the man two rulls for a necklace with a cat's head studded with emeralds in the eye sockets and moving on.

That thing is hideous, Trand said in his mind.

I know, but that wasn't the point.

If you wanted a better look at the man following you, why not simply ask me about him? I've been watching him for the past three blocks.

Remarin let the slightest smile flit across his lips. *That's pretty good, for cutlery, but he's been following me for ten blocks now, and is on his third disguise. I'm not surprised you missed him, though. Lacking eyes and all.*

Trand let the jibe go, seemingly embarrassed by the oversight. Remarin knew full well that his friend took great pride in his skill at observation, even if he was a disembodied spy tied to the magical blade.

Sorry, Trand said a moment later. *I don't know how I missed him.*

You missed him because he's good. Very good. And no one in their right mind would have followed us through all of Lowtown just to get to the Market. He's obviously known here, and just as obviously not someone to play with. I think it's time to go to ground.

I think that choice may have been made for you already. Guards up ahead.

Remarin glanced to the end of the row of stalls he was perusing, and sure enough, there was a pair of guards doing a terrible impression of lounging around. Peering behind him, Remarin saw a similarly "casual" pair of guards leaning against posts at the opposite end of the long tent covering that section of the Market.

Shit. I'm going to need an exit.

I don't know any of these buildings. They are all different businesses from when I had legs.

I think they're all different businesses from when we left, unless...yes!

What?

I know the owner of that spice shop.

Does he hate you?

Not every single merchant I've done business with hates me.

Name one that doesn't.

Gaither didn't hate me.

Dead.

Mara doesn't hate me.

You slept with her. And her sister. Both her sisters. Mara definitely hates you.

She does not! Besides, I slept with her the most.

The amazing thing is that you actually think that helps. Do I need to get Kit?

No! If they've recognized me, then they probably suspect Kit is with me. She needs to stay out of sight at all costs. I have a plan.

Those are the four most frightening words in my life.

Remarin ignored his friend and stepped into a short alley between two merchants. He beckoned a small boy over to him. "Come here, child."

The boy looked up at him, his face locked into a distrustful sneer. "I ain't into men, asshole. So be on your way, or I'll cut your giblets off."

Remarin shook his head and held up a golden rull at the boy. "I don't want your body, boy. I just need your feet. Can you run?"

"Like a gazelle, they tell me."

"Do you know what a gazelle is?"

"No idea. Guess it's something like a rat, but faster. Don't care. What you want me to steal?"

Remarin grinned. "That's more like it. All I want you to steal is attention. I need a distraction."

"Gimme that rull, and I'll give you more distraction than you ever seen."

"There are four guardsmen. I need you to distract the pair at the south end of this row. I don't care how you do it, just count to twenty and make a lot of noise between me and them."

The boy looked hesitant. "What's wrong?" Remarin asked.

"Can't count that high. I get lost after a dozen."

"Count to ten twice. Then take that rull to the Devil's Doorbell and tell the cook Remarin sent you to be her new scullery boy. She'll take the money for your first month's room and board, and pay it back to you with another besides."

"I ain't no whore!"

"That's why I'm sending you there to wash dishes. Mara will see you have a roof and food. She'll work you, but you'll be safe. Or you can take that rull and try to hold onto it with the bigger kids all trying to take it from you, and you'll get nothing but maybe a heel of moldy bread and a busted lip for your trouble."

The child thought for a moment, then his streetwise suspicion bubbled to the surface again. "Why you doing this?"

"You look like my nephew. Only dirtier. Now go distract some guards. I have a getaway to pull off."

The boy grinned and darted back into the main thoroughfare of the market, slipping between men and women like water. Remarin stepped out into the main thoroughfare, sidling up beside the man who had been following him. His pursuer was nondescript in almost every way, from his brown pants, dingy white shirt, and gray cloak to his perfectly forgettable face. Everything about him screamed "don't notice me," so, of course, Remarin noticed everything about him, particularly the muck on his boots.

"Does Inelle know you're freelancing?" Remarin whispered as he brushed shoulders with the man.

The assassin's eyes were hard, and a sneer pulled across his face as he turned to Remarin. "She has no idea, and you won't be the one to tell her. You're already dead; you just don't know it yet."

Remarin smiled at the man, a cold, thin smile that had frozen much larger men in their tracks. "I might be dead soon, but you're going to help me live just a little longer." He shoved the gray-cloaked man in the chest, shouting as he did. "Get your hands off me!" Remarin made a big show of patting his pockets, then pointed at the man, shouting, "Thief! Guards, help! This man has picked my pocket! Guards! Arrest this man!"

The assassin snarled a curse and turned to flee, only to find the burly man who owned the stall glaring at him with a scimitar in hand. The proprietor was huge, towering a full head taller than the assassin, with his gleaming brown pate shaved clean. Dozens of gold and silver rings pierced his earlobes, eyebrows, and nose, and his face was covered in the tattoos favored by the pirates from the Summer Seas.

Remarin heard a crash from the southern end of the market, and when he turned to look, he saw the entire contents of a silversmith's stall toppling into the aisle, clattering to the ground around the feet of guard and shopper alike. *Good distraction, kid,* Remarin thought as he slipped through the stunned crowd and worked his way north.

The crowd thinned out several yards ahead of the guards, so Remarin made the snap decision to choose brazenness over subtlety. He walked up to one of the guards and crooked a finger at the man. The guard bent over, and Remarin whispered a string of nonsense syllables in his ear.

The man stood up, a puzzled look on his face. "What did you say?"

"I said that no matter what that fellow says," Remarin pointed to the other guard, "your mother isn't really the worst lay in Bravis. I just left her, and she was perfectly serviceable."

"He said what?" The man's face reddened, then he turned back to Remarin. "Wait, what?" Remarin caught him on the point of the jaw with a sharp blow from Trand's pommel, and the guard's legs turned to water. Remarin spun, and using the larger man's momentum to aid him, tossed the guard into his partner. They both went down in a clatter of armor and spears, and Remarin vaulted over their tangled bodies and sprinted toward daylight.

The chase was on, and Remarin felt the old familiar adrenaline rising. A fierce grin stretched across his face, almost without him noticing. He dodged and wove between shoppers and vendors, striving to increase his lead on the guards, who had disentangled themselves from each other and were now charging through the market, simply bowling over anyone unfortunate enough to stand in their way, or be too slow in moving.

"Help! They're murderers!" Remarin shouted, grabbing the corner of a fruit vendor's table as he passed. He used the table's weight to help him take a right turn at full speed, then paused to flip the load of oranges and melons out into the walkway, further impeding the pursuit.

Remarin bolted for the exit into the main streets of Bravis, but the covered market had guardsmen posted at every entrance. He leapt over a woman pushing a child in a pram, tumbling forward between a pair of guards who immediately set off after him. The larger men carried not just more weight, but were dressed in full armor, so Remarin easily outdistanced them. He hazarded a glance backward, and no guards were visible.

But the assassin he left to sort things out with the tattooed vendor was hot on his heels. Remarin swore under his breath, then released the clasp on his cloak. The brown fabric billowed out behind him, hiding him from view for just a second, but it was enough to let Remarin leap from the ground to an awning over a nearby tavern. The nimble thief sprang from the awning to a second-floor balcony, then across the street to a clothesline. He swung on the clothesline twice to increase his momentum, then let go at the apex of his swing, flipping once in midair before slamming into the railing of a third-floor balcony next door.

That looked like it hurt, Trand said.

That's because it hurt like hell. Now go warn Kit. I'll lead them away from Inelle's place, but I think the Queen of Knives needs to know that she has a traitor in her midst. Remarin clambered over the rails and ran along the narrow balcony. At the end, he sprang up onto the railing, then leapt for the eaves of the next building.

Are you certain there's a traitor?

Is this really the time? But yes, I recognized the assassin. He was in the Guild Hall. I don't know how much he was paid, but he sold me out, and probably Kit as well. Now go, before the Guard catch me. I can hear their stupid mailed feet clattering down the alleys! Remarin felt the slight shift in weight on his side as Trand winked out of existence, presumably to reappear wherever Kit was. The enchanted blade's ability to return to whoever it considered its wielder was very useful, particularly since it thought of both Remarin and Kit as its wielders.

Remarin pulled himself up onto the roof, shooting a glance back over his shoulder at the guardsmen rushing through the streets, their heads turning this way and that looking for him. "Nobody ever looks up," the thief muttered to himself as he turned to walk across the rooftops to a nearby bolthole. Now if only his secret hidey-holes were still there after all these years.

A soft hiss was his only warning, and Remarin threw himself flat to the roof as something tiny whizzed overhead, passing through the spot where his neck had been seconds before. Remarin rolled over and saw the assassin standing on the north edge of the roof, a blowgun in his hand.

"Shit," he muttered, then sprang to his feet and sprinted southward as the man in the gray cloak tossed the blowgun aside and sprinted toward him.

CHAPTER 34

Remarin dashed across the rooftops of Bravis, his mind flashing back to the night eight years ago when he met Kit and his life changed forever. For the better, even taking into account the upheaval in his living situation, dealing with Taryn, and the constant threat of people trying to murder him. Thinking of just that, he made a quick turn to his right and ran down one side of the roof he was on, veering off the ridge beam onto the treacherous sloped slate surface. The boots he wore came from Inelle's stash, though, and the supple leather bottoms were perfectly suited to grip the tiles.

He tensed his legs and sprang forward just before he reached the gutter, vaulting over the narrow street below and slamming into the next roof. His foot crunched through the tar paper and wood roof, and he mumbled an unheard apology to the people living in the upper floors who would have a new leak come the next rainstorm. He scrambled to the pinnacle of this new roof and turned left to sprint along the ridge.

Remarin kept his head low, striving to present as difficult a target for his pursuer as possible. Without the blowgun, the assassin would have to stop, draw a knife, and fling it at a moving target, all while balanced on a narrow ridge beam. It wouldn't be easy, but Remarin felt no need to aid his would-be killer by running upright. As if called by his thoughts, a dagger whizzed by his left leg and buried itself in the roof. *Another leak*, he thought without breaking stride.

The roofs here were mostly tar paper and cheap wood, so even the slight thief had to take care where he placed his feet, for one misstep would send him crashing into an unsuspecting living room. Remarin cautioned a glance around and confirmed that he'd moved out of the depths of Lowtown and into the Merchant's District. A good mile from the main Market, this was where the shopkeepers lived, where the men and women who hawked their wares in stalls all day returned at night to feed and clothe the dozen starving children that everyone with a piece of fruit or hunk of overpriced jewelry to sell always seemed to have waiting for them at home. *It's funny*, Remarin thought as he jumped a narrow alley, *none of these homes look big enough to house all those starving children.*

Up ahead, a gap far wider than he could leap loomed directly in Remarin's path. He turned from side to side, but the house he ran across was the point of a promontory, jutting out into a split when one street became two, leaving him running into the juncture of a "Y" with nowhere to go but down.

"Well, shit," he muttered, coming to the edge of the roof and looking over. A good twenty-five-foot drop to the cobblestones, there was nothing below to break his fall. Remarin turned to look at his pursuer for the first time in several minutes and saw a smile creeping across the killer's face, some forty feet back across the roof. The nondescript man had the tip of a throwing dagger clutched between the thumb and forefinger of his right hand, and another three blades in his left in case he missed.

"I don't suppose we could discuss this, could we?" Remarin asked with a chuckle. He held both hands up even with his head, palms out to show the man he was unarmed. With Trand teleported directly to Kit, and his rapier safely back at Inelle's, there were no visible threats.

"I don't think so," the man said, the sibilance of his words making Remarin cringe.

Of course, he wouldn't just be a hired thug, he'd be a hired thug that worshipped Ketsin, goddess of snakes. Remarin's only hope would be if he knew nothing of—

"You are the defiler of our temple in Gorix, and the Dark Lady would withhold her blessings from me if I allowed you to escape justice again."

"Well, to be fair, blessings of anyone who answers to the Dark Lady aren't necessarily something you want, now are they?"

"You dare defile the lady's name with your tongue, blasphemer?" The assassin's eyes widened, and a flush crept up his neck.

"I've defiled a lot of things, with my tongue and with other parts, but I didn't say anything about Ketsin being a snake-humping whore, so I don't know how you think I defiled...Oops, I guess I did now, didn't I?" As the killer drew his arm back to throw his blade, Remarin snapped both hands straight down by his sides. The action of his wrists triggered the holsters on his forearms, and a pair of slim throwing knives dropped into Remarin's palms. He flung the blades underhand at the assassin as he dove to the left. One blade went wide, but the other buried itself in the killer's thigh. Remarin crashed into the roof and tumbled down, turning his fall into a roll that took him to the edge where he caught himself on the gutter by the fingertips.

Remarin listened to the footsteps creeping across the roof to the edge, clinging to the gutter by inches. As he heard the assassin stop less than a foot from where he dangled, Remarin heaved himself up into the air, snatched a knife from a sheath at the small of his back, and jammed it through the booted foot in front of him, pinning the assassin's foot to the roof.

The gray-cloaked murderer let out a shriek of pain, and the throwing knives fell from his fingertips to clatter on the cobblestones below. Remarin gripped his dagger with both hands, using the blade and the assassin's weight to anchor him to the rooftop. The assassin screamed and cursed in his ear as Remarin crawled up and over the man to the relative safety of the roof.

As he collapsed to the tarpaper surface, Remarin looked back with a fierce grin at the man who tried to kill him. "Sorry about your foot, old chap. But you won't have to feel it for long." Then he pulled another blade from the top of his boot and slit the man's throat. The killer's eyes went wide, and his lips moved as his lifeblood spurted out across the roof, but the dagger's edge left him with no windpipe to speak through.

"What's that?" Remarin said, leaning close to the man. "I'm afraid I can't hear you." He pulled away with a grin, but that vanished from his face as the assassin gripped the front of his shirt, and with the last of his ebbing strength, pitched himself, and Remarin, forward off the roof into the alley below. The last thing Remarin saw was the ground rushing up to him, and a nasty smile across the face of the assassin.

Remarin woke in agony, white-hot lances of pain shooting from his toes all the way to his eyelids, or maybe from his eyelids to his toes. He had no way of knowing where the pain originated—it was all-encompassing. His entire world was pain, and any tiny sliver of his consciousness that wasn't pain was terror.

His eyes sprang open, and light stabbed at his brain. He tried to flinch away from the invading light, to bring his hand over his face, but his hand wouldn't listen to his commands. He opened his mouth to scream, but no sound passed his cracked lips and parched throat. He sucked in air, huge gulps of breath, and blinked away tears that coursed down his cheeks and mixed with snot and blood.

After agonizing seconds that felt like hours of gasping for air and straining to see, Remarin's breath was slammed from him once more, this time by a faceful of brackish water. The foul liquid cascaded over his face and ran into his mouth and nose, sparking another fit of coughing and sneezing and spitting.

"Oh, do shut up," came a voice from behind the light, and a hand reached out with a filthy rag to wipe Remarin's face. The hand holding the rag scrubbed the water and bodily fluids from his eyes and cheeks, and when the hand drew back, Remarin could see.

He immediately wished he was blind once more. The man in front of him was a short man, bald and thin, the type of completely unassuming fellow that was either a simple tallier of sums, or the most dangerous man in any room. It didn't take more than a glance at the blood-spattered leather apron to tell Remarin which category this innocuous-looking fellow fit into.

A quick glance up told Remarin exactly where he was and the level of trouble he was in. He was hanging shirtless, probably naked if he thought about it, in what looked like a dungeon. Unless things had changed dramatically in the time he'd been away, there was only one dungeon in Bravis, so he was undoubtedly in the Keep, or under it. Which made the small man with the round lenses over his eyes the King's Torture Master. None of that, not the man's identity nor his current location, was good for Remarin.

"Now that you're awake, we can get started with our conversation," the torturer spoke, and his voice was a thin, reedy thing that wormed its way into Remarin's head and curled around the center of his fear. This little man was in control of this little piece of the world; that much was evident from his calm tones.

"Happy to chat with you, friend. Just cut me down from here and let's have a civilized talk. I like to talk over a nice ale, or maybe a whiskey. What about you?" Remarin put on as pleasant a face as he could muster, but his breath came in sharp, stabbing gasps, and his shoulders threatened to dislocate at any moment. It felt like there were some broken ribs, probably sustained in his fall from the roof, and he wasn't sure how he'd even survived at all.

"I seem to be out of whiskey, Sir Thief. How do you feel about wine? I have a nice red that I've recently developed a taste for." He held up a thin knife with a wicked hooked tip and ran it down Remarin's chest. A line of fire opened up across the thief's flesh, and he screamed as blood welled up in the valley left by the blade. "No? Not a wine lover? I understand."

The torturer turned and walked over to a small table, where he picked up another blood-spattered rag and wiped down his knife. "I used to be much more concerned about cleaning the blades, wanting to keep the wounds neat and prevent infection, but when I realized that none of the people I cut ever lived long enough to grow ill from any bad humors on my knives, I stopped worrying about it."

"What do you want?" Remarin gasped when he could speak again.

"I don't want anything. His Majesty has already sentenced you to death by impalement in three days' time. Nothing you do or say will change that. There is no information he needs or wants from you, nothing you can tell him to make the pain stop. You are a dead man walking, so to speak. Just a test subject for me to use in studying exactly how much pain a human being can absorb before they lose consciousness, or die. So I might as well enjoy the time I have with you."

The little man turned back to Remarin, and the smile he gave was both genuine and terrifying. "Now, how to feel about tendons? Do you think the tendons in the foot have enough tensile strength to hang from, or will they snap before carrying your full weight?"

CHAPTER 35

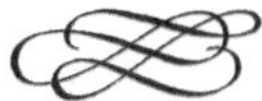

Remarin's eyes fluttered open at the sound of footsteps before him. This was a new one, not the usual torturer. The slight balding man was gone, replaced by a tall woman in a long black dress. Her red hair cascaded over her shoulders in luxurious curls, a stark contrast to the dark dress and her glowing pale skin. She looked achingly familiar, but Remarin's head was fuzzy from pain and hunger.

All sense of time had left him hours or days before. All he knew was hanging from his wrists, his feet barely close enough to the ground to help support his weight, but the slightest shift in his balance, or any of the blows that rained down upon him without notice would push him off-balance and threaten to tear his arms from the sockets. He knew he was bleeding from dozens of cuts and lashes from the whip. He could feel the scabs tear and fresh rivulets of blood run down his flesh with every movement.

When he wasn't being tormented by the bald bastard, all he knew was the stone wall in front of him and the drip of water from somewhere off in the dungeon. No matter how he twisted, he couldn't see anything other than the wall and some piles of straw scattered across the floor to soak up his blood, piss, and vomit. The whole room stank of him, his bodily fluids, his fear-sweat, and the damp, moldy smell of the Keep's dungeon.

"You reek, thief," the woman said, her deep voice cracking like a whip against the silence.

Remarin breathed out something, but no words would form. She gave him a languorous smile, curling across her lips like a venomous serpent, and leaned in to him. "I'm sorry, thief. I couldn't hear you."

Remarin breathed again, but still no sound came from his lips. The woman leaned in closer, almost touching his lips with her ear. Remarin drew in a shuddering breath, and as she inched ever nearer, he stuck out his tongue and licked the side of her face, smearing her with the last of his bloody spittle.

She stepped back and slapped him hard enough to split his parched lips. Remarin's balance wavered, and he slipped off his precarious perch, yanking his shoulders and pulling a gasp from his lips, but through it all, he grinned at the woman. "Was it good for you?" he said, his words slurred from pain and a mouthful of blood.

The woman drew back her hand, then slashed it down across Remarin's chest, her nails leaving four parallel lines of blood across his already battered flesh. The grinning thief just steadied himself once more on his toes and spit a huge gobbet of bloody spittle at her, landing on the side of her face and running down between her breasts, heaving in fury in a way that would attract Remarin's attention, were the setting different.

"You little bastard," she shrieked. "I'll have your balls for that!" She stepped forward, clutching Remarin's testicles in a grip so fierce that he thought she meant to make good on her promise right then.

"Do you think I won't, thief? Do you think you'll be the first bastard I've ever unmanned for insulting me?"

"I think I'll be the prettiest," Remarin said. He grinned at her again and puckered his lips. "But as long as you're holding them, how about a kiss?"

Her nostrils flared, and she squeezed his testicles so hard that Remarin faded into blessed unconsciousness.

W hen he woke, Remarin no longer swung from the ceiling, and his wrists weren't bound above his head any longer. He was far from free, as he now stood strapped to a table standing on its end, with his hands bound behind his back. But it was a marked improvement to his previous condition, as both feet were firmly on the ground.

His eyes fluttered open, but he feigned sleep to better assess his environment. That didn't last long, as a splash of freezing water cascaded over his face.

"Wakey wakey, thief." He recognized the woman's voice and wasn't sure if he preferred her to the bald man. But at least he wasn't hanging any longer, so that was something.

He opened his eyes. She stood before him, that same viper smile across her lips, but the bloody spit wiped clean from her neck and chest. She was dressed in the same black gown, but this time she held a cat-o'-nine-tails in her right hand. She gently slapped the short whip into her left palm, making a light *thwipp* sound as it caressed her skin. Remarin had no doubt that she planned to strike him much more firmly.

"I see you noticed my little friend." She waggled the whip at him. "If you behave, I won't have to use it. If you tell me what I want to know, I'll slit your throat and let you die quickly. If you try to keep information from me...well, eventually you'll tell me anyway, and I'll just let you die of infection and rat bites down here in the dungeon with no one but your fellow criminals and traitors to hear you scream."

"What do you want to know?" Remarin rasped.

"Where is the princess?" She stopped her lazy pacing and stood directly in front of him, an imposing woman with broad shoulders and strong jawline, she cut an impressive figure. In other circumstances, Remarin thought, he would definitely try to take her for a tumble.

"Water," he gasped.

"Talk and I'll give you water."

"Can't," he panted, working to exaggerate his actual difficulty.

She looked for a moment like she meant to deny him, then walked around behind him and returned with a dipper full of water.

It was warm, and none too clean, with the metallic taste of the dipper almost hiding the brackish flavor of pond scum, but not quite. It was also the most wonderful drink Remarin could remember, better even than the wines at his father's table in his childhood. He sipped, not wanting to cramp his stomach, but she still pulled the dipper away long before his thirst was fully slaked. She leveled an icicle smile at him and slowly turned the dipper upside down, letting the water pour out over the cobblestones.

"Now, where is Princess Kitarina?"

Kit burst into the room with Trand in her hand, startling the guards nearest the door and bringing Inelle to her feet. "They have him! We have to go rescue him!" She barged straight across the room and leaned over the desk, dagger in hand.

Inelle glared at her, closing a ledger she had been making marks in. "They have who, girl? And who is they? And why are you hearing anything in my Guild Hall before I do?"

"They caught Remarin! An assassin and the Guard chased him through the market and now they've taken him. We have to get him back! If they kill Remarin, our whole plan is lost."

"If Alexander and his people have Remarin, your plan is lost already. But that doesn't answer my other questions. How did you learn this before I did?"

"I...um...I...an informant?" Kit stammered and stumbled and finally shrugged.

"You have a grand total of one ally in this city, girl, and if what you're telling me is true, he's in the castle dungeon right now. So you don't *have* any informants, nor do you have the funds to pay them. You and your pet cutthroat haven't left the Hall all day, and Remarin wasn't supposed to, but I know there's no sense even attempting to cage him. So I am going to ask you one more time, and think before you attempt to lie to me again. Who told you about Remarin's capture?"

I did.

Inelle looked around for the source of the voice, but the only people in the room were herself, Kit, and the two guards. "Who said that?"

It's me, Nelle.

"I know that voice. It can't be…" Her eyes flicked down to the dagger on her desk, then back to the guards. "Leave us. No one comes in. No one. I will pluck out the eyes of anyone who disturbs us."

The guards nodded and left the room, pulling the door closed behind them.

Inelle sat down behind the desk, never taking her eyes from Trand. "Sit, girl."

"We have to—"

"SIT." The steel in Inelle's voice was unmistakable. Kit sat. The ruddy-faced Queen of Knives leaned forward, her gaze locked on Trand's pommel stone.

"Is that really you, T?"

It is, Nelle. It's really me in here.

"Prove it."

You have a scar behind your left knee. We were playing Archers and Invaders when you were ten and I was eight, and an arrow bounced off a stone in the woods and pierced your leg. You took an arrow to the knee, and your days of Archers and Invaders were over.

"You always were a terrible shot."

I've gotten better with time. But I'm a little short on arms these days.

Tears streamed down the Guildmistress's face as she reached for the knife. "May I…hold him?"

Kit's eyes went slightly blank, as if she were focusing on an object far away, and after a brief second, she nodded and passed Trand to Inelle. "He says you're his sister."

"I am. Two years older."

"Is that why you hate Remarin? For getting your brother trapped in a dagger?"

"You've traveled with the man for nearly a decade. Do you really think there is ever only one reason to hate Remarin?" She smiled when she said it, and her eyes grew wistful as she thought back. "It was never his fault that Trand got trapped in this blade. Hells, I never believed it completely until now. No, my relationship with Remarin was much more complicated than that."

Oh bullshit, sister. Your relationship was simple. You fucked him, and he wanted to keep fucking other women. You wanted him to fuck only you, so you decided it was easier to hate him than share him.

Inelle's eyes flashed up to Kit's face, and she knew by the look on the younger woman's face that Trand's words hadn't been for her alone.

"You and Remarin…"

"Were lovers, yes. Not for long, and not exclusively, much to my chagrin, as Trand has so kindly shared with you. But yes, we were lovers. Or at least, I thought we were lovers. He thought we were 'just having fun.' Then we were neither lovers nor having fun, and he went on a botched heist with my brother and had the audacity to come back while spinning some hare-brained story about Trand being trapped inside this magical dagger he stole on account of a dalliance with a sorcerer's wife. I didn't believe any of it, until now…"

It's all true, Nelle. This time it was my lust that got us in trouble, not Remarin's. And now we have to save him.

"Why, T? Why do I have to save him? Why shouldn't I just leave him to rot in the dungeon for breaking my heart?"

Kit opened her mouth to speak, but Trand's mental "voice" cut her off.

Because we can't take the castle without him. Because you aren't the type of Mistress to leave a Guild Member behind. Because without him, that bastard Alexander will hold the throne as long as he likes and will probably hunt this girl down and shove a pike up her ass. Because I'm asking you to. Because you still love him a little. Because he's my best friend.

"Well, shit." Inelle sat back in the chair and stared at the blade, ruby stone flickering in its hilt. "You always were a persuasive bastard, even before you were a magical weapon." She looked up at Kit. "So we're going to break into the castle to save my brother's best friend and my former lover, who you happen to be in love with. Do you have a plan?"

Kit looked for a moment like she might protest, then just said, "We've had good luck with sewers so far."

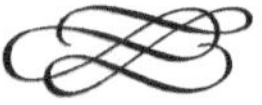

CHAPTER 36

I thought you wanted to be done with sewers, Trand sent into Kit's mind.

That was before your idiot friend got himself caught. She looked at Inelle. "I'm going to need a guide."

"I thought you were born in Bravis, Your Majesty," the Guild-mistress said with a teasing smile.

"Once we're inside the palace, I expect I'll be able to find my way around with no problem, but I never had to break in before. I spent most of my childhood and teen years trying to get out of the castle, not in. Most of the time when I entered the Keep, it was either in a litter or clutched tight to Uncle Drew's pommel as he dragged me back from some adventure or another."

Inelle laughed. "I see how you got along with Remarin so well. Birds of a feather, it seems. I'll send for a guide. I know just the thief." She rose from behind her desk and walked over to the door. She spoke in hushed tones to the guard who stood by the entrance, and he nodded and left the room. Inelle walked over to the bar, poured herself a glass of red wine, and one for Kit. She carried both of them back to her desk and passed the princess her drink.

"I don't think we should be sipping wine while Remarin is being tortured," Kit grumbled.

"Why not, dear? We're not the ones being tortured, and until Terrence gets back with Samir, you can't go anywhere. Might as well have a nice glass of wine while we wait."

Kit's mind whirled as she sipped the wine. How were they going to get Remarin out of the castle? If they could even get in, that is. She had no idea if there was even sewer access to the Keep. She had no idea if he was even still alive. Hell, for all she knew, her uncle was already storming the sewers with a battalion of Guardsmen ready to cut everyone there to ribbons.

Gods, you're a worrywart.

You aren't worried? Kit looked down at the flickering pommel stone. *He knows everything about our plans, our location, how many men we have...*

And I'm sure that's what has your stomach in knots, the tactical implications of Remarin's capture. Calm down, Kitten. He's been in worse scrapes than this before. Our boy will be fine. He always is.

When?

When what?

When has Remarin been in a worse scrape than captured by an evil fratricidal usurper to the throne who has no moral compass to speak of and unlimited resources?

Well, when you put it like that...never.

You are the very soul of reassurance. Kit lifted her head as a heavy knock sounded from the door.

"Come," Inelle commanded. The door opened, and the guard she sent away moments before entered, followed by a boy of perhaps fifteen. He was slight almost to the point of gaunt, with dark brown skin and a floppy mass of black, curly hair atop his head, spilling down into his huge brown eyes. He smiled at Kit, then dropped to a knee before Inelle in a swooping, overdone bow.

"My Lady," he said. "How may your most humble of servants be of use to you this evening? I can but hope that my unworthy talents can in some way serve the greatness that is my queen."

Kit started, openmouthed at the tiny youth and his huge display of obeisance, tinged with a hint of mockery. Inelle covered her own mouth with her hand, ostensibly out of modesty, but Kit could see by the crinkling of her eyes and the slight shake of her shoulders that the Queen of Knives was stifling laughter.

"Get up, Samir. I've already forgiven you for whatever it is you did this time." Inelle's voice held a heavy dose of amusement at the boy's antics.

"I promise, Your Queenly Knifeness, that it was not in any way my fault, and the shopkeeper is barely even mad. I expect he will forget all about the incident within a day or two of his genitals returning to their natural color."

Kit sucked in a deep breath as Inelle let out a long sigh. "Dare I even ask, Samir?" the thieves' Mistress said.

"Merely a misunderstanding between myself and a seller of lacy undergarments. Perhaps the dyes had not quite had an opportunity to set properly before I sold him a selection of the finest lace from Gorix," the young thief said, his face all innocence.

"Probably because you stole the lace from the dye pots directly, instead of stealing them from the saltwater soaking vats, where the dye would have been locked into the fabric," Inelle said, shaking her head.

"Your knowledge of dyes, and no doubt, lace, so far eclipses my own as to make me feel as though we were not even stars in the same firmament, My Lady," the florid little thief said.

"But why would that concern the man who sells the undergar-ments...oh," Kit said, a slight flush touching her cheeks.

"There is no need to blush, Lady," the thief called Samir said. "There is certainly no shame in wanting to look your best inside and out, top and bottom. We may not all be blessed with the abundance of natural beauty that you yourself possess, but we can all wear nice things. Paroot the merchant unfortunately has a tendency to wear his garments before he sells them to the public, and it has been unreason-ably warm this past week."

"And sweat makes unfixed dyes run," Inelle added.

"So the color ran, right onto Paroot?" Kit asked.

"Much to my undying shame," Samir said. "Not only onto Paroot, but also onto…ahem…'little Paroot' as well."

"What color?" Kit asked, her curiosity insatiable.

Samir looked at her, and his mien of obedient subject shattered as the true face of the mischievous thief broke free. "Purple, my lady. A pale lavender, if we're to be exact. But Paroot definitely had a purple tinge to his face as he shouted at me in the market."

Kit looked at Inelle. "This is the thief who's going to help us rescue Remarin?"

Samir's face immediately transformed, going from a whimsical rogue to a dark, scowling young man. "Remarin is in danger? Who is threatening him? I will gut the bastards myself." His hand dropped to the sword on his belt.

"Calm down, Samir," Inelle said, standing. "This is Kit. She is a friend of Remarin's. He was captured by the Guard several hours ago, and he needs our help to rescue him."

Samir laughed. "You have been told wrong, then. Remarin is the greatest thief in all Veosia! He would never allow himself to be captured, and certainly not by any so inept as the Usurper's idiot guardsmen!"

Kit shook her head. "As much as I wish you were right, Samir, Remarin was indeed taken by the Guard this morning. I fear that my —that the usurper Alexander has him and will torture Remarin until he reveals everything he knows about the Thieves' Guild."

"Not to mention what he knows about you. Right, Your Majesty?"

Kit let out an exasperated sigh. "Does every thief in Bravis know who I am?"

Samir shrugged. "Maybe not, but if not, it's only because they are very stupid. There are some stupid thieves in this city, but none of them belong to the Guild. Now, when do we leave to rescue Remarin?"

"Why are you so enthusiastic about this rescue?" Kit asked.

Samir looked away, his eyes darting over to Inelle, who gave him a tiny nod. The boy turned those huge brown eyes back to Kit, who spared a thought for all the women who would fall into those deep pools in a few short years. "Remarin saved me," the boy said. "I was very young when my mother died. I did not know my father, and when Mama died, the man who owned the building where we lived threw me out and told me never to come back. I lived on the streets for a few seasons, but when it got cold, I had to look for shelter."

"When was this, Samir? Was this before Alexander…was my father still the king?" Kit asked.

"Yes, Your Majesty. Your father was, by all accounts, a decent man, but he did not concern himself with the fate of one more orphaned urchin in Lowtown. Remarin is no king, and there are many who would dispute that he is a decent man." He glanced at Inelle with this, but she pointedly ignored the boy. "But when he came upon a large man carrying a struggling boy down an alley in the middle of winter, he stepped in and asked questions."

"I assume you were the struggling boy?"

"Yes, Your Majesty. This was nearly ten years ago, and I was a very small child of but seven years. Remarin came upon a brute hauling me off to be sold to a pleasure house and objected. He objected quite strenuously, with the dagger that wear at your side and a rapier that flashed like lightning. I will never forget the night he saved my life."

"So you are now ready to repay that debt?" Kit asked the boy.

"I can never repay that debt. I owe Remarin my life, and my liveli-hood. He took me away from the bruiser, put the dead man's coin purse in my hand, and led me here, to apprentice to the greatest rogues and rapscallions in the world. What I owe to him is something that will never be cleared from my soul's balance sheet, but if I can help you yank him from the clutches of that ignoble bastard Alexan-der, it will do some small part to balance the scales between us." The boy's eyes widened, and he stammered as he spoke. "I-I-I am sorry, My Lady. I forgot that Alexander is your blood. He is…"

"He is a filthy rat-buggering son of a poxy whore who murdered my father and tried to have me killed on more than one occasion. Now he has taken the man—" Kit cut her words short, then realigned her thoughts. "Now he has taken Remarin, and with him, all the secrets of our plans to overthrow the usurper. We must get him back at all costs."

Not even taking into account the fact that you're in love with him. Trand's "voice" held more than its normal quotient of snark.

I never said that, Kit replied.

You also have yet to deny it, child. Fear not, we've all known for years and not said anything. It's just nice to see you finally admit the truth. Now let's go get our boy so we can convince him of how much he loves you back.

It was with a red flush creeping up her neck that Kit bent to the desk to begin to craft a plan with Samir and Inelle. Every time she glanced at the gem on Trand's hilt, it seemed to wink at her, and she blushed anew.

CHAPTER 37

"This is ill-advised at best, Majesty," Taryn whispered.

"That describes almost every action we've taken for the past eight years, Taryn. Why should we change course now?" Kit replied, barely louder than a breath. She knew from the exasperated sigh behind her that Taryn heard her. The two women slipped through the deserted streets of Bravis barely three hours before sunrise, flitting from shadow to darker shadow as they crept ever nearer to the western wall of the Keep.

The front and rear gates were far from their view, and Kit recalled from her youth that the Temple of Caldar was the nearest building to the Keep, an accident of construction causing the bell tower of the temple to list eastward, putting the top of the tower much closer to the battlements of the castle than her father had considered comfortable. "Much closer" was still a good thirty feet, and the bell tower had no exterior access from street level, meaning that if they wanted to scale the tower and leap to the top of the castle walls, they would need to climb the marbled tower in the dark, with no tools that could make so much as a whisper in the night, then leap across a surely fatal gap to land atop a four-foot walkway.

"This is impossible," Taryn said when they finally reached the tower's base. "We can't climb this. You're good, Majesty, but despite Remarin's various nicknames, you aren't actually a cat."

"No, I'm not," Kit agreed. "But I am a thief. And every thief knows that when your first path is blocked, you move on to Plan B."

"What is Plan B in this case?"

"B is for bribery, my dear throat-cutter," Kit said. Then she put two fingers between her lips, and the piercing whistle of a diving falcon split the otherwise silent night.

Taryn slammed herself flat against the wall, her hands dropping to blades secreted around her waist, but no guards came running. Seconds later, a thick knotted rope dropped in front of them, and Kit gave her a fierce smile. "When in doubt, cheat." Then the slender princess grabbed the rope in both hands and scurried upward.

Taryn shook her head, muttered something about Kit spending far too much time with disreputable thieves, and followed. Moments later, the women slipped through a narrow window in the bell tower, and Kit clasped hands with a shaven-headed man who gave Taryn a short nod.

"Taryn, this is Marcus. He works here in the temple and has agreed to help us."

Ever suspicious, Taryn looked the man up and down. Dressed in a basic tunic and trews, he looked like a stablehand or builder, not a priest. "Why are you doing this?" she asked.

"Afraid I'll shout for the guards the second your backs are turned?" he said, a tight grin splitting his face. "I would, if the guards weren't the rightest bunch of pricks you've ever seen. Rightful heir or not, your girl here promised to get these bastards off the streets and in jail where they belong if she gets her throne back. That's all I needed to hear."

The bitterness in his tone gave Taryn all the confidence in the man she needed. He hated the guards with the passion of someone done a great wrong. "Who?" she asked.

Marcus looked at her, a piercing gaze that took the measure of the woman before him. "My boy. He took a loaf of bread. Wasn't even stealing, just picking through the baker's trash and taking the day-old leavings that he couldn't sell. But the guards called it stealing anyway and cut off his hand. It got the rot, and that took him. They murdered my boy for a hunk of moldy bread. So I want them punished."

"The gold I paid him didn't hurt, either," Kit added.

"Victor wasn't my only boy. That gold makes sure the rest of them don't have to steal to eat for at least a week or two. If you ain't took your throne back by then, you ain't going to."

"If we haven't taken it back by sunrise, our chances are far thinner than I'd like, Marcus," Kit said. "Now ready the hook. That's our signal."

The "signal" she referred to was a cart, rolling down the main thoroughfare toward the castle gates. Unmanned, the cart rolled pell-mell behind a pair of terrified horses at full gallop. The team and cart rattled and crashed against closed-up stalls and storefronts all the way up the hill leading to the Keep, heading straight for the front gates.

"That's the distraction Samir promised?" Taryn asked.

"Oh no," Kit said with a grin. "That's just the first part. Watch." Kit pointed to the cart, which was now engulfed in flames, spurring the horses onward to the gates. With nowhere to turn, the terrified animals headed straight for the main entrance to the castle and the quartet of pikemen standing there.

"I almost feel bad for them," Kit said.

"The guards?" Marcus asked, spitting on the floor.

"No, not at all. They chose this work. I feel bad for the horses. They must be scared out of their minds. Now get ready." At her words, Marcus dragged a heavy crossbow over to the window and aimed it down at the top of the battlements. A long, thin rope hung from the back of the quarrel, and Taryn realized that her mistress had finally, and unequivocally, gone mad.

Below, the horses crashed straight into the four pikemen, but the momentum and weight of the cart was too great, and the whole collection of horses, guards, pikes, and carts slammed into the closed gate in a tangle of limbs, hooves, and fire.

"Should we go now?" Taryn asked, watching the sally ports on either side of the main gate open and guards stream out to help their fallen fellows.

"Not yet. The upper guards are still at their posts," Kit replied.

"Of course they are," Taryn said. "They won't leave their posts for anything less than—"

A huge explosion tore the night asunder as the cart blew to splinters right against the gate. Flaming pitch splatted Greek Fire across the gate, and it began to burn. Chunks of cart, horse, and guard were blown several houses back from the main entrance, and every man atop the wall rushed into the towers to help their fallen comrades and defend against what looked for all the world like a major incursion at the gate. Samir had done his job well, indeed.

"Now!" Kit hissed.

Marcus fired, and the bolt streaked down to the battlements, crossing the distance in the blink of an eye and burying itself into the stonework there. Quick as a cat himself, Marcus took the loose end of the rope and tied it off taut around his waist. "Go," he said, leaning back with his feet braced on either side of the window.

Kit scampered out the window and wrapped her gloved hands and legs around the rope. Keeping her grip loose, she let gravity do the work for her and slid down the rope. Seconds later, before she even had enough time to feel the rope burn through her gloves, her feet slapped into the stone wall and she flipped herself onto the top of the castle walls.

Home, she thought. *I never thought to see her again.*

If you don't keep your head down and get out of Taryn's way, you still might not, Trand spoke into her mind.

Kit didn't respond, just took three steps to the left as Taryn leapt over to land beside her. "Grab my belt," Kit said, leaning over the edge with Trand drawn. With a little more support, the young woman was able to reach the rope, slicing it free for Marcus to pull up.

"There went our escape route," Taryn said.

"We never had an escape route," Kit replied. "This night ends with me on the throne, or all of us dead in the dungeon."

"So, of course, our first stop is the dungeon, just to make it easier on your uncle and his men."

"Exactly," Kit said, turning to walk down the battlement.

I like her more every day, Trand "said" in Kit's head.

That's because she sounds more like you every day, Kit replied.

Obviously that's the effect Remarin has on people. Now let's go save the great idiot so he can resume corrupting the poor child.

Kit led the way down the battlement, stopping about ten yards from the guard tower. "This is the riskiest part," she said to Taryn, peering over the edge into the courtyard. About twelve feet below was the thatched roof of the stables.

"That's not an insignificant drop," Taryn said, skepticism heavy in her voice.

"I'm less worried about that and more worried about remembering where the beams are. I think we could handle hitting the roof easily enough, but if we miss and fall straight through, I think we may have problems."

"Well, if you don't go soon, we're going to have problems of a different sort," the assassin said, pointing back to the gate.

Kit followed her arm and saw that the guards at the gate were arguing amongst themselves, but the general consensus was that many of the rampart guards wanted to return to their posts. Half a dozen men split off from the group at the gate and ducked into the nearest tower.

"They'll be up here in moments. Time to go," Taryn said.

"Follow me," Kit said, then vaulted over the stone battlement and disappeared from view.

Taryn followed with a muttered curse, diving over the edge with a brief prayer to any god that might be listening and inclined to look out for a pair of idiot thieves trying to rescue an even bigger idiot. The women slammed into the straw with a solid *thud*, but both of them spread themselves out to land as flat as possible, spreading the impact across a broader area, so they didn't punch through.

Kit was in motion immediately, with Taryn right behind her. They rolled to the side, away from the gate, and along the length of the stables instead of down the slope to the front of the building. Seconds after landing, Kit reached the edge, scrambled to her hands and knees, then reached under the edge of the roof to the eaves and grabbed hold. Using the eave as a pivot point, the lithe young woman rolled forward off the roof until she dangled by her fingertips from the edge of the roof. With a deep breath, she let go, rolling forward as she hit the ground, then darting back to the shadows beside the stable to check herself for injury.

Taryn landed in front of her like nothing more than the shadow of a cat, then pressed herself to the wall. "Are you alright, Majesty?"

"Nothing broken or sprained, but I'd rather not belly flop onto a pile of sticks and straw from a dozen feet up again if I can help it."

"When you are queen, you may outlaw the practice."

"When I am queen, I am also going to move the stables away from the walls of the Keep," Kit said. She knelt down and crept to the corner, peeking out to see the guards still arguing about who was going to clean away the mess at the gate. From what Kit could strain to overhear, they were all far less concerned with cleaning away the wreckage of the cart and more interested in avoiding mopping up the pieces of guard and horse that littered the entrance.

Waving Taryn along behind her, Kit crept along the wall of the stable, then ducked inside, closing the door gently behind them. Pressing her head near Taryn's ear, she whispered, "There's an enclosed walkway from the stables into the Keep, so my mother never had to walk outside in the rain or snow to ride."

"You never talk about your mother," Taryn said.

"I don't think about her much. I was very young when she died. I suppose being back here has brought a lot of those old memories back to the surface." She dashed away a tear and set her jaw.

"Well, let's go rescue Remarin and reclaim your throne so you can make lots of new memories."

"What's this, now?" a new voice came from the center aisle of the stable.

"Looks like the next memory we make will be a bloody one," Kit said, stepping out into the lantern-lit open area to face the sleepy stablemaster. He stood before them in his nightclothes, holding a sword in one hand and a buckler in the other.

"What do we have here? A pair of little thieves come for the King's horseflesh? Well, let's see what the guards have to say about that."

CHAPTER 38

Despite looking ridiculous in his nightclothes and armaments, the stablemaster held his sword and shield as though he was accustomed to their use, and his footing as he inched toward Kit and Taryn was sure and steady. "Ah yes, you must be the imposter princess His Majesty warned us might be trying to infiltrate the castle. I know he has your thief friend in custody already. I heard the screams filtering up from the dungeon this afternoon."

"I am no imposter, sir. I am Kitarina Rutvor, rightful ruler of Veosia and mistress of this castle and all within it. You shall put down your sword at once, or I will see you relieved of your duties and drummed out of Bravis." Kit stood straight and tall, every inch the noble.

The stablemaster just laughed. "That's a good one, girl. I almost believed you there for a moment. But you see, here's the thing—I don't care. I don't give one single ripe turd if you're really the long-lost princess here to reclaim your throne. I'm not going to let you. King Alexander has done right by me, putting me in charge of the horses here after that old fuck Barron dropped dead of a heart attack. One day I was shoveling shit behind these stupid beasts, the next day I had me a regular bed and a real salary, enough to buy some whiskey and rent a girl every once in a while at one of the good whorehouses. I ain't asking for nothing more than that, and I'll gut anybody who thinks to take that from me."

"I don't want to take anything from you, Mr...." Kit spread her hands and gave a little shrug.

"Me name's Kyle."

"Kyle," Kit repeated, taking a step forward and to her left. "I don't want to throw you out of the stables. As long as the horses are well cared for, there's no reason you cannot serve me as well as you have my uncle."

"But..." The man looked confused, but he kept his attention on Kit as she stepped to the left again, moving slightly closer to the man.

"But what, Kyle?" Kit's voice was all honey and sunshine as she smiled at the man. "We both want the same thing, don't we? We just want the best for everyone, right? And what's right is that the man who killed his brother and tried to kill his niece face justice for his crimes, not sit in a big castle surrounded by bootlickers and syco-phants while he sips on the finest wines and eats the choicest meats, all the while men and women who actually work for a living have to struggle by with watered-down beer and hard bread left over from the King's table. That's not fair, is it, Kyle?"

"I don't give a shit, girl. I sit at the King's table. I sit on the High Council, you ignorant bitch. I'm somebody important now. I'm a big damn deal around here since Alexander took over. I'm—" His eyes went so wide Kit thought they were going to roll forward out of his head, and after standing frozen for a long moment, he started to fall.

Kit darted forward and caught the shield before it could ring on the ground, and Taryn reached around from where she stood behind the dead stablemaster and held onto his shoulders as he collapsed to the ground. She pitched his sword into a pile of straw, then dragged the body into an empty stall. The slender assassin emerged a few minutes later, brushing straw from her hands and legs.

"There, that should keep him covered until we are finished with our business."

"What did you do?" Kit asked.

"I just covered him with some straw, then piled horse dung on top of the straw. I guarantee that will be the last stall to be cleaned. You want his sword?"

"No. I've never gotten the hang of curved blades. I always seem to be out of position for a parry. You take it."

"If I can find a sheath and belt," Taryn said, peering around the room. She walked over to a corner of the stable that had been converted into living quarters and rummaged around in the dead man's belongings for a bit. She walked back over moments later with a quiver slung over her shoulders, a short horse bow in her hand, and the sword hanging from a sheath on her belt. "Looks like he fancied himself an archer as well. I'll certainly make better use of these than he will."

"Especially now," Kit said, casting an eye back toward the stall. As they turned to go, a soft whisker caught her ear and she looked around again. A brown head with a white star emblazoned on its forehead stared back at her. "Apples!" she cried and rushed over to the horse.

The horse bent its head over the gate to its box, and Kit wrapped her arms around its neck. "Oh, Apples, I never thought I'd see you again," she murmured into the beast's brown neck. She stood for almost a full minute, just talking soothing nonsense to the horse before Taryn cleared her throat.

"I hate to break up this touching reunion, but if we don't get Remarin freed and kill your uncle, you're never going to get a chance to ride your horse again."

Kit straightened, patted the horse on the nose, and said, "I'll be back, old friend. I promise." Then she turned to Taryn. "Let's go. The walkway to the castle proper is over here."

Kit led Taryn to a door at the north end of the stables, barred on the stable side. "This way," she said, pulling open the bolts and easing the door wide enough to peek down the walkway. "The walkway is open on the sides above waist height, so we'll have to stay low. I don't know how often the guards patrol this section, but they used to leave it more or less alone."

"Let's hope they remain so careless," Taryn said. "Stay behind me. I will lead with the bow, and I would hate to have to shoot through you."

She slid past Kit to peer down the dark walkway. Just enough torchlight streamed in from the courtyard to make it apparent that no one patrolled the path now, but much could change in a hundred yards. She began to creep out into the darkness, walking in a deep crouch to keep her head below the level of the wooden panels that lined the sides of the walkway.

Kit slipped into the shadows behind her, scuttling on hands and knees to stay low. Both women were sweating even in the chill night air by the time they reached the door into the Keep. Taryn stood, pressing her body to a beam to hide her form as she nocked an arrow. Kit put a hand on the handle of the door, looked back at Taryn, and at a nod from the assassin, yanked the door open.

Taryn flowed through the open door like inky water, slipping inside and into a shadowed corner in seconds. Kit followed, drawing Trand as she pulled the door closed behind her.

Be careful. I can't sense anyone, but there's something interfering with my magic. I get only the faintest hints of people moving about in the castle, but nothing like what I should be finding.

Kit nodded, then tapped Taryn on the shoulder. Pressing her mouth to the other woman's ear, she whispered, "Trand can't see. Something is blocking his magic."

Taryn nodded, then motioned into the room ahead of them. They were in the main entrance chamber of the Keep, just inside the front gates. The grand foyer was twenty yards wide, tiled in marble, and lit by a pair of torches set into the wall by a door in the north wall. Huge columns lined the walls, and their shadows danced along the floor in the torchlight.

"Where are the guards?" Taryn asked.

"They'll be outside the main doors, a pair on patrol, and two outside the Great Hall. Others will patrol the upper floors, where their Royal Apartments are."

"So we only need to get past a couple of guards? Easy enough," Taryn said.

"We also have to avoid the cook and all her kitchen helpers and scullions," Kit added. "They will be getting up soon to bake the bread for the day, and we have to pass near the kitchen and their quarters to get to the stairs down to the dungeon."

"Lead the way," Taryn said, gesturing into the foyer.

Kit slipped from column to column like a wraith, Taryn on her heels. She stopped by a pair of double doors set into the north wall. "We can try to slip through here unseen, then duck through the library into the hall that will lead us down, or we can go to the far wall and take the long hall around the entire Keep. This way is much quicker, but has a higher chance of being seen. The other way is usually deserted, but will take us three times as long."

"Where does this door lead?" Taryn asked.

"A hallway with the library on the left, then the Council Chambers, then a double door leading to the Great Hall. There will certainly be guards there, but they may be asleep, or we may be able to bluff our way past them."

"Or we might not," Taryn said, tapping the bow in her hands.

"I'd rather not kill any guards if we can avoid it."

"I'd prefer that as well, but we may not have a choice. You said there would be another pair of guards on patrol. Where will they be? In the long hallway?"

"They could be anywhere, even in the kitchens or the dungeons for all I know."

"But we know there will be guards outside the Throne Room."

"There always were when I lived here before," Kit said.

"I say we take our chances with the two guards we can find. Keeps the element of surprise on our side."

"So just fling open the door and let you fill these men with arrows?"

"Well, I—" Taryn froze, holding up a hand.

At the same moment, Trand spoke into Kit's mind. *There are two coming. They're close. I'm sorry I couldn't give you more warning...*

Don't worry about it. "Trand says there are two coming from the far door. I guess that settles it," Kit said. "Fling and shoot it is." With that, she grasped the door before them and shoved it open, dropping to one knee in front of Taryn, who fired at the open-mouthed guard twenty yards down the hall.

Taryn's arrow took the man in the eye, and she had another one nocked before the body hit the ground. The assassin stepped forward and sighted on the remaining guard, who raised his shield a moment too late to keep an arrow from sprouting from his throat. He dropped wordlessly, but his shield fell to the stone floor with a thunderous crash.

"Shit," Kit said, dashing into the hall and yanking open a door to her left. "This way!"

Taryn followed her into a warm, well-appointed library with a roaring fire and chandelier full of burning lamps. Four guards sat around a table in the center of the room playing cards, but at the appearance of the two women, all activity in the room froze.

"Um, hello?" Kit said, working toward a smile but looking mostly as though her lunch was about to make a return appearance. "We were looking for the kitchen…"

One guard stood, and Taryn put him down with an arrow to the chest. He wheezed and clutched at the feathered shaft for brief seconds before he fell still. The other three guards sat wide-eyed, watching him die. A moist rattle escaped his throat with the last of his air making a bloody bubble on his lips, which popped soundlessly, sending tiny drops of blood across his face.

Then all hell absolutely broke loose.

CHAPTER 39

The remaining guards all stood at once, with one charging at Taryn, one at Kit, and the last running for the far door. He flung it open and shouted, "Intruders! Assassins! Assassins in the Keep!" before turning back to the women.

Kit drew Trand in her left hand and a throwing dagger in her right, flinging that blade at the oncoming guard. He dodged to the left and smacked the knife out of the air, earning himself a wicked slice on his palm but proceeding otherwise unharmed. Kit transferred Trand to her right hand and moved in on the guard, trying to close with him before he could get his sword out. The tight quarters were certainly better suited to the lightly armored women, but the chainmail the guards wore proved a good defense against daggers.

Kit got to the man as he tried to free his blade but staggered back when he slammed a heavy fist into the side of her face. He grinned at her and said, "You think to threaten my king, girl? Not going to happen. Not while I'm on watch."

I hate when they talk, Trand said to Kit. *I wish they'd just die quietly like good little idiots.*

Kit ducked under a sweeping roundhouse punch from the guard and jabbed him in the thigh with her dagger. The guard let out a yell, and one of the men engaging Taryn glanced over. That was his last mistake, as a knife suddenly protruded from his ear. He dropped to the ground, and Taryn took advantage of the momentary distraction to open the other guard's throat and kick him flat on his back.

She pitched a dagger at the guard attacking Kit, and when he ducked, he found his face meeting the princess's upraised knee. He dropped back onto his rear, blood streaming from his nose, and Kit stepped forward. She drove Trand into the man's left eye, spearing his brain with a sickening *crunch*.

The women stood amidst the bodies for a moment, panting and wiping blood from their blades. Taryn looked at the bow, then shook her head. "No point in that now," she said. "Which way to where they have Remarin?"

"He'll be in the dungeon, through that door." She pointed at the open door the guard just yelled through.

Taryn stuck her head out into the hall, then yanked it back and slammed the door closed. "That's not an option. Six guards coming down that hall at a run."

Kit turned and flung open the door they came through, recoiling from the face of a shocked guard before her. He was a young man, barely old enough to have earned his sword, with a splash of freckles across his nose and cheeks and a shock of bright orange hair sticking up all over his head. Kit reversed her grip on Trand and slammed the pommel down in the center of the youngster's forehead. His eyes rolled back in his head, and he sagged forward.

Kit stepped out of the way of the collapsing guard, then turned to Taryn. "Help me with him." Together the two women dragged the armored man over to the other door, sat him on the ground with his back pressed against it, and threw the bolt. "It won't keep them long, but it might earn us a few extra seconds."

"We'll need them," Taryn said. "Now which way?"

"Follow me," Kit said, and jogged across the room. She opened the door out into the hallway, then motioned for Taryn to be silent. Kit pointed to the end of the hall, by the doors to the Great Hall, where a white-haired guardsman knelt by the bodies of the two men Taryn shot earlier.

The women darted across the hall without a sound, but their luck ran out when they were almost to the far door. "Halt!" the guardsman shouted, and Kit heard his booted feet running across the polished stone floor.

"Run!" Taryn hissed, and Kit flung the door open, sprinting into a narrow hallway. The hall continued about twenty feet before it turned to the left, disappearing into the belly of the Keep.

"This way," Kit said. "These serving corridors will take us around behind the Great Hall and to the stairs leading down."

Taryn slammed the door behind her, looking around for some way to bar it or wedge it shut, but the door opened out and there was nothing to secure it with. The two women sprinted down the hall and turned the corner, their soft-soled boots making a quiet slap against the stone tiles. They jogged the length of the Keep and peeked around another corner at the end of that hallway.

Kit pointed to a door at the end of the long corridor that ran the length of the castle. "The stairs to the upper living quarters are through that door, then on the other side of another door is the staircase down to the dungeon. That's where they'll have Remarin."

"Halt!" came a shout from behind them. Kit and Taryn turned to see the freckle-faced guard leading several others down the corridor in their direction.

"Time to go," Taryn said, shoving Kit into motion. The women turned the corner and ran for the door, only to see it open ahead of them when they were still barely a third of the way down the hall.

"This way," Kit said. She yanked open a door to her left, and they dashed out into the castle's Great Hall. The throne of Veosia sat on a dais right in front of them, with a smaller, slightly less ornate throne to its right. Kit's throat tightened as she saw her parents' thrones, her mother's unoccupied for many years, but she took a deep breath and pressed on. "We can go out the front door, then cut through the Council Chambers to get to the back hallway by the kitchen."

Kit ran past the thrones and down the steps of the dais, skidding to a stop when the huge double doors at the front of the room opened. Four guards in mismatched livery stepped in, all grinning like the cat that ate the canary. A big man in a chain shirt and leather breeches stepped forward. "You've led us on quite the little adventure, ladies, but it's time to put an end to all this. Now put down your weapons and you'll be treated well enough before we hand you over to His Majesty."

An ugly little man with a huge boil over his left eye dressed in leather armor chuckled as he walked forward. "Oh yeah, Missy. We'll treat you real good. I don't know about your flat-chested girlfriend, but I'm happy to take care of you." He reached down between his legs and grabbed himself, then dropped to his knees as both women hurled daggers at his head. He fell to his side, the hilt of a knife protruding from each eye.

"Rush them!" Kit yelled, sprinting toward the guards, or mercenaries if they were to be named accurately. The Great Hall was a long, open space, with no furnishings but the thrones and a small desk for a court scribe. Kit bolted for the desk, using it to put some cover between her and the leader of the group.

"Come on, girlie," he said, leaning forward over the desk to swipe at Kit. "Time for you to put down your weapons and pay for your crimes." He leered at her, still grinning like a cat in cream.

Taryn ran straight at the other two men, one hulking brute with a shield and long sword, and one lithe man with a pair of curved short swords. She leapt high in the air, grabbing onto the front edge of the big man's shield with both hands, then pressing her feet into the center of the shield and throwing her body weight backward. She slammed into the floor, but flexed her legs, then straightened them, launching the giant over her head to slam into the stone steps of the dais. The thin carpet did nothing to cushion his fall, and the *crack* of his shattered skull echoed through the room.

Taryn came to her feet, shield in hand, and spun it through the air at the smaller man. He brought one blade up to ward off the flying hunk of metal, then went down in a tangle of black fabric and blades as Taryn dove into his legs below the knee, taking him to the floor.

Kit feinted left, then right, then left again, trying to make her foe overcommit. He refused to cooperate, so after another feint right, she planted her hands on the top of the desk and swung her feet around, aiming a kick for the man's head. He caught her leg under his left arm, and planted his right palm in her stomach, slamming her down to the desk and driving the air from her lungs.

Kit lay on the wooden desk, stars filling her vision as she struggled to draw breath. After what seemed like forever, she sucked in a great lungful of air and rolled off to the ground just as a mailed fist slammed into the surface right where her ribs had been. She drew Trand and flung the enchanted dagger high into the air, watching her opponent grin as the dagger whizzed by his ear.

"You missed, little chickadee," the man said with a grin. Kit saw a chunk of meat hanging between two of his teeth as his rancid breath cascaded over her.

"No, I didn't, big idiot." Kit grinned back as Trand flipped over in the air and streaked down, point first, to bury himself in the man's skull. The light went out of the guard's eyes, and he slumped to the ground, stone dead. Kit barely rolled out of the way in time to avoid getting buried under his bulk. She popped to her feet and yanked her dagger from the man's head, wiping it clean on his sleeve.

She turned to see the smaller man Taryn fought get to his feet, now holding only one sword. The other lay on the floor several yards away, with an angry female assassin between it and him. Taryn stood, blood dripping from her left arm and a dagger gripped in her right hand, her eyes locked on the small man's. They circled each other, never looking away from each other, sizing each other up and looking for openings.

Kit watched them for long seconds, then muttered, "Screw this," under her breath, and flung Trand into the little guard's back. He spun around, and Taryn was on him before he could take a step. She opened his throat from ear to ear, and he was dead almost before he hit the floor. Trand vanished from the guard's back to reappear in the sheath on Kit's hip, and the women shared a fierce grin.

"Shall we finish the rescue?" Taryn asked.

"We shall," Kit agreed, and the pair turned to the double doors at the end of the hall.

Where a dozen bowmen streamed into the room and knelt to form a barricade of archers. Kit whirled around, but another contingent of guardsmen poured through that door, at least a dozen strong. Behind them strode a tall man dressed in black silk with a circlet of gold on his brow. He stepped up onto the dais and stood there, his hand resting on the back of the throne he'd claimed for his own.

"Hello, niece. So good of you to return," King Alexander the Usurper said to Kit, a thin smile creeping across his flabby features, making him look even more disgusting than normal. "Kill the other one, but not a scratch on the traitor."

His voice carried throughout the Hall, and the air filled with the twang of bowstrings and the soft buzz of arrows in flight as the archers opened fire. Twelve arrows struck Taryn from the knees to the neck, many piercing her all the way through. The slender assassin jerked with each repeated impact, then looked over at Kit.

"I am sorry, Majesty. I wished to serve...better." Then the black-clad woman crumpled to the ground, her lifeblood pouring out onto the stones beneath her body. The last sound Kit heard before her uncle knocked her unconscious was her own screaming as her friend died before her.

CHAPTER 40

Remarin started to struggle in earnest when the guards dragged him into the Great Hall and he saw Kit's unconscious form slumped in the throne that had once belonged to her mother. Alexander Rutvor sat on the king's throne beside her, the smirk on his face stretching from ear to ear.

"Put him there," Alexander pointed to a spot on the floor directly in front of the dais. "I want my treacherous niece to watch his life's blood pour from him like the pitiful dregs of her dream to take my rightful place as King of Veosia."

One guard held Remarin by his bound wrists and his hair while another pressed a foot into the back of his knee, pushing him down by the shoulder. The thief dropped to the stone, adding the bruising of his knees to the list of injuries done to him during his time in captivity.

"Now, Remarin, isn't it?" Alexander asked. Remarin didn't reply. The king went on, rising from his throne and beginning to pace the front of the dais like a tiger stalking its prey. "I understand that you feel wronged by me. You feel that I used you improperly when I hired you to steal that gem so long ago. You think that I betrayed you, and that gives you the right to conspire with my niece to overthrow my rule."

Alexander moved forward, taking the three steps down to floor level and grabbing Remarin by the chin. "I used you just as well as you deserved, you filthy sewer rat. I used you like I use my shit-rags. I covered you in my waste, and I disposed of you. You are nothing, thief. You are not some dashing scoundrel, nor are you some revolutionary leader. You are a piece of trash, floating through the sewers like all the other shit of the city. And tonight, I will dispose of you and all the rest of the scum that lives beneath my feet."

Remarin's eyes widened as he realized what Alexander was saying. The king laughed, a cruel, mocking sound that made Remarin's blood boil. "Oh yes, I know all about your little den of thieves in the sewers of Bravis. I know about your little friend Inelle, and her rats. I've known all about her for years. I didn't care, as long as all they were doing was robbing the idiot nobles and merchants of my city. But tonight they raised their hand against me, and every soul that harbored even the barest thought of sedition will be hauled in here before your dear princess, and I will cut their throats myself. I will paint this entire floor with blood if I have to!"

Remarin looked up at Alexander, licked his lips, and tried to speak. Nothing came forth but a rasp, and he tried again.

"What is it? What could you have to say that I would care about, you filthy guttersnipe?"

Remarin finally mustered up enough spit to force out a single word. "Parley."

Alexander stepped back, shock flowing across his face like water. "What in the world? Parley? You have no right to parley, you fool. You are no noble! You are no foreign dignitary, with rights of state. You are—"

"Prince Remarin of Torin, Uncle of King Gareth and Ambassador to Veosia." Kit's voice was loud enough to be heard by everyone in the room, even those too far away to have heard Remarin's rasp. The guard holding Remarin's shoulder let go and stepped back, looking from his charge to the king as if searching for guidance.

Alexander spun around to glare at Kit, who sat on her mother's throne like it belonged to her. Awake and clear-headed, the young woman sported a spectacular bruise on the left side of her face, but her eyes were bright and her posture rigid. She looked every inch the queen as she gazed down upon the assembled men. "As His Highness's envoy from Torin, I claim diplomatic status for myself and my people and demand reparations for the death of my liege woman. You shall release His Highness immediately and provide him with medical attention and clean clothing."

The nearest guard knelt behind Remarin and began to untie his binds before Alexander collected himself and clouted the man on the top of the head. "Stop that, you imbecile! You do not take orders from this girl. You take orders from me! I am King of Veosia! I am in charge here!"

"Stamp your feet a little, Uncle. I think they'll believe you if you throw a bigger tantrum. That always worked when I was five, anyway," Kit said, her mocking tone sending a flush of red shooting up Alexander's neck to color his entire face.

He spun around and stepped up to where Kit sat, raising his fist to punch her again.

"Stop." There was no shout, no demand. Simply a word, spoken with such complete authority that Alexander froze. Remarin ceased struggling against his bonds. Kit stopped smirking up at her enraged uncle. Every guard in the Great Hall froze where they stood.

Remarin's heart sank as he recognized the woman who tortured him in the dungeons. She walked up onto the dais from the rear entrance to the Hall, her long black dress trailing along behind her like robes of state, if the state were dedicated to the darkest of the gods. Every eye save Kit's was locked on her as she glided toward the king and his niece, her crimson curls falling over her shoulders like a waterfall of blood.

"There is no need to strike her, Alexander. Not when we can use her," she said, walking up to where Alexander stood, still quivering with rage and a barely suppressed desire to pummel his niece to paste.

"How can we use this bratty little bitch?" Alexander snarled.

"Why, Alexander, she could be the perfect queen for you," the woman said, wrapping one arm around Alexander's waist and openly stroking his manhood through his robes. She melded herself to his back like a voluptuous cloak, pressing her mouth to his ear. "Look at her, my king. She is young, noble, and ripe for child-bearing." With the last, she reached out her tongue and licked Alexander's earlobe, drawing a shudder from the king.

And a groan from Kit. "That's disgusting," the princess said from her throne. "I wouldn't marry this murdering pig if he were the last man on Earth, and that is even if he wasn't my blood kin!"

"Oh, my dear," the woman said, a wicked smile curling across her lips. "I'm sorry. You are obviously of the opinion that I was asking you. I'm not. You will do as you're told, whether you like it or not."

Kit stood, and Alexander and the woman both drew back, still pressed together as though they were one person. "I do not take orders from you, no matter what perverse hold you have on my uncle. Because I don't take orders from him, either. I don't obey traitors and usurpers."

Alexander's hand started to rise, but the woman laid a hand on his arm. She moved left to stand beside him. "My dear, when I said you didn't have a choice, I didn't mean that you would choose to obey. I meant that *you don't have a choice.*" She reached behind her back and drew something from her belt. When she brought her hand around again, it held a familiar blade with a ruby set into the pommel.

"Trand!" Kit and Remarin both gasped at the same time.

Are you there, friend? Remarin asked through the bond he shared with the blade.

Trand? Kit's questioning was more tentative, but strong enough that even Remarin could feel her thoughts vibrating along the bond.

I'm sorry, Trand "said" to them both. *She has me. She controls me, and I fear she thinks to use me to control you.*

"That's right, Kitten," the woman said, her voice too low for anyone not on the platform to hear. "I have the blade, and I have the magic to follow its path into your mind. You *will* do as I say, and if I tell you to like it, you will *love it.*"

Kit's heart skipped a beat as she realized that she had heard the woman's last words inside her head as well as with her ears.

"I'll kill you, bitch," Remarin's words were barely above a whisper, but they carried through the entire Hall.

The woman spun on a heel and stalked down the stairs, grabbing Remarin by the throat and lifting him to his feet. He gasped for air as she hoisted him to his tiptoes one-handed, her strength out of all proportion to her size. She brought her face to within inches of Remarin's and dropped her voice so that only he could hear her words. "Little princelet, you should have stayed away. I was willing to forget your interference with my plans for your nephew, but now that you've come here, my patience is worn well and truly past to the breaking point.

"You've lost, Remarin. You're done. Your best friend is trapped in a prison of steel forever. Your brother is dead. Your assassin friend looks like a pincushion, and my man Alexander is going to be taking his pleasure from your dear little Kitten until his dying days. The woman you love will be nothing more than a brood mare for a rutting imbecile under my thumb. Everything you have ever loved is gone, and it is all thanks to me. Once I'm done here and Alexander's heir sits atop the throne in Veosia, I will take my leave to Torin, and I will slit your nephew's throat in his sleep, then throw dear Genevieve into the ocean to drown her grief.

"But I won't kill you, thief. I'll keep you alive, walled up in a room in the highest tower in Bravis with just enough sunlight so you can track the days of your imprisonment. And every time I kill another person you love, I'll force Trand here to shove the images into your head until you don't dare shut your eyes for fear of facing your dead."

"Why?" Remarin gasped. "What did I ever do to you?"

"You took something from me, thief. You took something you can never replace. You took my body, fool. You and your idiot partner here." She gestured with Trand, waving the dagger in front of Remarin's face.

Remarin couldn't speak, unable to draw enough breath with the woman's hand tight on his throat, but he could "talk" to Trand.

What the hell is she talking about?

I think we remember her looking different. Remember this? Trand sent an image into Remarin's head, a memory of the night Trand was trapped in the dagger. A memory of Remarin, sneaking through a powerful wizard's supposedly deserted workroom while Trand, still human, "distracted" the wizard's young wife. A voluptuous woman with long, full red curls...

Wait, what?

Yeah, buddy, Trand replied. *She's the wizard's wife.*

Remarin thought back to that night, to creeping through the wizard's workroom, finding a gleaming dagger with a huge ruby pommel stone sitting on a stand, light softly shining from it in the darkened room. He remembered putting his hand on the hilt, then a side door opening and a wizened old man barging in. In his memory, Remarin saw the old man raise his hands and fling a bolt of blue magical energy at him, saw himself hold up the dagger as if to take cover behind the slender blade, then he saw light and power course down the blade, wrap around his fingers and the hilt, then blast out the ruby to envelop the entire workroom in blinding purple light.

Remarin remembered waking up with the dagger clutched in his hand, and the wizard gone. A search of the building revealed an unconscious woman in the bedchamber directly below the work-room, but no Trand or mage in sight. It was later that day when the blade began to speak in his head.

You're saying...

I'm saying that the dagger disrupted the old man's spell to turn you inside out, or whatever it was meant to do, and trapped him in his wife's body, me in the dagger, and linked the blade to you.

What happened to his wife?

I have no idea, but apparently he doesn't like being a beautiful woman.

"Now do you know why you have to suffer, thief?" The woman growled at him, and Remarin could see the old wizard's hatred burning in the green eyes that used to belong to his wife.

"Because now you have the world's worst case of penis envy?" Remarin managed to croak, just before the doors to the Great Hall exploded inward in a shower of stone and splinters.

CHAPTER 41

Remarin dropped to the stone floor, gasping for air as rubble flew through the room. *Trand! To my hand!* he beckoned through the mental link he shared with the blade. An instant later, he felt the comforting weight of Trand's hilt in his palm. The nimble thief reversed his grip on the dagger and began to saw through his bonds as chaos erupted all over the Great Hall.

A pair of guards standing in front of the main doors was little more than boots and red soup in armor as they were crushed by the explosion of the doors and several feet of stone wall above and around the entrance. The other guardsmen ran toward the double doors, leaving Remarin and Kit alone at the dais with Alexander and the red-haired sorceress.

"Velisande! Do something!" Alexander shouted.

The sorceress turned to him, looked back at Remarin on the floor, then turned her attention to the conflagration at the entryway. She raised her hands above her head, muttered a string of unintelligible syllables, and a pulsating orb of red light materialized between her outstretched fingertips. Her chanting grew in speed and volume until it reached a crescendo, and she drew her hands back as if to hurl the orb over the heads of the guards running at the invaders.

Remarin kicked her behind the knee as her hands went back, and the orb flew high above the Hall, striking the nearest chandelier and exploding, sending shards of molten chain and metal cascading down upon the guardsmen. The woman, now identified as Velisande, fell back and landed on the steps leading up to the dais. Remarin felt the last strands of rope binding his hands part, and he pulled his wrists apart, shoving himself up from the floor as Velisande scrambled at him in a fury.

"I will drag out your guts and hang you with them, you bastard!" she shrieked, rage contorting her face into a frightful mask of gaping jaw and bulging eyes. The beauty was gone in her anger; only hatred remained, all of it directed at Remarin.

I'm starting to think she doesn't like me, Remarin thought to Trand.

He felt more than heard his friend chuckle over their mental link. *Somehow I wonder how you have remained unmarried all these years. Then you say something, anything, and I understand. 'Ware the king!*

Remarin looked to the throne, where Alexander and Kit struggled over the sword the king wore at his side. Remarin tried to leap over the crawling Velisande, but his body, abused at the hands of the torturer for several days, refused to cooperate, and he flopped on top of the sorceress, driving her to the floor in a heap.

Well, that's one way to do it, I suppose, Trand's dry voice echoed through Remarin's head.

Shut up and help the girl, Remarin thought, flinging Trand in the general direction of Kit and Alexander. The dagger blinked out of existence in mid-flight, reappearing in Kit's left hand. She raised her hand high above her head and brought the hilt of the dagger down on Alexander's skull. The usurper staggered back, and Kit used his motion to draw his sword from his belt with her right hand.

Remarin returned his attention to the task at hand, notably the sorceress writhing beneath him. He rolled himself over so he was facedown atop the struggling woman, then grabbed two fistfuls of her hair. He pulled her head back, then slammed her forehead into the stone floor, stunning her. An elbow to the temple later, and Velisande was unconscious.

"I'll deal with you later," he said, then struggled to his feet and looked to the sounds of pitched battle by the door.

His mouth dropped open at the sight before him. Eight guardsmen, some the worse for wear after being pelted with chunks of chandelier shrapnel, stood in a line facing down some two dozen thieves, assassins, second-story men, prostitutes, and Inelle herself. She stood in the center of a ragged formation of bandits and whores, a cloth tied around her hair and a cutlass in her hand. To her right stood a white-haired man who held a sword and shield like he'd spent his entire life in armor, and to her left stood a slender brown-skinned young man with a dagger in each hand. Remarin thought the man looked familiar but couldn't quite place him.

He's the remnant of one of your few good deeds, Trand "said," bringing memories of a little boy being hauled down an alley by a "recruiter" for one of the less reputable brothels in town.

I remember that! Remarin thought.

So does he, Trand replied.

The line of thieves and vagabonds advanced on the guards, who looked from man to man in confusion and fear. The gray-haired man beside Inelle stepped forward and lowered his shield. "Terrence, Philip, Eric…you three I know. You were good boys, if a little rowdy and lax in caring for your armor. You recognize me?"

One of the guards lowered the point of his sword and stood up straight. "Sergeant Drew?"

"Sir Andrew now, son. Her Majesty has knighted me, if you'll believe that crap." A smile split the old man's face for an instant, then his scowl returned. "Now put down your weapons and stand aside. There's a traitor in this room, and it's time he paid for his crimes."

The guards looked at each other, and Remarin's attention was drawn back to the dais behind him where Kit and her uncle still scuffled. He'd managed to get inside her guard, making the long sword useless, and had her knife hand in an iron grip above her head.

"Give up, little girl. You can't win. You're going to die in this room, at my hand, just like your imbecile father did," Alexander said, forcing Kit backward toward the edge of the steps.

Remarin charged then, a stumbling half-run, half-stagger that was far slower than he liked, but still ended with him crashing into Alexander's side with his shoulder and spinning them all away from the edge of the platform. Alexander twisted his left hand free and brought a sharp elbow down between Remarin's shoulder blades, driving the thief to the floor.

"Fool! I did my time in the Guard. I'm not some spoiled royal who's never fought a man before. You've been beaten and tortured for days, what did you hope to do against me?"

"Almost nothing," Remarin said from the ground. Then he wrapped both arms around Alexander's left leg and stood, throwing the other man to the ground with the last of his strength. Alexander crashed to the floor on his back, never letting go of Kit's wrist and dragging her down with him. Remarin swayed on his feet for several seconds before collapsing onto the nearby throne.

Kit landed atop her uncle in a heap, her knife hand still trapped in his grip and her sword flying across the platform to skitter uselessly across the floor. As Alexander's head rapped into the stone floor, she gathered herself quickly and drove a knee into the testicles of the man who murdered her father and stole her kingdom.

Alexander's eyes bulged in their sockets, and his hands flew to his groin. Her blade freed, Kit switched Trand over to her right hand and slammed it into Alexander's chest, slipping the blade under his ribcage to pierce his heart from the bottom. The usurper king looked up at her, shock all over his face. He opened his mouth to speak, but the only thing that came from his lips was a bubble of blood. His head lolled to one side, and he was dead.

Kit pulled her knife from the dead king's chest, wiped the blade on his shirt, and stood. She looked at Remarin. "How badly are you hurt?"

He just looked at her for a moment, then said, "That depends. Is that red-headed bitch still unconscious?"

Kit smiled, then her face paled in alarm. Her head whipped from side to side, then back to Remarin. "She's gone."

"Then I guess I'm not too hurt to join a witch hunt," he said, shoving himself to his feet. He stood for a moment, then the world went black, and he collapsed into the throne of the King of Veosia, completely unconscious.

EPILOGUE

Remarin woke, this time in a bed. He blinked a few times, then reached up to clear the sleep from his eyes. That proved to be more challenging than he expected, as his hand and arm felt ten times heavier than normal. After managing to pry open his eyes using a combination of fingers and eyelids, he struggled to sit up, but couldn't quite manage.

"Let me help you," Kit said from a chair in a corner of the room, then moved to help him upright. She leaned over him, pulled some extra pillows behind him, and between the two, managed to maneuver him into a sitting position.

She stood, then walked over to a washstand under a window. Moonlight streaked over her lithe form as she poured water into a basin, then dampened a cloth and walked back over to the bed. She wiped his face, removing the last vestiges of sleep from the corners of his eyes.

"How long was I unconscious?" he asked, smacking his lips to harvest what little moisture he had.

Kit saw him struggle and reached over to the bedside table where a plain metal cup with water sat. Remarin sipped the water greedily, then chased the cup with his lips as she pulled it away.

"Sit back, you greedy baby," she said, putting a hand on his chest. He winced as she touched a bruise, and she drew her hand back. "Sorry, I didn't mean to—"

"It's fine," he cut her off. "There's not an inch of me that's not all over bruises, except for the parts that are scabbed over wounds, or scarred up burns. Breathing hurts, but you touching me…I think I can survive the agony." He gave her that half-smile, and Kit's stomach did cartwheels even as her heart grew heavy.

"I'm glad you woke," she said, not meeting his eyes. "There was a time we feared you wouldn't."

"There was a time I feared that, too," he said. "Alex is dead, right?"

"Yes." She looked up at him now. "My uncle is dead, and the crown is mine. Uncle Drew has begun purging the Guard of the ruffians and criminals that Alex put in place, and Inelle has vanished, back underground I suppose."

"She won't go back to the same place," Remarin said.

"I know. I'm not inclined to look for her at any rate, but there will come a time when I am in fact chasing the Queen of Knives, and I don't expect her to make it easy on me."

"Don't worry, Kitten," Remarin said. "Inelle doesn't believe in easy. She thinks it's something like unicorns, that exist only in storybooks."

They laughed, and Remarin took another drink. "Taryn?"

"Dead. Alex murdered her before they brought you up from the dungeon."

"I thought so, but I wasn't sure. I'm sorry. She was a good one."

"Yes, she was."

They sat quietly together for several minutes, then Remarin broke the silence. "Go ahead, Kitten."

"I told you not to call me that."

"Go ahead, *Queen* Kitten. I know what you have to say."

"Then why should I say it?"

"Because you're the queen. You have to say the hard things."

"I can't be with you, Remarin."

"I know."

"I want to."

"I know. I want that, too. But I grew up in a castle, too. I know how it has to be. You have to marry a Prince Consort from a kingdom that needs its relations with Veosia shoring up. And I'm not the type to hang around the kitchen door waiting for scraps of attention. I'll be gone as soon as I'm healed."

"I wish it could be different." A single tear, caught by the moonlight, rolled down Kit's cheek. She fell on him then, sobbing into his chest, and he wrapped his arms around the girl he'd watched turn into a woman, now a queen, and the love of his life.

"I do too, my Queen of Kats. I do, too."

At least you still have me. Trand broadcast his thought into both their heads.

Kit sat bolt upright. "You know, there was a reason I left you in my chambers."

Oh, I'm sorry, did the two of you want some privacy? Too bad. Now get to healing, Remoron. We have a redhead to catch and murder, and then you have to find me a body.

"Tomorrow, butter knife," Remarin said. "I promise to start on that tomorrow. Tonight, I'm going to make love to a queen." Then he took Kit into his arms and did just that.

THE END

Did you enjoy Queen of Kats? Do you want to know when the next adventures of Remarin, Kit, and Trand will be? Would you like a free short story from one of my other series?

Go to the address below to sign up for my email list and you can have all those things, as well as updates on appearances, new releases, and sales!

https://www.subscribepage.com/g8d0a9

ACKNOWLEDGMENTS

Thanks as always to Melissa Gilbert for all her help, and for trying in vain to teach me where the commas go.

Thanks to Melissa as well for her amazing cover, and of course to all of you for reading!

The following people help me bring this work to you by their Patreon-age. You can join them at Patreon.com/johnhartness.

Sean Fitzpatrick
Sarah J. Ashburn
Noah Sturdevant
Mark Ferber
Andy Bartalone
Nick Esslinger
Sharon Moore
Wendy Taylor
Sheelagh Semper
Charlotte Henley Babb
Andreas Brücher
Sheryl R. Hayes
Amaranth Dawe

Butch Howard
Andrew Bolyard
Lawrence Nash
Delia Houghland
Douglas Park Jr.
Travis & Casey Schilling
Michelle E. Botwinick
Carol Baker
Leonard Rosenthol
Lisa Hodges
Patrick Dugan
Aloof Fox
Arthur Reisfeld
Darrell Grizzle
Kristie McKinely
Melissa Cole
Leia Powell
Noella Handley
Bob Dobkin
Jeremy Snyder
Candice Carpenter
Theresa Glover
Salem Macknee
Jared Pierce
Don Lynch
Jeremy Wilhoit
D.R. Perry
Andrea Judy
Anthony D. Hudson
John A. McColley
Mark Wilson
Dennis Bolton
Shiloh Walker/J.C. Daniels
Andrew Torn
Sue Lambert
Emilia Agrafojo

Tracy Syrstad
Samantha Dunaway Bryant
Steven R. Yanacsek
Scott Furman
Rebecca Ledford
Ray Spitz
Lars Klander

ABOUT THE AUTHOR

John G. Hartness is a teller of tales, a righter of wrong, defender of ladies' virtues, and some people call him Maurice, for he speaks of the pompatus of love. He is also the best-selling author of EPIC-Award-winning series *The Black Knight Chronicles* from Bell Bridge Books, a comedic urban fantasy series that answers the eternal question "Why aren't there more fat vampires?" In July of 2016. John was honored with the Manly Wade Wellman Award by the NC Speculative Fiction Foundation for Best Novel by a North Carolina writer in 2015 for the first Quincy Harker novella, *Raising Hell*.

In 2016, John teamed up with a pair of other publishing industry ne'er-do-wells and founded Falstaff Books, a publishing company dedicated to pushing the boundaries of literature and entertainment.

In his copious free time John enjoys long walks on the beach, rescuing kittens from trees and getting caught in the rain. An avid *Magic: the Gathering* player, John is strong in his nerd-fu and has sometimes been referred to as "the Kevin Smith of Charlotte, NC." And not just for his girth.

Find out more about John online
www.johnhartness.com

STAY IN TOUCH!

If you enjoyed this book, please leave a review on Amazon, Goodreads, or wherever you like.

If you'd like to hear more about or from the author, please join my mailing list at https://www.subscribepage.com/g8d0a9.

You can get some free short stories just for signing up, and whenever a book gets 50 reviews, the author gets a unicorn. I need another unicorn. The ones I have are getting lonely. So please leave a review and get me another unicorn!

FALSTAFF BOOKS

**Want to know what's new
And coming soon from
Falstaff Books?**

Try This Free Ebook Sampler

https://www.instafreebie.com/free/bsZnl

**Follow the link.
Download the file.
Transfer to your e-reader, phone, tablet, watch, computer,
whatever.
Enjoy.**